THE NARROWS

ALSO BY MARK ZVONKOVIC

A LION IN THE GRASS

THE
NARROWS

MARK ZVONKOVIC

DOS PERRO PUBLISHING

Go and catch a falling star
Get with child a mandrake root,
Tell me where all past years are,
Or who cleft the devil's foot,
Teach me to hear mermaids singing,
Or to keep off envy's stinging,
And find
What wind
Serves to advance an honest mind.

From "Song: Go and catch a falling star"
By John Donne

PREFACE

THE FIRST VERSION OF *The Narrows* was written in starts and stops during many years prior to 2008. During that time I was practicing law at a law firm, which, trust me, was not a good environment in which to write a novel. I managed to write a few paragraphs now and then during very early mornings, but only when I'd been able to sleep away the prior day's office rhetoric. Finally, in late 2008 I had finished a draft of the novel and I knew I had to do something with it. My alternatives were to burn it or to publish it in any way I could, which turned out to be only a little better than burning it. No publisher in those days was interested in a novel written by a lawyer unless it involved courtroom drama. And I was a corporate lawyer.

In 2008 that version of the novel was published as *When Mermaids Sing*. I hated the title from the start but I was talked into it by marketing people whom, I suspect, thought it sounded like a romance. What I'd wanted to title it was *Time To Go*, based on a passage where the protagonist is musing about the nature of time and wishing he could package it up and take it away, like take-out food. I spent ten years after that regretting the title I'd used and frequently disliking the book as well, until I retired from practicing law and wrote a second novel, *A Lion in the Grass*. Then, on the road to being a recovering lawyer, I decided it was necessary to return to the first version of this novel and fix all the parts I regretted, including the title. The novel is being republished now as *The Narrows*, a reference to the family home on Cape Cod where most of the story takes place.

The novel has changed in many ways. I've tried hard not to disturb Larry Brown's voice, but I've made many revisions to the text to integrate Larry and his cousins, Bradley and Herrick, into the world created in *A Lion in the Grass*. That novel is the first of The Raymond Hatcher Stories. Raymond was born in 1925. His father was an aide to Robert Lansing, the Secretary of State during World War I, and thereafter a career foreign service officer in Europe. Raymond was exceptionally intelligent. He graduated from college at eighteen and joined the Navy in 1943, where he was seconded to the Office of Strategic Services and served in the Pacific theater. He spent the rest of his life in government intelligence sectors until he died at age ninety. During his lifetime he affected many people in many ways. Some he killed. But others he befriended and a few he mentored. One man who influenced Raymond was a fellow OSS officer, Captain Bradley Wright. Sadly, Captain Wright and his wife, Betsy, were killed while serving as missionaries in 1950's French Indochina. Their son, Herrick, Raymond rescued.

The Narrows is the second book in The Raymond Hatcher Stories. Captain Wright's twin brother, Harold, married Betsy's twin sister, Adelaide Clements. After his rescue, Herrick was returned to Boston, where Harold and Adelaide raised him as a son, together with their own son, Bradley. The Clements's twins were from a family that owned a summer house in Chatham on Cape Cod. *The Narrows* takes place at that house in the 1970s and involves Herrick's first cousins, Bradley Wright and Larry Brown. Without giving away the story, I can say that the genetic connection between Captain Wright and his nephew, Bradley, is obvious.

In case it isn't apparent, my love of writing springs from my love of bringing characters to life. The Raymond Hatcher stories are, and will be, all about Raymond and the people he interacted with during his lifetime, as well as their descendants. Herrick will return eventually with his own story, as will his cousins. And Jay Jackson, Raymond's protégé in *A Lion in the Grass*, will reappear in 2021 in the third of The Raymond Hatcher stories. He will tell a story about Raymond that hasn't yet been told. That novel will be titled *Belinda*, unless the marketing folks talk me out of it.

1

I NOTICE THAT THE SEAT of Hal Green's pants is wet as I follow him out of the Venice Bar & Grill in Somerville, Massachusetts at almost 7:00 p.m. on a Friday in late October. The evening is in the waning moments of dusk, but the light isn't so bad that I can't see the wet spot.

"Hey, Hal. Your pants are wet," I say.

"Well, no kidding, Larry," he says, stopping so abruptly that I almost bump into the back of him. "You wouldn't be kidding, would you?"

He slaps both hands against his ass to emphasize just how wet he is, and then looks at me over his shoulder. It was I who had accidentally spilled the beer in his chair. I shrug my shoulders and walk around him toward the car.

"I'm not kidding," I say. "They're wet."

"Sweet Betsy," he says, pats the roof of his car, and throws himself into his seat. I always smile when he refers to his car as "Betsy" because Betsy is the name of one of my older sisters.

"Now the seat is wet, too," I mention to him as we roar out of the parking lot.

Hal and I have been good friends since September of 1968 when we met in our assigned dorm room as freshmen. One would never have guessed at the time that a friendship would develop. He was a jock and I was a book nerd. I still have a clear vision of him from that first day, standing in the doorway with a lacrosse stick in one hand, cleats tied together and slung over his shoulder, and other implements of sports warfare falling from his grasp onto the floor. Yet, we unexpectedly developed an appreciation for each other that transcended, and continues to transcend, our differences.

I suspect that the real glue of our friendship is a remarkable proclivity in each of us to be absolutely frank with each other. I don't have any idea how or why this practice developed, but it has been uncompromised and unwavering from its initial demonstration later that first day when I told him he reminded me of a gladiator and he responded that I should keep my books, which were piled three rows deep in the middle of the floor, on my side of the room. In those days I didn't go anywhere without my books; they were like the stuffed dog I had when I was younger. Actually, if the truth be told, I considered bringing that stuffed dog to college also, but at the last minute decided against it.

Frankness is not a quality one finds in any great abundance in most people. Actually, seldom in your life do you run across a person who is completely frank. I don't mean just an honest person, who may refrain from speaking his mind on occasion to spare your feelings. I mean someone who will step right up and tell you you're a dumb ass when you need him to. The problem is that most people, by their nature, are indirect. I don't know whether it's a matter of solicitude, by which I mean that people are generally reluctant to confront you with an observation that might distress you, or a matter of insecurity, by which I mean that when you make a frank, personal statement to someone, you often reveal as much about yourself as about the person you are addressing. The fact is that more often than not, even a close friend is reluctant to be completely candid with you, and you can waste a great deal of time beating around the bush just to get to a trusted intimacy that would have been best said at the beginning of your conversation.

Let me give an example. My cousin Herrick was in love with a girl who was a bitch of the worst sort. None of Herrick's or my siblings liked her, including my older sister Betsy, who has been a close friend of Herrick his whole life. In fact, as it later turned out, my aunt and uncle didn't care for her either. What was amazing was that none of us ever said a thing to Herrick about the girl. Of course, we would all talk about her in the worst way privately, but when they would come home together we'd be as nice as cherry pie. Finally, things went bad between them. The girl flipped out and broke up with him. I'm sure I heard an explanation at the time, but that's not important. About a month later, all of us were sitting on the lawn of the house on the Cape that our two families own and Betsy said to Herrick something to the effect that all of us had always thought the girl was a bitch. Well, Herrick became furious and demanded to know why we hadn't told him. None of us had an answer, of course, and we all just sat there with our fingers in our ears, so to speak. He didn't say a word to any of us for quite a while after that. It's hard to blame him. If just one of us had been candid with him about the girl, he might have been more cautious about getting as entangled as he did. And then, perspective is not always spawned by frankness. He could just as likely have ignored the observation.

My thoughts about Herrick dissipate when Hal swears at a guy in front of us who takes too long to make a turn. As he accelerates up the College Avenue hill, he nonchalantly proposes that we might just have one more beer over at George's Place, even though, as I point out, we're going in the wrong direction and we could have just stayed at the Venice. We were there for beer and pizza with several other faculty members from the school where we teach, the South Medford Junior High School. Hal teaches math and I teach English. We play volleyball with several other teachers in the school gym on Friday afternoons after the kids are gone, and then we all go to the Venice. I suspect Hal goes more on my account than because he enjoys hanging around with the other faculty. My suspicion grows out of my observation of his eyebrows while we're there. You have never seen eyebrows as thick as Hal's, although you don't notice them when you first meet him because he's such a big guy and the hair on his head is so bushy and unkempt. Anyway, at the Venice, usually about thirty minutes after we arrive, I always observe that his eyebrows appear to be moving toward the door. Of course, it could be I who am thinking about heading for the door. Whatever the case, he often suggests after we leave that we go to another place, and when we do he is noticeably more relaxed.

I tell Hal as we approach Veterans Circle that I think I am to meet Millie, my girlfriend, at my house, and he quizzes me about why I think I'm meeting her, as opposed to know I'm meeting her, somewhat in the manner that he would quiz one of his students about the basis for a solution to an algebra problem, although a bit more playfully. He knows me so well that he guesses that my meeting Millie at my house is actually wishful thinking on my part. As we drive along the side of the Medford College fields, I remember why she will not be meeting me, but I don't say anything to him. We turn onto Highland Street.

I live near the end of the street, up on the Medford Hillside. The three-story house is divided into three apartments, with one on each floor. Mine is in the middle. No lights illuminate my windows. He turns off the engine and we look at the dark house together.

"You want to go in and see if she left a note?" he asks.

"No. She hasn't been here," I say. "She's over at the Medford College Theater. She's in a show—*Guys and Dolls*."

He doesn't react for a minute, although even in the dusk I think I see his eyebrows rise. Then he glances sideways at me and suddenly twists his body to face me. He paints his face with an exaggerated look of dumbfoundedness.

"Of course," he exclaims, slapping his palm against his forehead. "Why didn't I think of that!" He looks out the driver-side window for a second, expels a breath noisily and asks, "Do you think you could have remembered this back at the Venice before we drove all the way up here?"

I'm not sure how to respond.

"She's one of the chorus girls," I say meekly.

"Oh, you're not kidding me, are you Larry?"

And then I remember.

"Oh, right," I say, feeling stupid. "You went with me last weekend to see the show."

He shakes his head, fires up the engine and turns the car around to drive back down the Hillside the way we came. It occurs to me that my forgetting he went to the show is not too surprising, as I spent most of the time in a dark funk, wishing I wasn't there. I'd like to tell him now, as we crawl through the traffic in Davis Square, how depressed the show made me the whole next week, but I can't. It seems that my propensity for frankness only applies to my being frank about his conduct, not about my own feelings. The chorus girls do a strip tease in the second act. I slouched down in my seat during the number. It drove me crazy to think about all those eyes on her body. It didn't bother her, though; her face broadcast a big, bright smile. "Look at me," the face said. "Look at my body." There were whistles from the audience. "More!" someone yelled. "Take it all off!" The smile became even brighter. "Anything you want," her face said. And Hal didn't see why her taking off her clothes up there should bother me, when I mentioned afterwards that it had made me a little uncomfortable. "It's just theater," he said. But he doesn't like Millie anyway, so I wasn't surprised. Perhaps he now remembers my remark, because he reaches over and slaps my shoulder.

"What you need," he says, "is a tall, cold brewski."

On Mass Ave the traffic is heavy. So we take a shortcut that avoids Harvard Square and will bring us up behind the Orson Welles Theater right around the corner from our destination. I start thinking again about old Herrick not seeing what a bitch his girlfriend was and that perhaps I could be doing the same thing. I admit, I sometimes struggle with perspective, and often I can't sort out whether my responses to self-questioning are arrived at objectively or only by way of rationalization. I frequently engage in narration and dialogue in my head as a self-perspective exercise, but the sorry truth is that I always hear what I want to hear. Perhaps that's not surprising. Think about how disturbing it is to realize something unpleasant about yourself from the words or actions of another person. How much worse would it be if you were the one conveying the message to yourself?

One easy way to demonstrate what I'm talking about is to pay attention the next time you hear someone describe you to another person, and then compare that description to your self-image. The dissimilarities should be remarkable. For example, I think of me as a tall skinny guy with somewhat baggy clothes and hair flopping over his ears. I'd also describe myself as a person who is always ready with a cynical observation and who believes that if in fact we are the creation of a god, then we are his idea of a joke. I am mostly serious about this; if Jonathan Swift were alive today, I could be a character of his. But other people describe me much differently. They say I am a reserved, polite young man who is scholarly and enthusiastic, like his father, who by the way, happens to be the Chairman of the English Department at Medford College. I do have in common with my father that we are both teachers, although his teaching post is certainly more lofty than mine. At the end of college I was somewhat ambivalent about choosing a career and I sent in my application to the Medford Public Schools because I could think of nothing else. And my getting hired was happenstance; an elderly teacher died over the summer and they were desperately looking for someone to replace her at the last minute. My guess is that my application just happened to be on the top of the pile. I suspect also that the school board lost my application photo, because I had not followed my father's advice to have a picture taken in a tweed sport coat. I don't even own a tweed sport coat. But that was five years ago, back in the Sixties.

My attention returns to Hal when he bangs his rear fender into a car in the parking space behind the one into which he has struggled to maneuver us. After he performs a perfunctory inspection for damage, we walk up the street and around the corner where there is a newspaper box that still has today's paper in the window. The headline says "Thrilla in Manila." The first doorway we come to is George's Place, which is a big, square room with tables all around. The ceiling is painted black and covered with a spongy material. Pipes that hang from the ceiling are at eye level when you enter because the floor of the room is below street level. Hal goes through the door ahead of me, down the stairs and then takes off toward an empty table, but a big guy with a Celtics hat stops me on the landing inside the door. Hal thinks they always card me because I'm so skinny, my clothes are too big and my hair is never combed, none of which is completely accurate. "You're twenty-six and you look sixteen," he said last week when the same thing happened.

"Hold onto this table, Larry," Hal says, after I finally get in the place. "I'll be back in a flash." When he returns, he bangs down two mugs. Then he turns his chair around so its back is facing his abdomen.

"Larry, do you remember Winkle?" he asks.

"Yep. Randall Winkle. But I haven't seen him since graduation."

"I ran into him the other day," Hal says. "He owns a house on the Cape. He inherited it from his grandfather last year."

"You're kidding!" I say expressively, always interested in the Cape because my family owns a house in Orleans. "Where is it?"

"It's in Chatham Port," he says. "Isn't that near your family place?"

"It is," I say. "What's the name of the street? Do you know?"

"Oh, hell. I can't remember that," he says with a grimace. "It's out in the car. He invited me out for the weekend."

If my memory is accurate, Randall had a face like a little dog, and he was only about five foot five. So I was always looking at the top of his head when I was around him. And he sniffed his food just before he ate it. He held it right up to his nose and squinted his eyes. Then he'd wrinkle the top of his nose when he chewed.

"Wrinkle Winkle," I say, remembering also that Hal and Randall had been good friends in prep school but had drifted apart at Harvard, particularly after Hal dropped out. "You used to call him that."

"Yeah," Hal says. "But he's changed. I wouldn't call him that now. He's become pretty sophisticated."

"Oh, no!" I exclaim. "He was such a goof. He would drive down Mass Ave in that old red Porsche convertible like a bat out of hell."

"I remember! I remember!" Hal roars. "He'd put the top down in the winter and wear that old aviator's hat and goggles."

"That's right," I say, my eyes leaking a bit from laughing at my image of Randall and his goggles.

Thinking about Randall's car unfortunately reminds me of Richard Bevins and his red Corvette. I saw Millie and Richard standing on her porch last night, not that I was spying on her or anything. I just happened to be walking by on the other side of a row of hedges. His car was in front of her house for quite a long time. I have an image, suddenly, of Bevins speeding up the coast road to his family's estate in Rockport that Millie and her friends talk about all the time. In my image Millie sits beside him with a scarf covering her hair, holding her arms up against the wind, exclaiming how wonderful the feeling is.

"That was the spring I was learning to play golf," Hal laughs, assuming I remember some other incident with Randall that I don't remember.

"I remember," I say, happy to continue reminiscing without asking what incident he's referring to. "Your golf balls kept rolling around the room."

"There was a hole in my bag," he says, resting his chin on his hand. "It wasn't my fault."

"Well, I stepped on one in the morning once, and almost broke my neck," I say, feigning indignation.

"You should take it up, Larry. It's a great game."

"No thanks."

"In fact, that's what Winkle and I are doing this weekend. He belongs to the club right there in Chatham. Or is it Orleans? I can't remember."

"It must be Orleans," I say. "There's a course on the other side of Pleasant Bay from our house."

"God, that's a beautiful place," he says, his eyes unfocused in a way that suggests he is looking at Pleasant Bay as he speaks. I close my eyes for a second and can see the part of Pleasant Bay that abuts our house, the sun glinting off the water and Strong Island just across the channel. Beyond the island are the flats, which are just below the water line if the tide is in, and then the dunes rise up, shining white with spots of waving green beach grasses. On the other side of the dunes the surf is roaring ashore from the Atlantic. I imagine white foam and spray, although I know you can't see it from our side of Pleasant Bay on account of the dunes.

"Most of the leaves could be off the trees by now," I say. "My cousin Bradley and I would usually rake them up on Columbus Day."

"How is Bradley?" Hal asks, his eyes snapping back into focus.

"Okay, as far as I know," I say.

"I'd forgotten," Hal says. "You and Bradley used to hang around the Cape during the summer."

"Every summer of our lives, until just a couple of years ago."

"I know this," Hal says, hitting the side of his head with his knuckles. "Don't I know this?"

I've repeated the story to Hal on numerous occasions, how the Browns and the Wrights, related through our mothers, own an old house in Orleans on the top of Pleasant Bay, not far from the Cape Cod National Seashore. The property on which the house is situated juts out into Pleasant Bay and extends back toward the north along part of a narrow channel that connects Pleasant Bay with Little Pleasant Bay. On account of this channel we often refer to the house as "the Narrows." There are seven children between the two families. My twin sisters were born first. Betsy was third, about three years after the twins, and I'm the fourth, born a couple of years after her. Herrick is about the same age as Betsy. He's the son of my deceased aunt and uncle who were missionaries, killed when Herrick was a boy. His mother and Bradley's mother, my aunt Adelaide Wright, were twins, both of them a part of the four Clements sisters, who included my mother. Bradley Wright is my next cousin, a year older than I, and our cousin Sally, the daughter of another Clements sister, is a year younger than I. So, the three of us—Bradley, Sally and I—were the youngest children in the Cape Cod household, until a little more than ten years ago when Carla, my kid sister, was born.

All of those summers growing up, Bradley, Sally and I were inseparable friends, although in some of the grade school years I'm sure Sally suffered through the role of Bradley's tag-along little sister. As young teens we became particularly close, sharing complaints regarding our parents, our older siblings—who we believed were always mistreating us—and just the Establishment in general. College was the breaking point. One at a time we drifted away, led by Bradley going to college in California. We came together for shorter periods in the summer during the college years, until one summer Bradley didn't return from California and a couple of years later Sally went into the Peace Corps for two years.

"So what happened?" Hal asks, after I mention to him that I have not spent much time on the Cape recently. "Did everybody just stop going to the house or what?"

"No. Our parents still go. And Carla goes, of course. And some of the older children and their families go. Bradley, Sally and I just got involved in other things, like the Peace Corps."

"And Bradley's still on the West Coast?"

"I think so," I say. "I haven't heard from him in a while. At least, not directly."

"So what does that mean?" he asks, wrinkling his forehead at me. "Do you communicate by rumor or what?"

"No. Well, that's not far off, actually," I say slowly. "Every once in a while a girl will show up at my door, tell me Bradley gave her my address and ask to spend the night."

"Now that's unique," he says, his features animated. "Who are these chicks?"

"It's not how it sounds," I say quickly, "These girls have all been a little different."

"Oh?"

"They're into macrobiotics," I explain. "They bring their own rice to cook. I think they were all from a commune out there. I don't know. They don't talk much, either."

"Too bad," he says, shaking his head. "Anyway, it must have been nice, growing up with all those brothers and sisters and cousins. All I had was the chauffeur, the maid and the nanny. I was an only child, as you know."

"I remember. But having all those siblings isn't so great all the time, either."

"Nothing is perfect," he says, banging his fist on the table. "That's what I always say."

"You're right," I say, banging my fist also, mocking him.

"Larry," he says in a serious voice. "You should come with me to Winkle's. I can pick you up first thing in the morning. It will be good for you."

"Golf is such a stupid game," I say, disgustedly. "You spend five or six hours chasing a little white ball through the poison ivy. What's so thrilling about that?"

"Well, there's more to it than that," he says, a little defensively.

"It's bullshit," I say, feeling a little feisty from the beer I've been drinking. "It's just a bunch of grown men walking around with long sticks, acting affected."

"That's ridiculous," he sputters, but then composes himself. "So come along for the ride. Bring a book to read while we're out on the course. I bet Winkle's house is beautiful. And it would be great to see him. We can talk about old times. And you can look across the bay and remember all the good times at your house."

"I can't," I say, and then turn my gaze out over the crowd, hoping he will drop the subject.

But I have no such luck. He's all over me in a flash, wanting to know what I could possibly be doing that was better than going with him to the Cape. And in a way he's right, if the truth be told. Nothing could be better than going to the Cape. I think about how I could spend a morning drinking coffee down in Chatham, reading a book, and then later sitting on a dune at the National Sea Shore. An awkward fact comes out quickly from his questions: I am expecting to see Millie. It's also a fact, however, that there exists no actual arrangement to meet Millie. She has the closing performance of the show tomorrow night, and I know there is a cast party afterwards. She hasn't mentioned that to me, but surely she's just been too distracted and will call me tomorrow. Hal shakes his head in exasperation and put his palms to his forehead.

"You are such an idiot," he says very quietly.

I protest. Why would he think so? He starts counting reasons, which, I admit, sound plausible. She has stood me up before. Then I remember how I met Millie in the first place and I stop him to say that, regardless of whether she calls me, I have to be in town on Sunday afternoon for my father's annual professor-student mixer at my parent's house. That was where I first met Millie. And he knows that I enjoy going to my father's party to get some chuckles from all the freshmen trying to impress the professors.

"Oh. Well, I can see that," he says in a disappointed manner. "I just thought you could use a good time."

He's on his feet, suddenly, stretching his arms and back, and then he's off to the bar with both of our glasses. When he returns, he rotates the chair around to its conventional position. He bangs the glasses on the table again.

"Yours was warm," he says, good-naturedly. "Who can drink warm beer?"

"The British. They drink bitters warm."

"Well, then, here's to you, old chap," he says quickly as he polishes off half a glass.

"Cheers," I say, taking another tiny sip.

The roar of all the surrounding conversations suddenly ebbs, and I feel as if we are hearing the guttural inhalation of a retreating wave. When I look over at Hal to see if he notices, his countenance makes me think that he has willed the relative quiet for the purpose of making a point. I look around but no one is paying us the least bit of attention. He leans forward over the table. I brace myself.

"Oh, shit, Larry," he says quietly, his eyebrows moving closer together with what I suspect is an internal struggle over what he is to say next. "You're such a smart guy about so many things. I'm going to level with you. You don't know it, but that bitch is two-timing you."

"What? Do you say that she makes me a cuckold?" I ask, trying to use some levity to defuse the bomb he is arming.

"A what?"

"A cuckold."

"Is that something like a turkey?" he asks, looking puzzled.

"A turkey? Yeah, that's good," I laugh. "In a slangish sort of way, I guess it could mean that. It actually means the husband of an adulteress."

"God, I hope it never gets to that!" he exclaims.

"To what?"

"To the husband part. Anyway, this isn't a joke, goddamnit," he says, irritably. "Be serious with me, why don't you?"

"Okay," I relent.

"I think she's making it with that Sky King guy."

"That's Sky Masterson," I say.

"Well, whoever," he sputters, banging the table with his fist. "What difference does it make, goddamnit? That's not the point."

"Oh?"

"What's his real name, anyway?"

"Bevins. Richard Bevins."

"That's the guy," he says. "That's who I'm talking about."

"You're crazy," I say. "So they're in a show together. They're just friends."

"Oh, bullshit!" he roars, rolling his eyes around like an epileptic. "Just friends! I can't believe it."

"Besides, how do you know this?" I demand.

"I know," he says smugly, now that he has my attention.

"Just like that? You just know? Like you're some kind of psychic or what?"

"I have my sources," he says, leaning back in his chair and appearing to enjoy my agitation.

"What's that supposed to mean? Your sources? If you don't want to tell me, just say so."

"A little defensive, are you?"

"Maybe. What do you expect? You just told me my chorus girl was balling the leading man. Do you expect me to say, 'That's great news, Hal'?"

"Listen, nobody wants to hear shit like this, but it's something you have to know," he says, leaning forward in his chair. "She's taking you for a ride."

"I don't know," I say, shaking my head. "I think you're mistaken. People always jump to conclusions about things like this. They watch too many soap operas. That kind of stuff doesn't happen in real life."

"You're crazy. You know it? Do you think everyone in the world is as straight as you? Do me a favor. Leave your wallet with me when you go out from now on."

"So what do you want me to do—become a cynic overnight? It takes practice," I say.

"Just get real," he says, ignoring the slight. "That's all I'm saying."

"I'm as real as I can be. I just don't believe you're right."

"Clair," he says, almost in whisper. "The costume designer."

"Clair?"

"She's my source. And don't you go running to Millie and tell her this. Clair will kill me."

"She lives in Millie's house."

"That's the one."

"I didn't even know you knew her."

"I know her sister. What difference does that make?"

"Why didn't she tell me herself? I see her all the time."

"Are you crazy?" he says, rolling his eyeballs. "Girls don't do that kind of thing. Besides, what was she going to do? Walk up to you in the living room and say, 'Oh, Larry. Did you know that Sky King is poking old Millie when you're not around?'"

"So she told you."

"Right."

"And told you to tell me."

"No. She told me not to tell you."

"Why would she tell you if she didn't expect you to tell me?"

"She did expect me to tell you," he says, looking confused.

"But she told you not to tell me."

"That's the way that girls think," he says, exasperated. "What difference does it make?"

"Maybe she's lying," I say, desperately trying to discredit his information, although I know, perhaps better than he knows, that Clair is a credible source.

"Why would she do that?"

"Why would she tell you not to tell me?"

"Who the hell knows why a woman tells you anything," he says, and bangs the table with the bottom of his glass, which causes foam to rise on the top of the remaining beer. "Maybe I just caught her at a weak moment and it slipped out. Maybe she just wanted you to know, but she didn't want to be responsible. Who knows? I'm not a goddamn shrink. I'm a math teacher. And what difference does it make anyway?"

"I don't know," I say after a moment, trying to keep my voice steady. "I don't want to talk about it anymore."

He doesn't say anything, and looks around at the other tables. The noise from the room washes over me. But the image of waves rolling onto the shore leaves me. Now the sound is only a hundred voices speaking at once and sounding like a motor that needs a tune-up. My instinct is to look off into the distance in order to push the closeness of the moment away from me, separating myself at least by a theoretical gap. I can look no further than the wall across the room, unfortunately, because all of the windowpanes are painted black. You never know whether it's going to be raining when you go out.

The windowpanes were painted white on the back door of the house Millie lived in last year. I remember that because I studied them for a couple of hours one evening from the outside when an old boyfriend of hers from Hartford unexpectedly dropped in. She pushed me out the back door right after one of her roommates told her he was at the door. "He can't see you here. He's a caddie at the country club and he'll tell my father you were here," she said. The next day when I mentioned to her that I'd hung around on the lousy porch all that time she said, "Oh, I thought you'd gone home, Larry. I never thought you'd be standing on the porch. Why would anyone stand on the porch in the rain for that long?" It was as if it were my fault that she had forgotten me out there. Why would I leave when it was only supposed to be a minute, and she was going to get rid of him, and with the rain crashing down like it was! But I never asked her that. I just shrugged my shoulders and said something about it being a misunderstanding. Now I wish I had said something. Suddenly I regret all the times I never said anything, all those times when it inexplicably became my fault that she had done what she did to me. And I start to wonder whether, through some fantastic turn of logic, Bevins is my fault also. The thought is so preposterous that my attention snaps back to Hal.

"I can't believe it, Hal. She wouldn't do that."

"Sometimes truth is harder to believe than fiction," he says, drumming his fingers on the side of his glass.

I suspect he is demonstrating a gruff manner in order to keep himself from sympathetically agreeing with me and backing down in his determination that I face what he is sure is reality. And I feel for him suddenly. It is hard to stand your ground in the face of desperate denial.

"But it's not the truth," I insist, weakly. "It can't be."

"Suit yourself," he says and looks around the room again.

Just a few nights ago she held me in her arms and whispered in my ear, "You're the only one." The funny thing is that when I first met her, she said I was only the next of many before me. She was as matter of fact about all her prior sexual experiences as she was telling me her favorite ice cream flavor. Then, as I got to know her, I began to suspect that her stories were not true. Finally, I decided she had fabricated them, and after that it was as if she had never told them. Instead, she whispered in my ear, "You're the only one." It's as if time rubbed her stories smooth, like the sea takes the sharp edges off a piece of broken glass.

"Suppose you're wrong, Larry," Hal says, interrupting my thoughts. "Suppose it's true."

"Okay, Hal. Suppose it is."

"You wouldn't do anything, would you? If you found out for certain she'd been making it with Sky King," he says, intensely.

"What could I do?"

"Well. You could stop shining her damn shoes," he says, vehemently. "That would be a good start."

"How's that? If it's true, she's getting the shoes shined someplace else, to borrow your metaphor."

"Save the English stuff for your students, why don't you!" he yells.

"Sorry, but it was a metaphor," I say, leaning forward and almost whispering, in an attempt to quiet him down.

"So what?" he says with lower volume, as he realizes from my hint and the stares of the people at the table next to us that he's attracting attention. "Oh, for Christ sake, Larry," he says, now in a normal voice. "I'm trying to be serious and you're talking shop. How would you like it if I started doing algebra on the goddamn napkins while we were talking?"

"Okay, I'll rephrase. If she doesn't love me, she won't be coming around," I explain.

"Is that what you think?" he asks, his voice rising again momentarily. "That all this is about whether she loves you or not?"

"What else would I think?"

"You are out to lunch," he growls. "Love has nothing to do with this."

"Well, excuse me, Master Lewis," I say sarcastically. "What is it, then?"

"Trust me on this one," he says, ignoring my literary reference. "This is about a spoiled bitch who has one thing and wants everything."

"You know what, Hal? I don't want to talk about this anymore. I mean, you're entitled to your opinion and all. But I don't want to talk about it anymore."

"Fine," he says abruptly.

He turns in his chair a little, so he's not facing me, and looks across the room at the people filing in the door. The place is starting to get crowded.

I think about Millie being at my place last weekend. I remember Sunday morning like it was a photograph. She lay on her back and counted strands of her hair. She had her two hands up close to her face and her fingers gingerly separated the hair. Her eyes focused so close to her face that they almost crossed. Her body hardly made an indentation on the sheets. "I think I'll wear my yellow sweater today," she said. She's always speaking her thoughts out loud like that, like she's delivering a little running commentary for my benefit. "It's time to brush my hair now," she'll say, or "I wonder if I turned the tea kettle off." It's her way of being intimate. The image explodes in a rush of steam from the kettle when Hal leans across the table suddenly.

"You know what I think?" he says rhetorically. "It's not Millie you love, it's the idea of being in love with Millie that you love. Millie just happened to be around when you got the silly idea that you wanted to be in love with someone."

"That's crazy."

"Maybe. Maybe not."

"Why would I be doing that?"

"I'm not a psychologist, Larry."

"Okay."

"But why else would you continue to chase after this two-timing bitch like a lost puppy?"

"Assuming you're right," I say, my voice cracking a little.

"Well, I'm wrong or you're wrong," he says, pointing in an exaggerated way first at himself and then at me. "One of us is wrong. But I've got all the evidence on my side."

"So what? It's a mistake," I say, trying to be calm, trying to act as if this was so clearly a mistake that it's not worth discussing any longer. "She wouldn't do it."

"Why not? Give me an explanation," he presses, refusing to be put off.

"Because she's a good person," I say, regretting the words as they leave my lips.

"Oh, no. Not that!" he exclaims, slapping both hands to his cheeks with feigned theatrics.

"Cut it out, Hal," I say, trying not to look at him.

He's rolling his head around in an exaggerated manner, looking like I just hit him with a baseball bat.

"Not the 'good person' routine!" he says.

I shrug my shoulders. I'm not going to say it again so he can slobber all over the goddamn table.

"Spare me," he says.

"Get lost," I say.

"O Mighty Oberon!" he says. "This poor soul needs the service of your gentle Puck."

"Oh, for Christ sake, Hal. Give it a break, why don't you!"

"Post your Puck to pour a sweet liquor to reverse the foul magic that clouds the vision of our poor Demetrius."

"Cut it out, will you?"

"Did you like that? 'Post your Puck to pour.' What's that called?"

"Alliteration."

"Pretty goddamn good for a math teacher, if you ask me."

He stands and leans toward me, with both hands, palms flat, on the table. A girl with curly red hair and a lot of lipstick watches him, talking all the time to her tablemate. She's a couple of tables away and my line of vision is such that I'm looking at her in a diagonal across Hal's forearm, and she's looking right at his left rear pocket button. When she notices me watching her, she looks away. In a second she looks back quickly, then away again.

"I have an insight," Hal says.

"Won't it work from a seated position?"

He squints. He raises an eyebrow. Then he shifts his weight and gathers the mugs together by their handles. The glasses crack when they come together. I hate that sound, because I always think they're going to shatter into a million pieces. And that would be a pain in the ass. We'd have people all around us suddenly, trying to clean up, just like when I spilled the god-damn beer at the Venice earlier. And everyone in the place would be gawking at us. Whenever I do something like that, everyone develops a rubber neck.

"First, we'll have another," Hal says.

I toss a couple of ones on the table and he slaps his hand down on them while looking at me, probably wondering if he should refuse them, given his sympathies concerning what he's just told me. I rub my fingers on my pants. You can't rub away the feeling of money. It's just like talcum powder.

"If you insist," he says, crumpling up the currency like it's a used piece of Kleenex, and then walking away. The girl with red hair watches his swagger, glances back at me, then quickly turns her attention back to her companion. She reminds me of a lion, with the way her hair waves back against her shoulders. As she speaks to her companion she leans forward in an exagger-ated manner, trying to emphasize that she's concentrating on her conversation and is not distracted by us. Some things are so transparent.

Hal returns and starts up a banter that is playful in a way but, I suspect, a cleverly disguised strategy to come back around to his point about Millie. It's the same as when we were room-mates, he contends, my seeing the world through a filter com-posed of all the novels I had read. True, I did, and still do, read all the time. And perhaps I am influenced, I admit, through some vicarious connection with characters and plots. As I explain to him, however, I'm not substituting a novelist's plot for what's happening to me. At most, it's a case of applying experience to interpretation, a case of analyzing precedent. I got the prece-dent idea, by the way, from vicariously experiencing Herrick's law school travails.

"With real life, there is no plot," he says.

"Sure there is."

"No, there's not!" he insists. "Every minute you live is a beginning for which there is no end. There's no plot. There's no meaning. It just is what it is."

"How can you say that," I demand. "Just look back over the time since we met. There's a plot there. There's meaning to what's happened to us."

"But you see, that's it. That's it, exactly. You're looking back. We've already been there. When you're talking about life, you have to look forward."

"So, there's still a plot going on now. We just don't see it yet."

"No. That's the difference. There's no plot until it happens. Every word a novelist writes, every action one of his characters takes, comes about in the context of the conclusion he knows will occur. And that's not life. You can't see into the future. And you can't draw your conclusions and then live your life to fit them. That would be stupid, right?"

"I don't know."

"It's stupid. Just think about it. You expect Millie to be good to you because you're good to her. You expect that doing the 'right' thing always wins the reward. You look into the future and you see her acknowledging how great you've been to her. But you're living by a code that is given short shrift by real people. It's a code you got from your goddamn books."

"You mean like the Bible?"

"Yes, Mr. Sarcastic," he says, shaking his head in an exaggerated manner. "The Bible. And all the other goddamn books that have all the answers."

"People have values," I say. "That's all you're talking about."

"Sure they do," he says. "But you have to remember that in real life, it's the people who determine the outcome, not the values."

"What?"

"What I mean is that, generally speaking, people merely pay lip service to values, and when a situation is contrary to their desires, they mostly forget what they've said. Then they rationalize what they've done, or they beg forgiveness so they can have it both ways. In day-to-day life there's not a clear-cut ideology like you have in a novel. There's no fairy tale for every circumstance, Larry. You think that there's always a fairy tale ending ahead."

"You really think there isn't?"

"No," he says. "There isn't. There's only what you make yourself."

"You're depressing me."

"Not me, buddy boy," he says, leaning back in his chair. "You're depressing yourself with all the make-believe."

"I'm just trying to put a good slant on things, that's all," I say, sounding a little desperate suddenly. "I'm just a poor slob trying to get by. Your approach seems so cold, so empty and futile."

"Oh, boy. The poor slob trying to get by," he says, rolling his eyes around in his head. "Talk about putting a slant on things. And empty? Not a chance. My tank is full of reality. Yours has only the fumes of imagination and irrationality."

"That's pretty good," I say, smiling at his imagery. "The fumes of imagination and irrationality. Not bad for a math teacher."

"You like that?" he grins, and then shakes his head. "I've been hanging around with you too goddamn long."

The girl with red hair is watching us again. I look right at her, and she looks away quickly. I wonder if there is some twist to the plot starting here, with her clumsy observation of us. Perhaps she is a jilted girlfriend of Bevins and, hearing his name, is wondering at the connection, calculating whether there may be here some opportunity for recompense for the misery she has suffered. I look at her more closely. No, she is not pretty enough for that plot, unless he never actually paid her any attention in the first place and her believing herself to be jilted is a fantasy. That would certainly make her the one in this group with the least perspective, I think smugly.

I deflect Hal away from his questions about Millie to a conceptual conversation on reality. I have some good points of reference that I try on him, the best one, I think, is Shakespeare, with Hal being Theseus trying to set me straight about Hermia. Of course, the question from there is whether it is better to mistake a bear for a bush or to mistake a bush for a bear. He falls into the trap and answers that it is better to mistake a bush for a bear, as the consequences are not nearly so bad as the other way around. I pounce, observing that in reality, making such a mistake is preposterous, that only a mind heavy with imagination could come up with a circumstance where a bear is mistaken for a bush.

"It was a trick question," he yells.

"No, it wasn't," I say, calmly.

"You asked which was better, not which was possible."

"Do you often make value judgments about the impossible?"

"I'm confused," he says, shaking his head.

"True."

"How did we get to bears and bushes from Sky King and your two-timing girlfriend?"

"We were establishing, I think, that there is a delicate balance between reality and illusion, and, since you claim I live in the worlds of the fiction I read, between art and life."

"Look," he says, leaning forward. "You say she's a bush, I say she's a bear. If I'm right, you're going to get mauled."

I shrug my shoulders. The game is getting old and it's time to go home, I'd like to say.

The girl looks at us again, but just for a second before she stands up and stretches. She points her elbows by clasping her hands behind her head, and for an incredibly long time she stands like that with her eyes closed and her chest pushing against her sweater. The effect is appealing, I have to admit. Perhaps Bevins *was* attracted to her.

"Let's talk about something else," I say, hoping that he'll just suggest that we go home.

"Fine," he says. "Did you have your tenure visit?"

"Did you?" I ask, after shaking my head no.

"I sure did. And I got a haircut for it, in case you didn't notice," he says, grinning and turning his head from side to side.

"So you did," I say.

"You could use one yourself," he says.

"It's not going to make any difference, Hal."

"Sure it is," he says seriously. "And you could also consider teaching a conventional lesson when they come, not one of your weird things where everyone sits on his desk and chants."

"That was a good lesson, I'll have you know," I say, indignantly. "We were reading *Siddhartha*."

"Oh, give me a break, Larry. When they come, teach grammar or spelling or somebody like Mark Twain, if you have to teach literature."

"That would be intellectually dishonest, Hal."

"Oh my god," he says, going through his repertoire of eye rolls and facial contortions. "I can't believe it."

"You have no principles," I say, trying to look disgusted, but not exactly sure that he isn't right.

"Sure, Larry," he says. "And next year, you won't have a job."

"All on account of Hesse," I say, slapping the table and feeling a little ridiculous. "They're going to refuse me tenure on account of Hesse?"

"Oh, please, Larry. You make huge accommodations for Millie and for your tenure review, you're irredactable. Now that makes sense," he says, glaring at me with wide eyes.

"Oh, good word, Hal."

"You like that?"

"I do," I say, hoping I've broken his train of thought.

"I've always liked the sound of 'irredactable,'" he says. "It reminds me of gum you can't get off your shoe."

"You know what, Hal," I say after a moment. "I liked the Sixties better."

"Are you changing the topic, Larry?"

"No. Really. At least in the Sixties you felt good about yourself, no matter what you were doing. Now everybody is too busy getting ahead to worry about whether they feel good about themselves. It's a different culture, almost, and it happened in just a year or two. That's what is so incredible about it. Woodstock was a fluke, if you think about it."

"Maybe you're right," he says. "I've never thought about it."

There's a kid standing at the door showing his license to the bouncer. I notice him only because he looks a lot like Bradley, only younger. He has the same curly blond hair. I wonder if he'll get in.

Suddenly, the red-haired girl stands next to us.

"Hal?" she says. "Is it Hal Green?"

When he stands up, he towers over her.

"Sure is," he says.

"I'm Mary Ann McGuire."

"Mary Ann!" he says, enthusiastically. "How are you? Sorry I didn't recognize you, but it's been so long."

"Oh, don't apologize," she says, with a tiny laugh. "I've been sitting over there with a friend for a hour trying to remember where I knew you from."

"Well, sit down. And your friend. Where's your friend?" he says, looking around as he pulls out the chair to his left.

"Oh, he had to go," she says and sits down.

"Meet Larry Brown," he says. "We're teachers together at a public school in Medford."

"Nice to meet you," I say, feeling low suddenly with the evaporation of my hypothesis that Mary Ann had been cast off by Bevins.

"Likewise," she says.

Meeting old acquaintances always involves a ritual of establishing the circumstances by which you are acquainted. Hal and Mary Ann get right to it. They met at the Boston University School of Education. After graduation, he got his position in Medford and she became a guidance counselor in Roxbury.

The kid I saw at the door earlier sits down at the table next to us. He sits there by himself without a drink, staring at the wall. Some of the people at the neighboring tables gaze at him quizzically, as I do, but then my attention is diverted back to Mary Ann and Hal, whose conversation has moved on to Mary Ann's summer trip to England. I should keep my mouth shut, and just smile and nod. I know I should.

"Mary Ann," I say. "You didn't go to Oxford when you were in England?"

"No. I ran out of time. I really wanted to go. I wanted to go to the Cotswolds too."

"There's a great place near Oxford called Port Meadow," I say. "Have you heard of it?"

"No."

"It's this big meadow. Every year the Oxford sheriff is required by law to collect taxes from those who graze their animals in the meadow. So he nails up an announcement the day before, that he will collect the annual tax for all animals in the meadow the next day."

"Oh, that's smart," Hal says. "I bet half the cows are mysteriously missing the next day."

"Actually, all of them are. On annual tax day there's not a cow in the meadow."

"Really!" Mary Ann exclaims, her eyes so wide that I wonder, for a second, whether she is mocking me.

"No kidding," I say, deciding that she isn't. "In fact, most of the cows are standing right outside the fence in the road. And the whole town is there. The sheriff goes into the meadow, looks around and says, 'No tax this year,' or something like that, and the crowd cheers."

"Then what?"

"Then, they put all the cows back in the meadow and they all go to the Trout to celebrate."

"The Trout?"

"It's like a bar. It's down at one end of the meadow, next to the river. Of course, the sheriff doesn't pay for his own drinks."

"That is so incredible. I wish I'd made it to Oxford," Mary Ann says.

"You are so full of shit, Larry," Hal says.

"It's a true story. I swear to god. It happens every year."

"I'll never understand the English," Mary Ann says. "You'd think they'd just repeal the tax."

"You'd think so," I say, trying to duplicate the stupid look on her face, and finding it difficult. "Some people never want to change anything, do they?"

"It's so silly," she says.

"Even when it's completely stupid, they don't change."

"But you'd think someone would do something, anyway," she says.

"I suppose there's a moral to this story, Mr. Smart Guy," Hal says.

"I don't know. Maybe."

"You jerk."

"What? I don't get it," Mary Ann says.

"Well, maybe there's something to be said for tradition," I say.

"Oh," she says. "I see. I think."

Two guys walk up to the table next to us, where the kid is sitting by himself. I notice them right away because they look so straight. They're wearing perfectly ironed white shirts and their hair is really short. One of them actually has a crew cut. The other one reminds me of the Beaver's brother, Wally, from the television show. The kid just looks at the table in front of him, not acknowledging them. It occurs to me that he may have come into George's in the first place to evade them, figuring a bar would be an unlikely place to find him. None of them look like beer drinking types. The guy with the crew cut puts his hand on the kid's shoulder.

"Jeremy," he says, "we've been looking all over for you."

"I'm not going back," Jeremy says, pushing the hand away.

"Misha is disappointed," the guy who looks like Wally says.

"Fuck Misha," Jeremy says.

Old Wally and Mr. Crew Cut don't like that. I can see the displeasure in their faces. Jeremy clutches the end of the table, like he's afraid they're going to drag him away. He grips so hard that his knuckles turn white. He is clenching his teeth and still refuses to look up.

"You must come with us," Wally says softly, bending down close to Jeremy's face. "The devil is with us in this place."

"We must return to the Path," Mr. Crew Cut says, putting his hands on Jeremy's shoulder in a paternal fashion.

He tries to help Jeremy up, but Jeremy refuses to let go of the table.

"Oh, dear," Mary Ann says. "I'm afraid there's going to be trouble."

Hal leans over and taps Mr. Crew Cut's arm.

"Hey, Buddy," he says. "Why don't you leave the guy alone?"

"We are not here to make any trouble," Wally says quickly.

"Good," Hal says, "because we're all trying to have a good time here."

Wally and Mr. Crew Cut look at each other.

"Jeremy has lost his way," Wally says. "We're only trying to take him home to Misha."

"So what's the matter with him?" Hal says. "He can't find his own way?"

"You might say that."

"Come on home, Jeremy," Mr. Crew Cut says. "Come on home to Misha."

But Jeremy doesn't let go. His face is red and he grimaces.

"Oh, they're hurting him," Mary Ann whispers.

Mr. Crew Cut looks at her in a threatening manner. Hal pushes back his chair a little.

"Doesn't look to me like he wants to go see Mishy," Hal says in a loud voice. "What do you think, Larry?"

"Doesn't look that way to me," I say without looking at either of the men, wishing Hal would leave me out of this.

Hal looks at Mary Ann and raises his eyebrows. She shakes her head. Then he looks at a group at a nearby table.

"What about you guys? Does he want to go see Mishy?"

"Mishy fishy!" someone from another table yells.

Nervous laugher rocks the place. Mr. Crew Cut's neck turns red around his collar, and his lips press together, tight as a clam.

"That's Misha," he says, strictly.

"Okay," Hal shrugs. "Misha, then."

"Fuck Misha," Jeremy yells suddenly.

With the flash of his hand, too quick for the eye to follow, Mr. Crew Cut slaps Jeremy's face. Hal's body blurs across the distance between them, like the close passing of a speeding car. Chairs fall, a woman screams, several men yell, all amidst a general scramble to back away from our tables. Hal, with both hands about Mr. Crew Cut's throat, swings him in a circle.

The melee moves to the right, toward the wall. Hal's eyes are wild. He's going to hang Mr. Crew Cut on a hook like a coat, if no one stops him. The bouncer yells and pushes his way through the crowd.

Mary Ann screeches at me, like some kind of prehistoric bird. She pounds her fist on my shoulder. Wally advances toward Hal with a chair over his head.

"I should have gone home an hour ago," I say to no one in particular.

"Do something, Larry," she screams.

I never think clearly in situations like this. I just do the first thing that occurs to me. I have my hands on the table, so I give it a running push at Wally. It slides across the floor. I'm amazed by how easily it slides, almost like the floor is greased. I wonder if it's adrenaline, if this is one of those circumstances where I couldn't move the table to save my life if none of this commotion was going on.

The whole thing works better than I planned. I hadn't intended to push the table as hard as I did, and I didn't notice that the corner of the table was exactly groin-high on Wally. He falls to his knees and someone in the crowd grabs the chair that falls from his hands.

"Oh, I'm sorry," I say, sincerely. "I didn't realize."

Mr. Crew Cut's head hits the wall with a thud, like the sound of a basketball off a rim. Hal holds him in place, poised to give his head another slam. The bouncer is closer. I run over and tap Hal's shoulder.

"Sorry to interrupt, Hal," I say, as calmly as I can, "but I've got to get home."

"What?" he screams.

"For Christ sake, Hal. Let's go," I yell.

"Fine," he says and releases Mr. Crew Cut, who slides down to the floor.

People mill around now. Someone slaps Hal on the back. People in bars love this kind of thing.

Mary Ann stands aside, a bewildered look on her face. The bouncer leans over Wally. Hal pulls me by the arm.

"Nice to meet you," I say to her as we pass.

The air is so cold outside that it feels like water from a hose on a hot day flowing over my head. It's the same as when I was a kid and I got so hot playing baseball that I would put my head under the spigot.

"Are you going to stand out there all night, Larry? Let's go, already."

"Keep your pants on," I say, refusing to be hurried through my brief flashback of my childhood moment.

He gets the car moving before I even get the door closed.

"People park so goddamn close," he says. "How do they expect you to get out?"

He bumps a few fenders. Then we're out and driving down a dark side street, weaving our way home.

"Who were those guys, Larry?"

"Krishna people, maybe?"

"No," he says. "What makes you say that? They didn't have those little pony tails."

"Some other religious group, then," I say, just wanting to forget the whole thing. "There are lots of them."

"I don't remember them saying anything religious."

"Do you think someone named Misha is the leader of a motorcycle gang? Did they look like bikers?" I ask, sarcastically.

"Maybe it was a fraternity or something," he says, ignoring my insolence. "They were sort of dressed like fraternity guys."

"Fraternity guys don't dress like that anymore."

"Well, how would I know?" he asks, his voice showing his frustration.

"No, it was some weird religious thing," I say. "That guy was talking about the devil."

"You ever heard of Misha?"

"No."

"What about nonviolence? Don't all these guys preach non-violence?" he asks, his voice strained, almost to a shout.

"The violence was yours, Hal," I say quietly, knowing what I say will raise his hackles.

"Wait a minute," he yells, his eyes flashing at me. "He smacked the kid. What was I supposed to do?"

"Turn the other cheek," I say. "And you could watch the road also."

"It was his goddamn cheek, not mine," he rants.

"You're right. It surprised me too," I say in a conciliatory way.

"What about goddamn freedom of religion? What's hap-pened to that?"

"I don't know," I say, quietly, seeing that he's raving, all pumped up from his physical struggle.

"The kid didn't want to be in their club, did he?"

"Didn't look that way to me."

"Oh, never mind. What do I care."

"I'd forget it," I say, staring out the window and trying to appear disinterested.

"What happened to that other guy, anyway?"

"He bumped into the table."

"No, not him. The kid."

"Jeremy?"

"Right. Jeremy."

"I don't know. He disappeared, I guess, when the commotion started."

"Well, isn't that something!" he sputters.

"I'd forget it, Hal."

"Yeah. I'll forget it. In just a minute, I'll forget it. But here I stand up for this kid and he just beats it."

"What was he supposed to do, Hal? Hang around and kiss your ass?"

"Okay, Mr. Smart Guy. A simple thank-you would have been sufficient."

"Just forget it, Hal. That's my advice."

"You can't just forget it. What do you mean, forget it?"

"It was a fight in a bar," I say, a little irritably. "Aren't we too old for that?"

"Are you kidding? Speak for yourself."

"I'd forget it."

"It will make a great story on Monday."

"Looks like good weather on the Cape tomorrow, Hal."

"I'll say."

We drive along the soccer field, just after Veterans, and the moon is up over the tops of the houses on College Avenue. There's a starlit, clear sky, which is a harbinger for clear weather for the weekend.

It will be nice to have a crisp day for my father's party on Sunday. Professor O'Neill, an old friend of my parents, will make a big deal about it. He'll come banging into the house in his tweed coat and his pipe. Then he'll kiss my mother and yell "What about this fine weather!" And she'll say, "Luck of the Irish." That's what she'll say.

"Well, a good time was had by all," Hal says, as he pulls the car up in front of my house.

"I'd have had more fun sticking my head in an airplane propeller," I say grimly.

"Oh, come on, Larry," he says, punching my arm. "We had a good time."

"Just kidding," I say, giving him a weak smile.

"Okay, then, champ. Sure you don't want to come to the Cape? Last chance."

"Some other time."

"Your loss," he says.

"My loss."

He drives off. I don't feel like going inside, suddenly. The windows are dark. I think about how I'll describe my feelings in my journal later tonight, how I'm thinking that Millie, if she were upstairs, would have the lights on, how the windows would be aglow, her fear of being alone in an empty house in the dark all too strong, as I know from earlier occasions for which my way was lighted and my tardiness met with grave displeasure. My journal entry will sound like I'm old Leonard Bloom come home to look for his Molly.

I walk up my street to the top of the Medford Hillside and look back toward my house. The empty street reminds me of the strange visitor I had this morning. It was 6:00 a.m. and the early morning light was coming through the windows. A frail girl in old clothes and long, straight blond hair pounded on my door.

"Oh, you're not Bradley," she said, after I swung the door open.

"Who are you?"

"Is Bradley here?" she asked, trying to look around me.

"No, he's not."

"Are you Larry Brown by some chance?" she asked after she dug a wrinkled piece of paper out of her pocket.

"Yes."

"Bradley gave me your name, and, I'm sorry, I thought he might be here."

"He's in California. At least, that's where he was the last time I heard from him. And that was six months ago, or more."

"Oh."

"So, why don't you come in and sit down," I said, opening the door wider and standing aside.

"Oh, I can't," she said after she stared at me for a moment. "It's six in the morning!"

"Well, you knocked, didn't you?"

"I'm sorry. I thought he would be here."

"Why?"

"What?"

"Why would he be here? He's in California, like I said before."

She looked around, as if she'd forgotten where she was.

"You're right. I mean, I don't know. I'm sorry I bothered you."

She started down the stairs.

"Wait. What should I tell him?"

She stopped, suddenly, and turned around.

"But you said he wasn't here."

"He's not. But if he shows up, what's your name?"

"He probably won't," she said, waving her hand.

"But if he does, I should tell him you were here."

"I have to go," she said as she ran down the stairs.

"Wait," I called after her.

I paused because I didn't have my shoes on, but then I ran after her anyway.

"I'm sorry I woke you up," she yelled.

By the time I got to the porch, she was already a couple of houses away. I watched her run down the hill toward Highland, the same hill I'm now looking at. I remember wanting to yell to her to come back so she could tell me something, anything, about Bradley: what he's doing, how he's feeling. But I didn't know her name. So I couldn't.

2

THE MORNING LIGHT PEEKS AROUND the window shades. The night seemed endless, and my rehearsal of my call to Millie inexpedient. I let the dial go and listen to the phone click into the connection.

"Residence," Hannah says.

That's the way they answer at the house where Millie lives. They do it so that a caller knows right off the bat it's not a business, like Joe's Garage or something. But I don't believe it does any good. Someone looking for Joe's Garage isn't just going to say "sorry" and hang up. No one thinks that fast. He's going to say "Joe's Garage?" And then what is Hannah going to say? Will she say, "No, you fool, this is a residence. Weren't you listening?" Of course she won't. She's going to say, "No. I'm sorry. You have the wrong number." So, she might as well have just said "Hello" in the first place.

"Hannah."

"Hi, Larry. I knew it was you."

"You did?"

"The phone rings a certain way when you call."

"It does?"

"Yes."

"Oh."

"She's not here, Larry."

"She isn't?"

"No, she isn't."

"Have you seen her this morning?"

"I'm not the house mother, Larry."

"Sorry. I didn't mean it like that."

"I don't know where she is."

"Oh."

Millie sometimes calls her "Homely Hannah." But it's not true. It's just that she has a strikingly plain face, and her hair is the exact color of her skin, making it hard to distinguish the eyebrows and eyelashes without close observation.

"Was she expecting you?"

"No. Not really."

"Well, you can come on over and wait for her if you like," she says.

"No, I'd better not."

"Hmmm. I don't know when she'll be back. I'll leave a note if you want."

"Okay."

"Anything else?"

"No."

"So where are you going to be?"

"What?"

"For the note. Where should I tell her to find you?"

"Oh, right here. I'm not doing anything."

"Seems a waste," she says. "Such a nice day."

"Really. And what are you doing on this fine day?"

"Reading, what else."

"Such a waste."

"Okay, okay," she says. "Maybe I'll go out and sit under a tree."

"That's an idea."

"But I have to go get Clair's sister's cat first."

"Cat?"

"She's out of town."

"And where's Clair's sister?"

"Funny, Larry," she says. "Real funny. The cat is in Brookline."

"A good place for a cat."

"Not a bad place for Clair's sister, either. Want to go for a ride?"

"I don't know."

"Come on. I don't want to go all the way over there by myself."

"I really should stay around here and get some things done," I say, wondering suddenly why I'm looking for an excuse not to go. I do this sometimes—decline an opportunity before I consider it. Curious.

"You said you had nothing to do. Sounds like a brush-off to me."

"No, it isn't."

"Well, come for the ride then. If you come and hold the cat, I can put the top down. It's a pretty day, you said so yourself."

"Just over and back?"

"Back by lunch. I'll put in the note that you'll be back by lunch."

"Forget the note," I say quickly, imagining Millie's displeasure with discovering the reason for my suddenly being unavailable to her. The telephone is slippery in my sweaty hand.

"Okay. Whatever you want. I'll pick you up in about thirty minutes."

"Thirty minutes?"

"Well, I have to finish this chapter and put on some clothes," she says. "Relax, why don't you. Have some tea."

After I get dressed and make the tea, I stand at the window, watching for Hannah. This is the same place I stand when I'm waiting for Millie to walk up the hill. Normally, I don't have a mug of tea in my hand and I cross my arms across my chest and lean my shoulder against the window frame. Sometimes

I imagine that I'm wearing a long leather coat with the collar pulled up and a hat with the brim pulled down. I could be Heathcliff leaning against the gatepost waiting for a glimpse of Cathy.

I've always thought that folding your arms across your chest was a signal that you were not a receptive person. At the beginning of our junior year in college, my cousin Sally started doing it all the time. Every time I'd see her from across the room, when she didn't realize I was watching her, she'd have her arms folded. At first I thought it was just that she was self-conscious about her breasts. Those were the days when girls stopped wearing bras. But Sally wasn't that modest. I started to worry about her. I thought she had a secret problem that she couldn't solve, and that as a result she was retreating from everyone, particularly me. It was like I was watching her slowly sinking into a pool of quicksand. It sounds crazy now, but at the time I was convinced I was right.

So I started asking her if something was wrong. Every time I saw her with her arms folded, I'd go over and ask her. My strategy was that if I confronted her often enough, she would eventually open up. I became a madman about it, and finally she got a little pissed off.

"Larry, why do you keep asking me if something's wrong?" she demanded one day.

"Well, is there?" I asked innocently.

"No," she said. "Is something wrong with you?"

"No. Well, yes, there is," I said, in a rush of candidness. "You're always standing around with your arms folded across your chest."

"You're kidding," she said, pushing her eyebrows together with incredulity.

"No, I'm not."

"You have to be kidding," she said, starting to laugh.

"I'm serious," I said, a little hurt that she thought my concern so funny.

"It's that I'm cold, Larry," she said in an exasperated way. "I'm just cold. That's all that's wrong."

After that she wore sweaters, and stopped crossing her arms. But I still regarded her with some suspicion. For a month every time she'd see me she'd hold her arms out away from her body and say, "See. Okay?" She didn't have to make such a big deal about it, actually, unless, of course, I was right in the first place and she was trying to cover it up.

Hannah's car comes up the street. She has the top down and the sun shines on her blond hair. If it weren't for the car, she'd look like an advertisement in a magazine for shampoo, what with the sun so bright, the sky so blue, and her hair blowing out behind her like it is. The car is a Corvair, and it looks like a square dull green box without a lid.

Hannah waves at me. She knew right where to look. If I ask her, she'll tell me that she felt me standing here looking at her, same as she knew that I was calling when her phone rang. But I don't believe in clairvoyance. She probably thought of ten people when her phone rang, and I just happened to be one of them. I'm not saying that she's disingenuous. Sometimes the mind just plays funny tricks on you.

She wears a red and white serape that matches the car's seats. As we drive down the street, she adjusts the mirror.

"It's loose," she says when she notices that I am observing her. "Every time someone gets in or out of the car, it goes out of whack."

"Okay. If you have a screwdriver, I could tighten it."

"You can't. It doesn't have a screw. It has a weird bolt that you need this long skinny thing for."

"Oh. Where do you get one of those?"

"You can't. I think they stopped making them when they stopped making the car."

"Okay."

"Stupid, isn't it?"

"There must be something you can do," I say. "There's always a solution."

She shrugs her shoulders.

"I like it better this way," she says.

The air is dry and cool. We leave the side windows up to cut down the breeze, but that works only as long as the car is in slow traffic. When we speed up near the Harvard Business School, going by the stadium, I get cold and stay that way until we're going up Harvard Street in Allston. The traffic is lined up at the signal at Coolidge Corner.

My father says "Coolidge Corner" with his long double "oo" and his emphasis on the "l" so that the accent is on the "cool," and not the "lidge." When I was a kid, he'd say to my mother, "My only son and I are going to Coooool-idge Corner for the afternoon." It was one of our family idioms. What it meant to her was that he was taking charge of me for the day, and she was free to do as she wished. To me it often meant a late breakfast or an early lunch, whichever I liked, at Jack & Marion's, followed by an afternoon of reading in the Boston College library while he did research. Occasionally, we went to a ball game at Fenway or to the Aquarium.

"Are you hungry, Hannah?" I ask, inspired by the memory of having lunch with my father.

"I'm always hungry, Larry. It's a way of life."

"Good. Let's stop over there," I say, pointing to an empty parking space.

"Are you kidding?" she asks, looking over at me.

"You said you were hungry, didn't you?"

"I said that I'm always hungry. You said that you were in a hurry."

"So, I'm always in a hurry. Let's eat," I say, grinning at her.

"Okay, Larry. Boy, a psychiatrist would have a field day with us."

"A field day?"

"That's a Midwestern expression. Translated into your Yankee dialect it means 'a good time.'"

"You're from Pennsylvania," I protest. "You told me so yourself."

"That's Western Pennsylvania," she says, as a smile sweeps across her lips. "We're proud of our frontier heritage."

The empty parallel parking space is directly across from Jack and Marion's, but an incredibly long Buick is in the space ahead, its bumper hanging over the line. The car ahead of us slows down while the driver calculates his odds. Hannah gives him plenty of room, goading him almost to give it a try, and the split second he determines not to make the attempt and moves forward, she zips into the space. It's really quite a show. She gets the car about an inch from the curb.

"Pretty good, huh?" she boasts, as she twirls the key ring around her finger.

"It was okay," I say, feigning nonchalance. "But do you think you could get a little closer?"

"Don't scrape my door, smart aleck," she snaps. "This is a delicate machine."

She stands on her seat and hops over the door to the pavement, like a gymnast doing a floor exercise over a horse. I catch up to her at the line coming out of Jack & Marion's door.

"Have they said how long?" she asks the couple we stop behind.

"Ten minutes," the woman says.

"Which means twenty," the man says.

"That's not bad," I say. "Either way."

"It's okay with me," Hannah says, giving me a suspicious glance. "You're the one in a hurry."

Two couples squeeze their way out the door. They're in high spirits, and I guess that they're neighbors, out for a late breakfast. Maybe they live across the hall from each other in one of those old apartment buildings just around the corner on Brookline, although they could have just met for all I know. Sometimes I make up lives for strangers that I see. My sisters used to do it in restaurants. It would drive my father crazy, because before he even got his salad they would have everyone in the whole goddamn restaurant in a category. "You can't judge a book by its cover" is what he said every time. But they didn't care. There would be a doctor at the table next to us, and a stockbroker at the table in the corner. Of course, it depended upon the restaurant. Sometimes they were auto mechanics and bus drivers. And I always wondered if someone on the other side of the restaurant was doing the same thing to us. I mean, someone could have been sitting a couple of tables away saying, "Oh there's a family whose grandparents left them a house on the Cape and a small trust fund. That's how they can afford to eat in this restaurant on two professors' salaries." It's unlikely, but I was always suspicious when I caught someone looking at us.

Once we're inside, the line breaks apart into a chaotic group. A dowdy hostess stands on her toes to see into the back of the restaurant and then turns to scan our eager faces. There's not even something that resembles a line. She's doing it all from memory. If I were she, everyone would look the same to me. We could just as well be sheep, and she a shepherd, and just beyond the first booth is a cliff that she's going to herd us over, like the poor, unfortunate beasts in a Thomas Hardy novel.

"How many in your party?" the hostess asks me.

"Two," I say.

"Follow me."

Hannah walks in front of me. A girl at a table we approach watches her, and then leans to the man on her left. Her lips move, and his head turns toward Hannah. He then makes a nod of assent.

A booth in the back is where the waitress takes us. We are the envy of the huddle at the door. The hostess slaps the shiny cardboard menus on the table.

"The luck of a girl from the Midwest," I say, shaking my head.

"It's my moment for the month," Hannah says.

"Usually they make me wait for the table by the kitchen door," I say. "That's what Millie says, anyway."

"Maybe it's her they're looking at."

"Oh, no," I say, struggling to ignore her incorrect use of the personal pronoun. "For her, when she's with anyone else, it's the table up front."

"Oh, come on, Larry," she laughs.

"I'm not kidding. I'm the awkward companion," I say, trying to look serious, but not able to prevent the infection from Hannah's radiant grin.

"No way. You're your father's son," she says, raising her almost imperceptible eyebrows.

"That's family resemblance you're mistaking for eloquence and charm. There's no such thing as family eloquence," I say, raising my eyebrows in return.

"You're crazy," she says, continuing her laughing.

The waitress comes back.

"What'll you have?"

She's a large woman wearing a dumpy blue uniform and a black hairnet.

"Blueberry pancakes," Hannah says without looking at the menu. "And tea."

The waitress scribbles in a pad and then glares at me.

"Ditto," I say, holding out the menu to her.

"What's that?" she snaps, ignoring the menu.

"The same," I say, meekly. "I'll have the same as she."

"Original," she says, grabbing my menu. "Very original. Two blueberry pancakes. Two teas. You want lemon?"

"Yes," says Hannah.

"And you too, I suppose," she says to me.

"Yes."

"That's it?"

"That's all," Hannah says politely.

"It'll be a few minutes," the waitress says as she walks away.

"See what I mean?" I say to Hannah.

"Oh, you're too sensitive, Larry."

"Maybe."

"I'll guess you have an older sister and you were the baby brother," Hannah says, looking at me seriously but then wrinkling her nose.

"Not a bad guess."

"Child Psychology 101. Was I far off?"

"Only by two. Three older sisters is the right number."

"Wow. And you're the only boy?"

"Right."

"Four children. I wouldn't have guessed."

"Five, actually," I say in an offhanded manner.

"What?"

"Five. I have a baby sister."

"You're kidding. A baby sister," she exclaims.

"Well, she's eleven."

"Oh. That's different."

My older sisters are convinced that Carla, our kid sister, was an unanticipated child. I agreed with them at first, but recently I've changed my mind, because I've come to believe that things are seldom what they appear on the surface to be. And I don't believe it's possible for us to untangle the intricate web of thought and emotion in which our parents' lives were ensnared during the years we were growing up. Everything looks deceptively simple to us now, when we're looking back. But we easily forget all the mundane and trivial occurrences that, often appearing momentous when they occur, shape the decisions that we make. It's the impact of the day-to-day ebb and flow of our lives that we fail to consider, we who look back in time to decipher how a circumstance came to past. As hard as it may be to accept, it may have been no more than a passing twinge of loneliness, or a heated moment of passion, or a glimmer of optimism, or any one of a number of fleeting emotions, that was the catalyst for my kid sister's, or for that matter my, conception.

"How about you, Hannah?" I ask. "What about your family?"

"Oh, we have the typical Midwestern household," she says. "Three children. Two boys and me."

"Older or younger?"

"I'm the middle child. One brother two years older, and another brother two years younger."

Carla was born in the dead of winter. I'll never forget it. It was on the eve of that huge snowstorm that shut down Boston. My father was stranded at the hospital by the snow, and he was worried about Betsy. He had to worry about Betsy. She was wild. So he wouldn't worry anymore, Betsy and I finally walked to the hospital. It took us about three hours. That was eleven years ago.

"What about your father, Hannah. What does he do?"

"He's a doctor," she says. "A country doctor."

"What's the difference between a country doctor and a city doctor?"

"Attitude, mostly. And he makes house calls."

"I should have guessed your father was a doctor," I say, enjoying, suddenly, the way she sometimes watches my lips when I speak. "That explains your fascination with microbiology."

"I don't know about that," she says, wrinkling her forehead. "Do you like literature simply because your father is an English professor?"

"No. You're right. In fact I'd say I like it in spite of him."

"Oh, Larry," she says, feigning a look of disapproval. "You haven't taken any of his classes, have you?"

"Well, that's true."

"Well, he's an inspiration," she says, leaning across the table, looking into my eyes and for a moment putting her hand on my shirtsleeve. "He pulls you in, heart and soul, to what you're reading. You must see it at home. He has this ebullient personality, it seems to me, just bursting with excitement about what he's teaching."

"He can get worked up on a topic."

"Oh, well," she says, rolling her eyes and sitting back. "Maybe you're too close."

"I'll admit that," I say.

"So, what about your baby sister? What's she like?"

"Ebullient. Like her father," I say with a grin.

"Don't make fun of my vocabulary," Hannah laughs. "I've worked very hard on it."

"Sorry."

"What's her name?"

"Carla."

"Watch your elbows," the waitress says.

"Oh, this looks good," Hannah says.

"Need anything else?" the waitress asks.

"Not I," Hannah says.

"What about you?" she asks me.

I shake my head no.

"Good," the waitress says, "because I'm busy. Look at this place. You'd think all these people would have something better to do on a nice day like this than eat pancakes."

She rips the check off her pad and puts it in the middle of the table.

"Pay at the cashier," she says and walks away.

I cut a triangle, like a miniature pie slice. My second triangle is in the shape of a sail. It reminds me of the sail on our boat at the Narrows. Betsy would always make these picture-perfect turns into the wind. It was uncanny how her sail never luffed.

"Carla is an unusual name," Hannah says between bites.

"They were sure she was going to be a boy," I say. "Probably just based on the odds."

"So she was going to be Carl?"

"That was my great-grandfather's name, on my mother's side."

"Do you call her Carla, or is there a nickname?"

"Carly, lots of times. Why do you ask?"

"Oh, no reason. Lots of times the baby in the family has a nickname."

"Actually, my sisters and I called her 'Oops' for a short time. When she was still a baby," I admit.

"'Oops,'" Hannah says. "Whatever for?"

"We thought she was a mistake. You know. Something my mother and father hadn't planned on. It was a big joke with us. One day when we were playing with her we got silly, and one of my sisters called her 'Oops.' I can't remember whom. It was probably Betsy."

"That didn't bother your parents?" Hannah asks, a concerned look on her face.

"Well, that's why we stopped, actually. At first, we were careful not to call her Oops when they were around, but of course, one day it slipped out."

I push the pancakes around my plate. I'm not really hungry anymore. That's the trouble with pancakes. I can't ever finish them.

I'll never forget my mother's startled and hurt expression when she overheard us that day. We hadn't noticed her walk into the room. She looked at us for a moment, and then she just turned around and walked out. It was like the sun going behind a cloud. And now, I sometimes relive that moment when I detect even a small measure of disquietude in my mother's face, in the same way that I experience a twinge of pain after a glance at a scar on my hand.

"So, what happened?" Hannah asks.

"Well, nothing at first. When my mother heard us, she just walked out of the room. Later we made up this story that Carla so liked the expression 'oops-a-daisy' when we tossed her around that we were calling her 'Oops' for short. It might have worked too, except that my father ignored us, picked up Carla and said in his French accent, 'Oh my little mistake. Where would we be without you?' You had to be there. He often used the same expression, only substitute 'cabbage' for 'mistake.'"

"That doesn't sound bad," Hannah says, smiling and now pushing pancake pieces around her plate also.

"My mother didn't take it well. It's hard to explain. My father's expression was one problem. Also, at the time my older sisters and I were complaining, in a joking way, but not really joking, if you know what I mean, that we were all grounded because of this baby."

"Grounded?"

"We weren't going anywhere. In particular, there had been some talk some years before about a family summer in Provence, which was a thought my older sisters couldn't forget. I don't know. I think my mother, when she heard what my father said, concluded that where we would be, if not for Carla, was in the south of France, and that we were all blaming her for this baby."

"But it was just as much his mistake as hers," Hannah says.

"Oh sure, but I don't think he meant it that way, anyway. I don't even think Carla was a mistake, to tell you the truth."

"So it was only a misunderstanding."

"Yes, but it made a big impression on me, I guess, because I think it was the first time I ever saw a strain between them. It scared me, I think, because I didn't really understand why she was so sensitive about the whole thing. I still don't."

"Maybe she resented Carla herself, and wanted to be in the south of France as much as anybody. Resenting your baby would be a hard emotion to deal with."

"I guess so," I say. "I don't know."

"Or it could be that Carla wasn't a mistake, as your sisters assumed," Hannah says in a pensive voice. "It could be that Carla was the product of your father's insistence, and who your mother really resented was him."

"I don't know about that."

"Why not? Do you think only women want to have children?"

"No, but, I don't know, it seems a little out of character to me."

"That's funny, because it doesn't seem so out of character to me."

"But you've only seen him in the classroom," I say.

"He's different?"

"Well, not exactly. He's just more assertive in the classroom, I guess."

"Too docile at home to insist upon a baby, you think?"

"Maybe. Not docile, exactly. I always saw him as going along with things that my mother thought of, as opposed to instigating them."

"So you never made it to Provence?"

"Actually, a few years ago, they went."

"Really."

"For a whole year, in fact. They spent the school year in Paris, and went to Provence for the summer. I was in college, and only made it for a month."

"What about your older sisters?"

"Same as I. They had graduated, and were working. In fact one of them was only there for two weeks. Betsy was there the whole year, though. She spent the school year at the Sorbonne on an exchange program."

"And your father taught?"

"No. He was on sabbatical, and only did research. My mother taught."

"Your mother?"

"Yes," I say. "At the Sorbonne."

"Really," Hannah says, a look of surprise coming over her face.

"Really. She's a professor at Brandeis," I say, shaking my head in response to the look of incredulity on her face.

"No kidding. I didn't know that. How long has she been doing that?"

"As long as I can remember."

"What does she teach?"

"French history, actually."

"Wow."

I'm overwhelmed by the heaviness in my stomach. A full stomach makes me think of myself with my belly hanging over my belt and my cheeks rubbing against my collar, even though people are always saying I'm as skinny as a rail. I abhor the fat feeling. And suddenly it seems as if all the people at the neighboring tables are pushing into their faces vast quantities of sausages, cakes, coffee, toast, raw fish on bagels and whatnot, smacking, slurping, sighing and stretching, finally, against the backs of their chairs to see if one or two centimeters of space can be freed up in some corner of the rib cage for one last bite. It's revolting.

My disgust reminds me of a date I had with this very pretty girl who wanted to go to a hamburger joint in Allston named Ken's. All the way over there she kept saying, "I'm so hungry." When the waitress brought us our burgers, my date took this voracious bite of her hamburger and was transformed into an ogre. I couldn't look at her for the rest of the night, because I couldn't forget the contortions all over her face when she took that bite.

"Delicious," Hannah says. "I'm stuffed."

"Me too."

"Well, you have a regular academic family, don't you? Both of your parents are professors."

"Oh, it's worse than that," I say. "One of my sisters is teaching law. As it turns out, I'm the slouch."

"Oh, Larry," she exclaims, and then wrinkles her forehead. "That's not true."

"Yes, it is," I insist. "I'm the only one with just a B.A. All the rest have one graduate degree or another. Except Carla."

"What grade is she in?"

"Fifth. It won't be long before she's ahead of me, too."

"Do you like what you're doing?"

"I love it."

"So what's the difference, then?"

"I don't know. Millie says I'm wasting my brains."

"How's that?" Hannah says, tilting her head to the side in a manner that says she disapproves.

"She says it's a dead-end job. I should go on to something else."

"Like what?"

"Law school has been suggested."

"Do you think you'd like that?"

"I don't know. My sister likes it. And one of my cousins is a lawyer," I say, thinking about Herrick. "But it seems like he's given up everything else in his life."

"So why change?"

"Why? Because that's the ethic, isn't it? Ambition. Get ahead. That's what an education is for. To get ahead," I say, looking as serious as I can.

"A little cynical today, aren't we?"

"Maybe," I say. "Yes, you're right, I'm being cynical."

"Whatever happened to 'Be what you want to be'?"

"By taking the phrase literally, you misinterpret it," I say, raising the eyebrow that is over the cheek I have my tongue in. "What it means is that you should exercise your opportunities to advance to something better. It's the same as, 'Be happy with who you are,' which means resign yourself to your inability to advance."

"Oh, boy, have you got a bad case," she says, rolling her eyes.

"Maybe so," I say, laughing.

"Well, even if you're right about all these things being expected of you, nobody is holding a gun to your head as far as I can see. Why not step out of the crowd, Larry? Go to India or drive a taxi or something."

"Wow. You've been reading paperbacks behind your micro-biology texts."

"No. I read it last semester in your father's class."

"Which one?"

"Survey of Modern British Fiction."

"That's a new course for him, I think."

"You couldn't tell. He would recite whole paragraphs without opening the book."

"He does that at home, too."

"That must be nice," she says wistfully.

"Only if you like living in a classroom," I retort.

"Oh, come on," she exclaims.

"Really."

"I don't think I'd get tired of it. Ever."

"Well, you can take Romantic Poets next. He teaches that in the spring."

"I plan to."

"Incredible," I say, shaking my head.

"And why not? Professors are like ice cream," she says seriously. "If you liked it the first time, you should order it again."

The waitress walks around our table, looking at me out of the corner of her eye. I could see her giving me the elbow in the ribs, just because I'm not eating my lousy pancakes.

"So you think I should be a Larry Darrell? Is that what you were saying?" I ask Hannah.

"Well, maybe so. Maybe it would put some harmony in your life."

"Oh, yes. Harmony," I say, sarcastically. "I could use a dose of harmony."

"Smart ass," she says, pressing her lips together and looking at her fingers, turning her hands in a rotating motion. "I wish I didn't bite my nails. My fingertips look like carrots."

I am not persuaded that after only a small effort, a person obtains a harmonious existence, as many religious sects now promise. Enlightenment, which must be the cornerstone of a harmonious existence, is not a commodity that you acquire suddenly by wandering around Paris and Tibet, or saying prayers at dawn. Life is a puzzle, it seems to me, and to put the pieces together is a lifetime's work. It's as straightforward as that. My hope is that before I die, I'll be able to decipher the picture. But that's the problem. There's not a box top to go by.

My parents each have a philosophy about obtaining peace of mind. Once when I was particularly discouraged about something, I can't remember now what it was, my father said, "Dip the bucket into the well of knowledge and use the cool water to calm your despair. Overcome your skepticism as if it were superstition." I'll never forget that.

And my mother once told me that, to her, harmony was like two clocks ticking in unison. She got that from Voltaire, of course.

The waitress comes back and slaps a wet dishcloth down on the table.

"You gonna sit here all day," she says.

"Oh, it hasn't been that long," says Hannah.

"It appears that it's time to go, Hannah," I say.

"You bet it is," the waitress says.

"Well, thank you for your pleasant company," Hannah says.

"Anytime, sugar," she says. "Come back when he's hungry, next time."

We walk single file to the cash register. The man at the cash register is jolly.

"How was everything?"

"Fine. Just fine."

He makes change. Then he impales the green receipt, and counts the bills and coins into my palm.

"Thank you, and enjoy the day," he says.

The vinyl on the seats is hot from the sun. When the car moves I lean my head back, and, with eyes closed, the sky is a red expanse. When I open my eyes I expect to find us gone farther, and to see the Chestnut Hill Reservoir to my right. But that's not the case. Closing my eyes befuddles my brain's capacity to judge the distance covered by moments elapsed. We make a quick turn onto Short Street.

I stay in the car while Hannah goes in for the cat. When she comes out, the cat is draped over her arm. She drops him into my lap, and he curls up in the concave space.

"Ahhh," she says. "He likes you."

"Swell," I say, shaking my head.

"Loosen up, Larry," Hannah says as she walks around the car. "He doesn't bite."

She shakes her head, and starts the engine. After she tugs at the gear lever, the car moves forward.

"Have you ever been to the little park around the corner?" I ask.

"No. There's a park up here?"

"Turn left on Summit Ave," I say authoritatively.

"Yes, sir."

The park is a small grassy hill with a swing set and a few trees on the uphill side near where we stop. Even if the park were flat, you couldn't play a baseball game on it. That's how small it is. But it has quite a view. You can see the trolleys crossing Harvard Street at the Commonwealth intersection. In fact you can follow North Harvard Street up all the way past the Mass Pike overpass to Harvard Stadium. The cars crossing the Larz Andersen Bridge look like ants.

"What a nice place," Hannah says.

"I like it."

"How did you ever find it?"

"My sister's friend once lived right over there," I say, pointing to a gray house across the street.

I came up here once on a dark, frigid night to find Betsy. The stars were so sharp they looked like ice crystals. And the Harvard fields were a deep, black abyss. Betsy's best friend had called around midnight to tell me Betsy had been sitting in the park for an hour, and she wouldn't come inside. "Let's go home, Bets. It's cold," I said after I found her. But I knew it wouldn't be that easy. That's why I had brought a blanket with me. I wrapped it around her. "It *is* cold," she said, but she made no motion to leave. "Well, at least let me under the blanket if we're going to stay," I said, and we huddled there until the sun rose.

I can't remember the name of the guy she was distraught about. He was inducted into the army, which we all believed was tantamount to a death sentence. He never saw combat, however. He had a desk job in Japan. Derek, that was his name. They drifted apart after he went into the service. So the whole crisis turned out to be for nothing.

"Gosh, this is a beautiful place," Hannah says.

The Larz Andersen Bridge looks like an intense little circle, like the point of focus under a magnifying glass, emphasized by the blur of all things around it. It reminds me of a close-up photograph of a leaf on a tree, the camera lens having been set with a depth of field that causes the leaf to appear clear and sharp, while the branch from which it springs retreats into an opalescent mass of green, brown and white, as if the leaf and forward end of the branch had pushed their way through a small seam in a large hanging sheet of muslin.

"I've tried to bring Millie up here a couple of times," I say, while staring into the distance. "But we never have the time."

"Millie's a busy girl," Hannah says.

"Too busy sometimes."

"I don't know."

"Often I feel like the odd man out," I say, suddenly feeling like I have to tell somebody these thoughts. "You know what I mean? It's like Millie and her activities have a life of their own, and for haplessly being in the wrong place at the wrong time, I've been swept up in their vortex and can't extricate myself."

Hannah looks at me a moment, but doesn't say anything. So I keep talking. I tell her how I met Millie, and then before I know it I'm spilling my guts. I tell her how I sometimes feel like the puppy who keeps returning to the master who kicks him. At first she is reluctant to say anything and she just listens. Then I refer to Millie as a bully and she jumps in.

"Now that's a great description," she laughs. "Millie the bully."

"I didn't exactly mean it that way," I say, fighting off the defensiveness that springs up inside of me. "I was only drawing a comparison."

"If the shoe fits," she continues.

"Really. I don't think you can mix up aloofness with impudence."

"Aloof? Is that how you would describe her?" she asks, the incredulity coming back into her voice.

"Well, yes."

"I wouldn't. I don't know how you got me into this conversation, Larry. Let's talk about something else."

"Wait," I say, urgently. "Tell me how you would describe her."

"Okay. Not aloof. Indifferent maybe. Insouciant. How about that."

"Insouciant?"

"I've been studying my vocabulary. Remember?"

"Do you really think so?"

"Well, Larry. It's not necessarily a rank. She's just not somebody I would seek out to talk to if something bad happened to me, not someone I would expect to receive a lot of empathy from."

"I don't know."

"You and she are so different. It's amazing to me. You're so diffident and warm hearted. Oh, a little sarcastic sometimes, and then there's some of that put-on cynicism. I knew all that after talking to you for five minutes. And she's so . . . Well, she's not someone you'd expect any empathy from, about anything."

"Some of it is that she's so damn competitive," I say. "You know, like she always has to be in front of you."

She shrugs and looks out over the Charles River landscape. The sky is bright blue.

"Larry, let's talk about something else," she says in a determined way. "What are you doing for the rest of this beautiful weekend?"

I don't want to tell her that I am basically just waiting around for Millie to invite me to the cast party, so I talk about the Cape and how nice it would be to go down there for the night. In fact, before I know it I am trying to persuade her to come with me, describing how we could go sit out on the beach at the Cape Code National Seashore and watch the moon rise. I explain how Bradley and I would do that all the time.

"Oh, I've heard Millie talk about Bradley," she says.

"Probably disparagingly," I say. "They didn't hit it off when they met, though neither one gave it much of a chance. There was a conflict from minute one."

"She wasn't disparaging. What did she say? Something to the effect that he was a little mixed up, I think. That he was living on a commune in California and picking grapes with the migrant workers."

"Well, you see, that's not exactly it. He's working with an organization that is providing medical services to the migrant workers. At least, that was what he was doing the last time I heard from him."

"I would say that's a commendable thing to do."

"I envy him for his responding to his social conscience."

"What you're doing isn't too shabby either, Larry."

"Not really. It's just another job."

"What are you talking about?"

"A dead-end job, really. I look at some of the older guys and I think, 'Do I really want to be doing this in twenty years.'"

"And what would be wrong with that?"

"I don't know," I say.

"No one should worry about twenty years, anyway," she says, rolling her eyes.

"Millie worries about twenty years from now."

"Oh, Millie, Shmillie," she says, disgustedly, "Let her worry."

"You know what? I couldn't go to the Cape anyway," I say suddenly. "Tomorrow is my father's mixer. I told them I would go."

"Oh, well," she sighs. "Who wants to think about tomorrow anyway? I could just sit here all day in the sun."

"Besides that, I haven't heard from Millie. Tonight is closing night for the show, and I can't remember if I'm supposed to go someplace."

"Like to a cast party, for example," she says, leaning back in her seat and looking up at the sky.

Small clouds sail along on the jet stream, as if they were launched from below the horizon behind us on an eastward trajectory. We used to lie on the lawn at the Narrows and watch them. Rogue clouds, Bradley called them. I remember that Sally had a cowboy shirt. It had smooth leather on the fringes going up and down the arms and across the back. When she wore it, she would wear her hair in a long braid that would rest across the front of her left shoulder. The three of us made a pact to brave the frontier together. I remember how, when we got a little older, our pact changed. Then we talked about how we would break away from the system, and make a mark on the world with our lives. That's why Sally went to Africa with the Peace Corps. She begged me to go with her, and I wouldn't.

"I've never been to a cast party," I say.

"And this one won't be typical, will it?" Hannah says, still looking at the sky.

"What?"

"Oh, since it will be at the Richard Bevins family house in Rockport. Excuse me. What did he call it? The 'Bevins Estate,' or the 'BE' for short," she says. "That's what he said. As in the 'place to be!' I can't do a very good imitation of him. He's a real snob."

"What are you talking about?"

"The cast weekend," she says, looking over at me. "It's been the hot topic at the house for a whole week."

"Oh."

"You didn't know," she says, the corners of her mouth turning down.

"I guess I forgot," I say, looking away, trying to comprehend, or to keep myself from comprehending, I don't know which, the import of the information just given me.

A cloud passes in front of the sun. I've never had surgery, but I've always imagined that the feeling you get from the sun going behind a cloud suddenly is the same feeling that a patient on an operating room table feels when the anesthetist's drug starts to seep slowly into his blood. He's apathetic and lethargic and he knows that the blackness will come next.

"Sorry," she says, softly.

I look at the park and remember the night I was here with Betsy. The place is bad karma.

"We should get back, Hannah," I say, quickly.

Hannah senses my disquiet, I'm sure, but she doesn't say anything. She starts the car and drives down the hill.

"You should go to the Cape," she says when we're at the stoplight at Commonwealth Avenue.

"No. I have my parent's mixer."

"Blow off the mixer, then," she says, her voice rising in determination. "I'll go to the Cape with you."

The sun comes back out.

"You're nice to say that, Hannah," I say. "But I'd better not."

3

ON NORTH HARVARD STREET THE insides of my eyelids make a bright red screen, which reminds me of the way the horizon looked the time we drove up to Wellfleet to the drive-in. There were ten of us in the old station wagon, and I sat on the tailgate as we drove along the dunes road. Over the last tall dune Duck Harbor retreated. Then I felt the sunset on my back, and Sally started jumping up and down in her seat. "Oh, forget the movie. Let's stay till this ends," she said. And Bradley responded in his typical nonchalant way, "But it never ends. You can't see it, but it never ends." We saw a sheet of red stretched out across Cape Cod Bay, as if the mainland were ablaze.

"Now, what's happening here?" Hannah says.

We're in a slow-moving line of traffic coming up to the Larz Anderson Bridge. Several policemen stand together in a semi-circle on the grassy embankment next to the Weld Boat House.

"Can you see what's going on?" Hannah asks. "I can't see around."

The traffic stops. I hold the cat against my hip and stand on the seat.

"Hold on," Hannah says.

She inches the car forward with the traffic. The seat is a little wobbly.

"You look silly, Larry."

"You don't like my orthogonal position," I say, trying to act casually, although my position on the car seat is a bit precarious.

"Your what?" she asks, looking quickly from the road to my shuffling feet and back to the road.

"My orthogonal position," I repeat. "I'm orthogonal to the vehicle's horizontal. Put that on your vocabulary list."

"Oh, swell. How do you spell it?"

"It's perpendicularity, that's what it is."

She shakes her head and then focuses her attention back on the traffic, which has started to move. I can now see over the railings on the bridge. One late winter night I walked one of those railings like it was a balance beam. Millie was with me. "Don't be a clown," she said, standing below me, huddled in her coat from the cold wind blowing along the river. But the cold incited me, and I threw her my coat. "Come down, Larry," she said. "Oh, Millie, lighten up," I urged. She scowled at me for a minute and then she retorted, "Well, if you're so light, Larry, you can flap your way home by yourself." Then she threw my coat on the ground and stormed off.

When I was six, I walked on a log over a stream. My mother was with me. "Ladies and gentlemen," she said to our imaginary audience, "I give you the Amazing Larry Brown, high above the ring." I did a turn in the middle. "He defies gravity," she said. I turned again but lost my balance. "He falls into the water," she said. "Why, Amazing Larry, now you're soaked." In front of my mother, I lost my perpendicularity.

The cat meows displeasure, which snaps me back to the scene in front of us.

"Don't drop the cat, Larry," Hannah urges.

"Don't worry," I say, gripping the top of the windshield a little tighter.

Four firemen carry a heavy bundle up the grassy bank from the river. I can tell they're firemen because they're wearing these black shiny overcoats. You'd think the coats would be some bright color, like the trucks. How do you find your buddy in a smoky building if he's wearing a coat like that?

We come over the crest of the bridge. There's a traffic cop at the Memorial Drive intersection. An ambulance comes screaming around the corner. Hannah slams on the brakes. The Amazing Larry Brown topples onto the hood.

"Oh, Larry! Are you okay?" Hannah shrieks.

"Oh, shit," I exclaim, realizing that my hand is empty. "The cat!"

"I'm sorry," Hannah cries.

"Which way did she go?"

"Over there," she says, pointing to the right. "Toward the firemen."

I see the cat go under the ambulance, but when I get there she sprints under the police line. I go after her.

Her tail is in a straight line with her back when she runs. When she walks the tail is up, almost perpendicular, except for the tip, which flops over, first one side, then the next. She stops on the downhill side of a group of men and presses her belly flat against the ground.

"Hey, buddy. What the hell are you doing?" one of the cops yells at me.

I sprint to the cat, trying to scoop her up, like a shortstop fielding a hot grounder. But she wiggles free, gone like a firefly into the night, and I skid across the ground, my face in the grass.

"Get him up. Quick," a voice says, as two cops grab me under both arms and lift me up.

When I stand up, I see that the men are loosely gathered around a corpse. The eyes are open and lifeless. The body is white and bloated. A drowned person's body swells so much, someone once told me, that its limbs turn gray and split through the clothes. But this guy is so white, he looks like the frosted interior of a freezer. And I've seen the face before. It's the face of the kid from George's, or someone who looks just like him. My knees buckle and a cop has to grab my arm to keep me from going over.

"Never seen a stiff before?" he asks in a manner that tells me his question is rhetorical.

He walks me a few yards from the corpse to a man in an old suit coat. The man's tie is loose, the knot pulled to the side and the button undone. His eyes squint while his hands strike a match and hold the rushing flame up to a cigarette protruding from the corner of his mouth. Everything is occurring in slow motion.

"What's happening here?" he asks.

"This one almost fell on the stiff," the guy who is holding my arm says.

"Didn't you see the police lines?" the man with the cigarette asks me.

All I can do is shrug my shoulders and shake my head, because I can't make my voice work.

"They're plain as day," he says, looking back toward the bridge.

He pinches the end of the cigarette between his thumb and forefinger and returns his gaze to me. His eyes watch me intently. The corpse is slid onto a stretcher, and then covered by a black blanket.

"I was chasing my cat," I say finally.

"Really," he says, without smiling.

"This what you're looking for?" asks a fireman who appears suddenly from behind me and hands me the cat, which is meowing frantically.

"That's one of our jobs. Recovering cats," the fireman says to the man with the cigarette.

But the man's countenance doesn't move. He watches me for another moment. I don't know where to start.

"Go on," the man commands. "Watch where you're going next time."

The firemen hoist the stretcher and walk with knees bent toward a police truck. The detective flicks his cigarette down toward the river. A tiny billow of smoke appears on the grass where it lands. The cop gives me a nudge.

"Let's go. What are you waiting for? An invitation?"

He leads me back to the intersection. When I'm in the car, the cat wiggles to escape. A policeman stops traffic so we can pull out and cross Memorial Drive.

"Thanks," Hannah yells to him as we cross the intersection.

"That guy told me they just pulled a body out of the river," she says when we're around the corner.

"It's true," I say. "I almost tripped over the corpse."

"Oh, you're kidding," she gasps.

"No joke."

" Oh, I'm sorry. You didn't hurt yourself, did you?"

"No. Only my pride was injured."

"Oh, come on," she laughs.

"Really," I say. "I shouldn't have been standing up there."

"Was it gross?"

"What?"

"The corpse."

"Oh. Well, it wasn't pretty," I say, trying to appear disinterested.

"Was it gray and puffy?"

"More white than gray."

"My father took me to the morgue once to see a cadaver," she says. "It was very gray."

"Maybe the cold water made this one white," I speculate.

"Poor guy. Did he drown?"

"I don't know. I didn't ask any questions. I think they were mad that I ran in there."

"What did you say?"

"That I was chasing the cat."

"Oh, poor kitty," she says, looking at the cat.

"Oh, swell," I protest.

"And poor Larry too," she says, smiling.

She rubs her hand up and down my sleeve, the same as the way she strokes the cat. Someone behind us blows his horn. Her eyes flip to the rear-view mirror.

"All right, all right," she mutters.

Hannah inches the car through the Saturday crowd in Harvard Square. Up ahead of us a bus comes out of the underground and there's a pop of electricity when it passes under a joint in the overhead electric cable.

"Hannah, let me out here, will you," I say quickly. "I think I'll go over to the Coop bookstore."

She looks at me quizzically, and then pulls alongside the curb in the middle of the Square. After I get out of the car, I hand her the cat, which starts to meow frantically again.

"Oh, poor kitty," Hannah says.

The moron behind us blows his goddamn horn again.

"Hold your water," I yell at him.

"I'd better go," Hannah says and drives off, looking at me in the mirror and waving.

The moron pulls up beside me.

"You have a problem?" he demands.

"Not I."

"Well, fuck you, buddy. You hear me. Fuck you."

"Yes sir, captain," I say, giving him a salute as a moron behind him starts blowing his horn.

"Fuck you," the first moron screams as his car squeals away.

I shrug my shoulders at the second moron, and then cross the street toward the Coop. Life's too short to get excited over assholes like that. Tomorrow the cops could be pulling my bright white body out of the river, and what would people be saying about me, that I got upset over a couple of morons?

I walk up Church Street to the Coop. Inside I go upstairs to the fiction section. Looking at the familiar titles and authors' names makes me feel better.

When Carla was three, I watched her look at a picture book one day. All of a sudden, out of the blue, she got this terrible look of disquiet on her face. It wasn't the pictures. I looked at them. There was a picture of a cow and a rabbit, and some other things like that. She got up and ran off for a minute and then came back with this stupid blanket she always slept with. It wasn't even a blanket really. It was only a piece of cloth material she had manipulated so much that it looked like an old rag. She folded it over three times into a neat little square and held it against her face, just staring out into space. After a few minutes, she put it down and went back to the pictures.

I pull out a book and turn it over in my hands. Stephen Dedalus is a hero of mine. One of my favorite passages in the novel takes place right after a priest tries to convince Stephen that he should accept the calling of the priesthood. Stephen stands on a landing in front of a church, shaking the priest's hand. At that moment a group of singing young men pass by and a segment of time no longer than the glance of Stephen's eyes is stretched over eight lines of prose. I look up those eight lines now, and I feel suddenly like Carla must have felt after she folded her blanket over three times and held it against her face.

Bradley, Sally and I went through a period of adolescent "artistic apprehension," just like Stephen does in Joyce's novel. We would walk around Walden Pond and talk about the nature of things. How did we apprehend a fallen tree beside the path? Would it matter that no other human eyes ever see it? Those kinds of things. My father thought it was pretty goddamn funny.

We'd come back from a walk and he'd say, "Why, look. It's Emily, Henry and Little Bill."

The summer before college, at the Narrows, an equinoctial event occurred that marked the conclusion of our Walden Pond phase. It happened at the summer solstice. A big summer moon had risen from the Atlantic and a shadow from the flagpole in the middle of the lawn cut across our feet. We sat on the grass looking at Pleasant Bay. Then Sally and Bradley got into one of their little squabbles.

"I love the shadows that the moon makes," Sally said musingly. "Don't you guys agree? The flagpole makes a moon dial."

"But it's the beginning of the end, Sally," Bradley said.

"What?"

"The shadow," he said. "Pretty soon the moon will be directly overhead and the shadow will be gone."

"But it won't be dead or anything," Sally said, urgently. "Soon it will come out the other side."

"But there it's just the backside of a shadow," he said in a manner that sounded like he thought Sally didn't know what she was talking about.

"Oh, bunk," Sally cried. "The glass is always half empty to you, Bradley."

"It's not bunk. On this side time is our ally," he said calmly. "It's the fuel for our experience. The shadow is the gauge. On the backside time is our foe, for its only purpose is to mark the passage to the inevitable."

"The inevitable?"

"When the daylight comes, and we depart, Sally," he said, looking up at her with an expressionless face.

"Oh, please, Bradley," Sally cried. "Let's think about that in August."

"We will, Sally," he said coolly. "We will."

So we watched the shadow shorten until it was no more. Then we watched it lengthen until daylight captured it, and hid it from us. And that was the end of our existentialism.

The sales clerk, who sits behind a desk with a sign that says "Information," clears his throat to get my attention. There's a sign on the wall behind him that says "No Reading." I flip some pages to distract him and then slide back into my thoughts.

A few nights ago I had a strange dream about Bradley. We were at the Narrows and I was standing on the big rock at the end of our lawn, looking out over Pleasant Bay. Bradley soared over the water, wearing wings made of feathers and wax. Right away I thought, of course, that the wax was going to melt and Bradley was going to fall into the bay. What happened, however, was that Bradley kept zooming by me with this look of glowering persistence on his face. He was trying to go higher, circling like a hawk, but not making progress. He was flapping his arms like a crazy man.

I knew that look. I'd seen it hundreds of times. When we were kids, he manifested it every time he thought I was about to say we should quit doing something, or that it was time for us to go home. And that was exactly what I wanted to do in my dream. I wanted to yell to him that it was time to go, that he should come down now. So his look indicated more than recalcitrance. It was his defiant refusal to go. It was his resentment over my caution, his anger that I was going to tell him that he couldn't go any higher. And finally in the dream I yelled at him, "It's time to go!" I screamed it at him, in fact. I screamed so loud and hard that I woke myself up.

I'm startled back to the present, either from my dreamed scream at Bradley or from the presence of the old clerk, who is standing next to me all of a sudden.

"Excuse me, young man," he says in an irritatingly nasal tone. "Can I help you find what you're looking for?"

"I doubt it," I say, absentmindedly slamming the book closed, unhappy to be distracted from my rumination about Bradley.

I notice a small cloud of dandruff particles that fall from the his head to his shoulders as he hops back a step from my retort.

"Well, if you gave me a chance, I might be able to find it," he says indignantly.

"Oh, yes. I'm sorry. I was distracted," I stammer trying not to look at the dandruff now, and not really wanting to be rude.

"I can see that. Do you need some help?"

"Well, no. But, yes, actually. Yes, I do. I'm looking for a book about Breughel."

"I don't know that author," he says. "We can look him up."

"Oh, he's not an author," I sputter, incredulously. "It's not a book by Breughel. It's a book about Breughel."

"Breughel?" he says, wrinkling his eyebrows, like an old dog.

"He was a painter."

"A painter, you say?"

"Yes. A painter."

"Well, the art books are downstairs. There may be something there. Why don't I look for you?"

"Oh, that's okay," I say quickly. "I'll go down and look myself."

"Well, if you don't see it, come back and I'll check the catalog."

"Yes. Definitely. If I don't find it, I'll come back."

But he follows me down the stairs. I look around the art section, if only half-heartedly. After a few minutes, he's helping a customer at the cash register near the door. I try to slip past him while he's ringing up the sale. But his bulging eyeballs flip up at me.

"You didn't find it?" he asks, and then looks back at the cash register.

"No, sir."

"If you'll wait a moment, I'll look for you."

"Thank you very much," I say, "but I have to go. I'll come back later."

"Well, I'm here until five," he says, pushing a book into a bag.

"Thank you, sir. Thank you very much."

"Well, good day, young man," he says, nodding at me and then giving his customer a meaningful look.

I walk down the bricked alley. The bricks are so old, they're worn smooth. When I'm walking over them, each brick looks unique. But when I get to the end of the alley and look back, all the bricks look the same.

I turn toward the river like I used to when I was an underclassman. At Mt. Auburn Street I angle left. That's where all the Harvard dormitories start. Actually, at Harvard they call them "houses." It was supposed to be a big deal, that I was in a particular house, and I was supposed to end up being bosom buddies for the rest of my life with the other guys in my house, like Hal and Winkle. It all seems rather contrived, all of a sudden.

I walk along a path worn smooth to the dirt across the corner of a lawn. The next house was mine, and I stand in front of it for a while, trying to conjure up the old feelings. But I don't feel anything, except, maybe, a distant familiarity. I cut across Mill, take a right, and cross Memorial Drive at the footbridge.

People stroll along the banks and over the bridge. A crew rows up the Charles at an even pace, the pacer's beat just barely discernible over the breeze. I lean over the railing and watch the Charles flow under me. Drowning must be pretty horrible, I think, what with the cold water all about you and the last gasp of stale air in your lungs, burning to be free. I don't know how I know this. I mean, I've never drowned, of course. But I have a very clear image of that last second before you give up. In your mind you think for a moment how a mountain climber would cling to a small outcrop of rock on a sheer face, his feet dangling, his fingers slipping ever so slowly, imperceptible to the eye but precise to the feel. Then, your throat burns and the pressure in your chest pushes so hard that the muscles around your rib cage ache. There's a foul gurgle in your stomach. Your eyeballs are hot against the cold water. A last glimmer of hope flashes through your brain that a great wave of your legs and a thrashing of your arms will propel you to the surface. But your arms are too heavy to move, and your legs so limp they can only point the path to the bottom. You think, suddenly, about the mountain climber again. His fingers slip another centimeter. There is snow on the tops of the mountains over his shoulder. The sky is blue and the air is crisp and clear. You close your eyes and you think it's you on the mountain. Your fingers slide off the rock, and in a rushing quiet you glide through the air, the blue of the sky and the white of the mountaintops whirling into magical shapes. And while you're falling, you imagine a man drowning in a river. He slips beneath the surface, the cold water rushing into his throat, squeezing, squeezing, until his buoyancy is gone and his body plummets toward the river bottom.

It's an ugly image, and it makes me think of that poor kid from George's. I wonder, suddenly, whether Hal and I were not somehow indirectly responsible for his death. If we had let the goons take him back to Misha, that is where he'd be right now, instead of on the morgue table. Of course, the opposite could be true. The goons may have finally caught up to him, and that's how he came to be on the river bottom. I'm rationalizing now, I decide. I'm squashing a ridiculous guilt with a preposterous hypothesis.

The crew comes back under the bridge from the other direction. I've been here a long time. The sun is going down. My hands ache from the cold air sweeping down the Charles.

The Medford Square bus is about to leave when I get to the Harvard Square underground, which is lucky because the Medford buses don't run that often. I've waited as much as an hour a few times. Someday they'll extend the Red Line all the way to Davis Square. When they do, I'll only have to walk over the hill.

On the bus I start thinking about Sally, probably because she and I used to ride the bus to Medford Square on weekends when we were in college. Medford Square is where we transferred to the Winchester bus.

A couple of years ago our families spent the Christmas week together at the Narrows. I was in my third year of teaching. Herrick was working in the Office of the General Counsel at CIA. Sally had finished her master's degree the summer before. She was going to Africa with the Peace Corps in March. Bradley was there, also. He had just come from California, from his camp with the migrant workers, we thought, although no one was inclined to ask him.

One afternoon a group of us sat in the living room in front of the fireplace looking at old photo albums.

"Oh, will you look at this," my mother said, pointing to a picture of Sally, Bradley and I when we were very young. "You guys were the three inseparables."

"Looks more like we were the three untouchables," Sally said.

"Let me see that one, Sally. How old were you guys then?"

"About six, I think," Sally said.

"What is that all over you?" my mother asked.

"Mud," Sally said. "We painted ourselves with mud. That was the beginning of my artistic aspirations."

"Your what?" I asked.

"My artistic aspirations. I'm going to be a body painter when I grow up."

"Oh, look at this, Larry! The prom," Sally exclaimed and held up the book.

"Sally was the only girl with two dates," my mother said.

"I was also the only one who knew what was going on," Sally laughed. "Look at Bradley's tie."

"You never did get it right, Bradley," I said, nudging him in a friendly way.

"You mean perfect," Sally said. "The first time he tied it, it was fine. But it wasn't perfect. That's how it got so wrinkled. He kept pulling it out and tying it over, the whole night. Once when we were dancing, he left me standing out there for about five minutes while he fooled with his stupid tie."

"Did you expect me to go with a bum tie?" Bradley asked, scowling.

"Oh, this must be graduation," my mother said. "Here's Sally with Herrick."

"Let me see," Sally and I said together.

"Herrick was always the big shot," Bradley said as he walked out of the room.

Bradley was sullen the entire week, as it turned out. We all tiptoed around him, as if he were a terminal patient in a cancer ward. And the night before we left, when we were sitting in front of the fire, Sally lost it. I can't blame her. She was anxious about going to Africa and he had been particularly obnoxious toward her.

"Bradley," she said. "You've been here for three days and you've hardly said a thing."

After a minute and without even looking at her, he said, "So what."

That really got her going.

"So what!" she yelled. "So why'd you come if all you were going to do was to sit and mope."

He gave her this incredulous look.

"You wouldn't understand, anyway," he said.

"That's because nobody can understand you, Bradley," she retorted.

We were quiet for a few minutes, watching the fire, and then Bradley said, as if to try to explain himself, "You both have something I don't."

Sally refused to speak, she was so pissed off.

So I asked him, "What's that?"

He looked at her when he answered my question.

"You have your teaching, Larry, " he said. "And Sally has her Peace Corps now."

He stood up and leaned against the mantle.

"I don't have anything really. It's like I'm just awash in the bay," he said and waved his hand in a dramatic fashion in the direction of Pleasant Bay.

Sally couldn't keep quiet any longer.

"Should I go get out my violin, Bradley," she said.

"Oh, thanks a lot, Sal," he said.

"Don't thank or blame me," she said quickly. "If you're stuck, sail yourself to shore, Bradley. Grab the line, and pull it in. Wasn't your father in the Navy? What do you expect?"

He sat down, looked at me this time, and smiled.

"Well, the mast line is snapped in the middle, and the pin has fallen out of the rudder joint," he said slowly.

"Oh, give me a break," Sally laughed.

He shrugged and looked away from both of us.

"I know. Pull up the centerboard and paddle in," I said.

"I've lost it," he said.

"Then the tide will carry you in," Sally said.

"The tide is going out," he sighed.

So the whole thing became a big joke. And we could have left it at that, except that Sally can be incredibly stubborn. A little later she came back around at him again.

"So, what's happening with the migrant workers, Bradley?" she asked.

He shrugged.

"Nothing. It's futile. Nothing ever gets finished, and nothing ever gets better," he said.

"Well, sometimes progress is hard to detect," Sally said, trying to sound positive.

But he turned to her suddenly, with his fierce, sardonic look.

"Come on, Sally. That's just an excuse. Save it for Africa, why don't you."

She jumped to her feet and glared at him for a moment before announcing, "I'm going to bed."

He shrugged again.

At the foot of the stairs she turned back to us and said, "You're wrong, Bradley, to think that everything you try to accomplish in life is like running a footrace. Making progress can't be measured that way. Lots of times it happens all at once, at the end."

When he didn't say anything, she whirled around and dashed up the stairs.

After she was upstairs, he looked at me and said, "Maybe she's right. But it doesn't make any difference." Then, suddenly, he flung the magazine he had been reading into the fire and walked out the door.

After the flames died down, I looked out the window and saw him standing in the cold on the big rock with his hands deep in his pockets. I left him out there and went to bed. Maybe I should have gone out to him. But I didn't. I'd heard my mother telling my father once that Bradley's uncle, Captain Bradley Wright, had most likely been a manic depressive. That had made me wary.

When Bradley got angry with himself, he raged like a madman. As kids we accommodated him. We called his manic episodes the "BTs," which was short for "Bradley Tantrums." And we were cruel about it, just like kids can be. The BTs became a family joke. When Carla was three and would throw one of her snits, someone inevitably would say something like, "Man, she's got a bad case of the BTs."

4

THE BACK OF THE THEATER isn't as dark as I hoped because there are two big spotlights at the top of the wall above the stage door porch. A storm is brewing, and I can hear the rumble of thunder in the distance. About thirty minutes ago, when I was still at my house, the moon was brilliant. I turned off all the lights and used the moon's glow to pick out the darkest clothes I had. But by the time I left my house, the clouds had rolled in, and on my way down the hill it looked like a dark cloth had been draped over the landscape.

If I stand in the middle of the theater parking lot, she'll see me as soon as she starts down the stairs from the stage door. The advantage to taking up such a position is that it will give her plenty of time to get used to the fact that I've been waiting for her. Millie isn't the sort of girl who likes surprises. Of course, the disadvantage is that, if she's the last one to leave, all of the cast and crew will see me first, which doesn't appeal to me. So I sit down on an old tree stump in the shadows behind the bushes against the wall of the Drama and Dance Building. When I see Millie on the porch, I can stroll out into the middle of the parking lot before she comes down the stairs.

I can hear on the breeze the orchestra playing the final number. Bevins is an awkward Sky Masterson. His legs are too stiff when he crosses the stage, as if his knees won't bend. In fact, the director had to cut out all but the simple dance routines for him. I know that from hanging around the rehearsals. But Bevins can sing. I have to say that for him.

His red TR3, with its top down, is parked about fifteen yards away from me. It's backed into the space that's just below the stage door porch. I imagine him bursting through the door at the end of the performance. He'd be wearing a leather aviator's jacket and a red scarf, its tails blown back behind him by the breeze. Taking a deep breath, he'd fling his arms out, look at the sky, and then leap over the railing, landing perfectly in his car. As his car roared down College Avenue, just before the darkness enveloped him, he'd hold up his arm and wave a detached farewell to his fans, all of who would have gathered on the back stairs to swoon after his departure.

And where would Millie be when Bevins did his hero stuff? She would run out with the other chorus girls into the parking lot just in time to see the hero disappear into the College Avenue shadows. They would all sigh and wave the elbow-length white gloves they used in their last nightclub number. Suddenly, as the moon appeared from behind a bank of clouds, I would emerge from the bushes and put my arm around Millie's shoulders. The other girls would look at us knowingly and then go back up the stairs into the theater. "Let's go home now, Millie," I'd say in an understanding voice. "Oh, Larry," she'd say. "I'm glad the show is over so things can go back to normal." Then we'd turn and walk, arms around each other, up the hill to my place, the glow of the moon lighting our way.

A breeze shakes some mulberries loose from the bush in front of me. This is the time of year that the berries get ripe, fall off the bushes and stain the bottom of your sneakers red. Bradley and I used to flick them at things. There was a giant mulberry bush in Bradley's yard, right next to his porch. We would sit on the porch and flick mulberries onto the driveway.

Bradley was particularly good at flicking. He showed me his technique once, although I could never do it as well. He cocked his finger back behind the thumb joint and nestled the berry there by bending the thumb over slightly. At the instant before he flicked he straightened out his thumb to make a smooth plane. Your timing has to be perfect. If you forget to straighten out your thumb, you squash the berry against it. Or if you straighten it out too early, the berry rolls around and your shot will wobble off to the side.

Once Bradley and I flicked a few handfuls of berries onto his brother's car. I don't know why we did it, except that the car just happened to be parked in the driveway near the porch. Herrick got really sore when he caught us. Bradley shrugged off his brother's rage in a manner of casual indifference.

"So what's a few dots on the roof, Herrick," I remember him saying.

"A few dots," Herrick screamed, pushing berries off the roof, where most of them had landed. "There's a million of them."

"Who looks at the roof anyway?" Bradley said calmly, rubbing at one of the spots on the trunk with his finger.

"Damnit, Bradley, I spent my own money on this car."

"It's not like it cost a million dollars or something."

"Well, it might as well have, as far as I'm concerned."

"Besides, Herrick. Dad paid for part of it."

"So what? Did he tell you to throw mulberries on the car?"

"We didn't throw them. We flicked them. You want me to show you?"

"Oh, for Christ sake, Bradley! No. Just get lost, will you."

"There's more to life than having a car with a perfect paint job, you know."

"You're incredible, Bradley. You're goddamn incredible."

"Besides, if you weren't standing up there, you wouldn't be able to see them."

"Just get lost, okay! Just get the hell away from me!"

The problem with Bevins's car is that it doesn't have a roof, because the top is down. So, when I flick at it, the berry lands in the passenger-side seat. Pretty soon, I'm experimenting to see how high I can flick the berries and still make them land in the passenger seat. The higher the arc, the worse my accuracy, although my hits far exceed my misses.

The security guard opens the door on the landing, and I can hear the curtain call. He leans over the railing and lights a cigarette. His posture intimidates me, and I decide that emerging from the hedge to clean the berries out of Bevins's car would look suspicious.

After a few minutes, the musicians come out. On Broadway the orchestra plays the reprise while the audience leaves. But they don't do that here. Right after the curtain goes down, the musicians beat it out of the theater, like there's a fire inside. Next, most of the cast and the stagehands trickle out. The guard smokes several cigarettes as he watches them disperse. Some stroll off toward the dorms; others get in cars and drive off.

Soon there are only two cars left in the parking lot, the TR3 and a Plymouth. The security guard flicks his cigarette out over the parking lot. He looks at his watch, then turns and walks into the doorway.

"Time to close up," he yells.

He stands with his hands on his hips. Nothing happens. He turns back toward the lot and folds his arms across his chest for a few minutes. Then he goes inside.

The breeze kicks up for a moment. A car roars by on College Avenue. Just before Veterans Circle, the taillights glow. After a right turn at the Circle, it accelerates along the top of the fields, up toward the Hillside.

Bevins and Millie walk out onto the landing. Behind them are Nathan and a chorus girl, then the guard. They're crowded together at the top of the stairs.

"I missed that line," Nathan says, in a voice that suggests that he's displeased with himself. "Completely missed it."

"So nobody noticed," the girl says, patting his shoulder. "We didn't stop for more than a second. It's as if the line wasn't there."

"It was a whole page of lines," Bevins says, giving Millie a meaningful look. "He skipped over a whole page of lines."

"It wasn't that bad," Nathan says with a defensive tone.

"Well, it confused the hell out of me for a second," Bevins says.

"It was quick thinking on your part," Millie says to Bevins, "to pick right up where he skipped to. If you'd said the response to the line he was supposed to say, everyone would have been confused."

"Guess I saved the show, then, didn't I?" Bevins boasts.

"Oh, it doesn't make any difference now," the chorus girl says, scowling. "The show's over, isn't it? Closed. We can all forget it."

"Hard to forget the missed ones," Bevins says, running a finger down the crease line on the sleeve of his shirt. "They live on in your psyche, don't they?"

"My psyche has more interesting things to do," the chorus girl says, looking at Bevins incredulously.

The security guard wants to close the door, but Millie and Nathan are standing in the way. Bevins moves over to the railing and extends his arms in a broad dramatic gesture.

"What a night!" he says exhaling. "Tomorrow will be a beautiful day in Rockport."

"What are you talking about?" Nathan sneers. "It feels like rain."

Bevins looks at him quickly, and then looks up at the cloud cover. They all look up at the sky.

"Oh, no," Millie cries. "It was so beautiful this afternoon."

"Well, a lot can happen overnight," Bevins says, irritably.

"It sure can," the chorus girl says, saddling up to Nathan. "And who cares if it's raining."

"Goodnight kids," the guard says.

"Oh, sorry," Nathan says, and moves out of the way of the door.

"Wait," Millie says anxiously. "My overnight bag."

She bangs on the just-closed door with her fist.

"Wait a minute," she yells. "I forgot something."

The security guard pushes the door back open. Millie bolts into the darkness.

"Back in a sec," she yells.

"Let's make it snappy," the guard yells after her.

"We're going to go on ahead," Nathan says to Bevins. "We'll see you and Millie at the party."

"Fine," says Bevins.

He turns against the railing, his left foot on a lower stair than his right, his two hands wrapped around the rail that crosses him at an angle, hip to elbow. Nathan and his chorus girl get into their car. Nathan backs it up and the red lights shine on me. I try not to move, suddenly feeling circumspect.

"She'll only be a minute," Bevins says.

"I hope so," the guard responds.

With his hip, the guard bounces the door impatiently. Bevins leans back across the stairs, extending his arm to keep his balance. He lets the other arm dangle free.

"Great football game this afternoon, wasn't it," Bevins says.

"Didn't see it," the guard says.

Millie appears in the doorway and leans with her left hand against the door jam, her arm out straight. She's breathing hard from running up the stairs from the dressing rooms. She looks at the guard, and then at Bevins.

"Richard," she says, puffing. "I should call my mother before we go to the party. There's a pay phone right in here. It will only take a minute."

The guard and Bevins look at each other. Millie tosses her overnight bag to Bevins. The force of the bag hitting him makes him sway a little.

"Hold this for me while I call," she says as she turns to go back inside.

"Let's go, Millie," Richard quickly says. "You can call her when we get there."

"I can't do that, Richard," Millie says coolly, glancing at her watch.

"Gotta get this place locked up," the guard says sourly. "Call from somewheres else."

That was good enough for Bevins. He plods down the stairs. But Millie doesn't move. When he doesn't hear her behind him, he stops. She's clicking her teeth, irritably, like a rattlesnake manipulating its tail.

"Come on, Millie," he pleads. "We'll find a pay phone on the way."

She still doesn't move. He did better getting Sister Sarah to Cuba in the show. What he should say to her is, "Come on or find your own way to the lousy party." That's what I would say.

"There's one right over there," the guard says, pointing at an angle across the side of the parking lot to a wall on the ticket building that's next to the fields. "Works just the same as the one inside."

"Okay," she says, as soon as she spots the phone. "Thank you. Good night."

The guard slams the door. Millie runs down the stairs and across the parking lot. She's wearing a cardigan sweater around her shoulders, buttoned at the top button, with the sleeves dangling free. Beneath that is a white dress with a flappy short skirt and a halter-top. The top of the halter is tied in a bow that sticks out above the sweater. On the back where the dress comes together are two bright red buttons. It's a dress you'd more likely see in July.

Bevins swaggers toward the car, looking like a man who's just killing time. He looks at his watch. He looks at Millie. He sits against the trunk of his car with his arms folded.

"Hurry it up," he says.

She turns around, leans over and squints her eyes. Her hand goes up over her eyebrows. He looks the other way.

"Richard," she yells. "I have to call her tonight."

At first, he acts like he didn't hear her. Then he shrugs his shoulders.

"So go ahead," he says.

"What," she yells back. "Did you say something?"

"I said, go ahead," he yells.

She rubs her arms with her hands. It ruffles the front of the halter, which has three blue buttons down the front, shiny like the red ones on the back, but smaller. The top one is unbuttoned, and the front hangs open seductively.

"If I don't call her tonight, she'll try to call me in the morning," Millie says.

Bevins keeps his mouth shut. He looks up at the sky. He should just tell her he's leaving without her. That's what he should do.

"To find out how the closing night went," she continues.

Still nothing from Bevins. Millie waits. She squints her eyes at him again.

"Since I won't be at my room in the morning, I can't take the chance," she says.

"Okay, okay," he says. "Just call her and let's get going."

She puts a dime in the phone and dials the operator.

"Collect call, please."

She recites the number. The breeze whips her skirt around her legs and she sways her hips to accentuate the effect. But Bevins isn't paying attention.

"Hi Mom," she says. "It went just great."

A gust of wind blows some leaves across the parking lot. They make a scratching sound, which drowns out Millie's conversation. Bevins stands up and slides the leather bottoms of his loafers across the pavement. They make a scratching sound too, just like the leaves. He stands on one leg and bends back his ankle so he can see the shoe's underside. It's amazing how expressive his face is when he runs his fingers across the bottom of his shoe. Just by watching him, I feel the roughness of the sole with my fingers.

I suddenly have a bad feeling about my hapless presence behind the bushes. Whatever is going to happen next, I don't want to be its witness. But I don't see a good escape route. I could scramble out to my left without Millie seeing me, because I could go around the corner and up the dark side of the theater. But Bevins could recognize me. And I can't take that chance. I imagine him saying to Millie, "I just saw that crazy friend of yours running out from behind the bushes and around the corner." Even if he didn't remember my name, she would know exactly who it was.

He bends over the back of his car and looks at a mulberry sitting on the trunk, one of the mulberries I flicked over there earlier. He gets his face so close to it, I think the next thing he's going to do is pull out a magnifying glass. But he backs away and then very priggishly picks it up with his thumb and forefinger and drops it on the ground, like it's a piece of bird shit. Maybe he doesn't know what a mulberry is. I don't know. He pulls out his shirttail and rubs at the spot on the car left by the berry.

The problem with using his shirttail as a rag is that it's hard for him to get close to the car without bending his body into a weird position. He has to bend his knees and arch his back. That's what Millie sees when she looks up from the phone, only she sees it from the back and, unlike me, she didn't see what went before, so it looks like he's taking a piss, right there in the parking lot.

When she coughs loudly, I can see by the look on his face that he realizes he must look funny to her, although I don't think he has a real clear picture of what it looks like he's doing. He stands up straight quickly and starts tucking his shirt back into his pants like a madman. Of course, from Millie's perspective that is only a confirmation of her suspicion. She coughs again.

"No, I don't have a cold, Mom," she says.

Bevins is walking around now with his hands in his pockets.

"I know I was coughing, Mom. I'm just a little hoarse from all the singing."

That makes me smile, despite my anxiety, because I know that Millie can't sing a note. All she did was move her lips, and squeal occasionally. But, it occurs to me, at this point she probably believes herself that she was singing. It's a phenomenon I come across with my students. "So what about your homework," I'll ask one of them. "I did it," he'll say. "Okay, so where is it," I'll insist. And with a blank but solemn look on his face he'll say, "I don't know, but I did it. I really did." They lie about something so much that they convince themselves eventually that what they're saying is true.

"Gotta go now, Mom," Millie says. "I'll be late for the cast party."

She listens to the phone for a second.

"No, Mom. Larry's not going with me tonight. He's out of town this weekend."

She listens again.

"Oh, I'm wearing my long-sleeve madras blouse with my blue skirt," she says.

She looks over at Bevins and holds up a finger, as if to say, "Wait for me. I'll be right there."

"Okay, Mom. I will. I love you too. See you soon."

She hangs up the phone and walks across the parking lot to the car, looking around for a puddle on the pavement. She has the look of a woman about to confront a puppy about his incontinence.

"What in the world were you doing, Richard?"

"Standing here waiting for you. What do you think?"

She looks around at the ground some more. She's got some nerve, actually. Most girls, if they saw their date urinating in the parking lot, would pretend that they didn't see a thing. But not Millie. She's acting like he pissed on her shoes.

"You were standing in such a strange position," she says.

"I was wiping a spot off of the back of my car with my shirt tail."

"Oh, Richard! With your shirt? You should carry a handkerchief. Didn't your mother teach you that?"

She skips over to his side of the car, all smiles, and before he can say a word, she throws her arms around his neck and swings around him in a full circle. He holds her waist. How she changes her mood so quickly is stunning.

"Well, let's go," she says.

Her voice has an impatient tone, as if it were he who caused the delay. But he doesn't say a thing. He just releases her and follows her around the car. He's going to open the door for her, obviously. But at the back of the car she turns around suddenly so that he bumps into her and she falls into his arms.

"Oh," she says.

"Sorry."

"Don't be such a gentleman," she laughs. "I can open my own door."

"Fine," he says as he shrugs his shoulders and releases her.

"Beat you in," she yells.

They scramble to their doors and throw themselves into their seats, like two ducks landing in a pond.

I once saw a lady sit down in a puddle of water on the seat of a bus. When she realized the seat was wet, she looked above her, as if she expected to find a hole in the roof with the rain pouring through. It's what I expect Bevins and Millie will do when they feel the berries.

Just when I expect Millie's face will register that something is wrong, the lights up on the theater wall go out. The parking lot isn't completely dark, because the light on the pole at the other end is still on. But the visibility is suddenly much worse, and until my eyes adjust I can't see their faces.

"What was that?" she asks.

"I guess the guard turned off the lights," he says.

"No, I mean the sound."

"What sound?"

"Like I sat on something wet."

"Can't be. I just had the car cleaned."

"Did it rain while we were inside?"

"There's no water on the hood."

"I need to look."

"We're never going to get there."

"I have to look," she says.

They both get out of the car. Millie walks back a few feet, out of a shadow and into a bright circle of light under the lamp pole. There's a mass of red blotches on the back of her white dress, looking something like a pattern on a batik or a tie-dyed tee shirt. Bevins follows her. His pants are spotless, of course.

"I don't believe this," Millie shrieks.

She twists her torso to look at the back of her skirt. Then she pulls it around with her hands and holds it up to the light. Bevins walks in a little circle trying to see the back of his pants, like a dog chasing his tail.

"Don't you ever clean out your car?" she screams at him.

Because the light is behind her, I can see spit coming out of her mouth as she speaks.

"I cleaned it out this morning," he says. "I don't know how this happened."

"It's ruined," Millie sobs.

"Hey," he says, as he gently puts his hands on her shoulders. "We'll take it to the cleaners on Monday. They'll get it clean."

He strokes her arms and she puts her head against his shoulder, still holding the hem of her dress.

"We're late for the party," she moans. "And it's your house."

"We'll swing by your room on the way so you can change," he says, talking in his theater voice. "It will only take a minute."

I wish suddenly that I were sitting on my couch eating an apple and reading a book. I'm not a person who regrets many things, but I regret intensely my coming to the theater. And I regret the day three years ago that I went to my father's cocktail party and met Millie. I regret the day I was born, in fact.

Millie stands up straight, suddenly, and looks around.

"There's a mulberry bush over there," she says, pointing right at me.

"Too far away," he says.

"The wind, maybe."

"No," he says with an exasperated tone. "They don't fly. They fall."

"Well, I don't know," she says, irritably. "Maybe some kids were playing a prank."

"What's the difference," he says. "Listen to us. We're crying over spilled milk. The damage is done. Let's go on to your house and change."

"No need to do that," she says brightly. "I brought some extra clothes."

She goes to the car, takes off her sweater, pulls out her overnight bag from behind the seats and opens it. Bevins opens the trunk, removes a little whisk broom and brushes off the seats. He's just the kind of guy who would have a whisk broom in his trunk. Always prepared. Millie throws some clothes over her arm and looks around.

"You can go right over there behind that mulberry bush and change," he says, pointing in my direction.

I can see myself when she walks back here and finds me sitting on this tree stump. "Oh, sorry, Millie," I'll say. "I was just passing by." It's a ridiculous situation. My mouth is dry from the thought of having to make such an excuse.

"Oh, I don't need a changing room," she says. "Stand up straight, with your back to the street. You're my curtain."

Her fingers tug at the bow at the back of her neck. She puts the side of her face against his chest and reaches around to the small of her back to undo the two buttons. With her elbows out, and the white dress below, she reminds me of a swan stretching her wings. When she stands back, the dress falls to a ground and looks like a white puddle around her ankles.

Bevins is Mr. Polite. Millie is naked in front of him, yet he only stares at the wall behind me. He doesn't look down at her until she's tucking her purple shirt into her pants.

"Do you want to put that in your bag?" he asks, pointing to the white dress on the ground.

She looks at him. Her hands reach in behind her ears and pull her hair out from under the shirt's collar. She shakes her head around.

"No, silly. It will just get everything dirty."

"Oh."

"I'll worry about it later," she says in Scarlett O'Hara fashion, as she scoops up the dress from the pavement and walks over to the car, where she tosses it into the trunk like it was an old rag.

And before I know it, I'm walking up the hill toward my house. It took them only a second to get back into the car and drive away. Or at least that's how it seemed. I did have a moment to notice as they were driving out of the parking lot that he had his Sky Masterson look of sincerity on his face. But Millie, her purple shirt flashing in the light of the street lamp and her hair blowing out behind her, was no Sister Sarah.

At the top of the hill, the night appears suddenly serene. The thunder that had been rumbling in the distance ceases and the College Avenue intersection is deserted. The silence startles me. Only a few minutes ago, the world was wildly spinning in its rotation. But time is fickle. When I look up into the dark sky, the lightning flashes suddenly, and I see Millie's naked back and Bevins staring at the wall. I will carry around that image in my mind until I die.

5

I DIDN'T EXPECT TO SLEEP after I came home, but I did. Soon after I got in bed, where I had expected to stare at the ceiling and replay Millie's nakedness in the parking lot, the rain began—a hard, driving rain that beat against the windows. And then I slept, although not before I had one bittersweet moment of contentment from the thought that somewhere along the road to Rockport, Bevins had pulled over and was frantically trying to put the top up.

For me, rain can be simultaneously soothing and traumatic, if that is possible. The soothing part is best depicted in memories of the warmth of my small room at the Narrows on those cold summer mornings when I would stay in bed to listen to the rain pound the roof and the ocean rush through the channel that is just outside my window. The trauma occurred when I got out of bed, and the world suddenly seemed dim and my body was a shadow slinking through a heavy shade cast upon the hallway outside my door. I would clutch the rail along the stairs as I made my way down to the living room into a dim daylight seeping through the windows. There my shadow became detached from my body, where it would lurk behind me until the sun came out. The shadows of an overcast day were not my friends.

Perhaps on account of these memories before I fell asleep, I dreamed last night that on a bright, sunny day I sat in a white chair on a lawn that sloped to the beach. Without being able to identify any specific objects or occurrences that gave me the impression, I remember the atmosphere as surrealistic. If a rabbit in a butler's outfit had come around and offered me a cocktail, I wouldn't have been surprised.

I remember the dream quite well, actually. Several couples lounged on the grass beneath a tree off to my right. They were gathered around a large blanket, in the middle of which was a picnic basket. Plates were stacked to the side, a bowl of fruit was in front and a bottle of wine protruded at an angle from the top of the basket, all in the fashion of a still-life painting. A couple played croquet on the lawn to my left. The man wore a baseball cap, and the young woman, who faced the ocean, wore a provocative two-piece bathing suit, with the straps holding up the top being no more than strings tied in a bow behind her neck. She addressed the red ball, the mallet between her ankles, taking aim at a wicket ahead. A short distance from them, a boy was throwing rocks into the waves.

The boy suddenly turned and threw a small rock that hit the woman playing croquet in the head. She dropped her mallet and the man in the cap ran to her. She laid her head on his shoulder, turning her face toward me. Her hair was red, which I hadn't noticed before, and it slanted gracefully down across her cheek and around her chin, making an oval frame for her eyes, which were the color of clover in a meadow. The resemblance was stunning. I say resemblance because one moment I was sure it was she, and the next moment I wasn't.

The dream girl lifted her face off the man's chest to look into his eyes. The top of his cap touched her head when he looked down at her. His hands held her at the small of her back. She smiled at him. Their lips touched gently, like a bee landing on a flower's petal. Then, standing back slightly, his hands slid up her shoulder blades and grasped the loose ends of the bow.

A wave crashed against the rocks, throwing up a plume of white spray. The boy on the beach threw back his head in laughter. The skin on his face was as white as the ocean's foam, his eyes as steely gray as the shoreline rocks. The man pulled the strings. The woman turned her back to him quickly, and the suit fell forward. Caught by the wind, it flapped in front of her. Bare-breasted, her arms glided out like a dancer to a full open position, and she executed a small curtsy. The people picnicking under the tree applauded.

I tried to get up out of the lawn chair and I couldn't. I started kicking my legs in a panic, and suddenly I was on a bicycle roaring down a hill, going so fast I couldn't keep my feet on the pedals. It was my trying to get my feet on the pedals that caused me to wake up, when I realized that I was kicking against the underside of the sheets in my bed.

The sheets were tucked in tight, and now that I think about it, it was the sheets that changed the course of the dream, for they were the restraint that made me think I couldn't get out of the chair. If they had been loose, maybe the dream would have continued and I would have discovered that the bare-breasted girl was Millie and the guy throwing rocks was the dead kid they pulled out of the Charles. With this dream a psychologist would have a field day, as Hannah would say.

My father once described the dreaming process to me as a bucket going down into a well. Dreams happen near the top, he said, which is on the bucket's way down and then again on the way up. When the bucket is in the water, you're sleeping deeply and not dreaming. But what about the water in the bucket, I asked him, although I can't remember what he answered. I hate incomplete metaphors.

Just before the rain started last night, the girl across the street came home, and I heard her talking to her boyfriend. The two of them are as predictable as the dawn. On Saturdays at midnight when I hear a car pull up, I know it's they.

I didn't have a curfew when I was growing up. I have Betsy to thank for that. She gave my parents so much trouble in that respect that they had given up by the time I started going out at night. Betsy never made it in by midnight. In fact, it was almost always about two when she rolled in. Then she and my parents would have a big shouting match and wake up the whole neighborhood. I often wondered why they just didn't change the curfew to two o'clock. I said to Betsy once, "Why don't you just sneak in the window or something. It's your coming in the front door that wakes them up." And she said, "Why should I do that? It's my house too." That shows what the problem was, actually. It wasn't just the curfew.

During my few minutes of consciousness after the girl across the street came home, I recalled Millie's disrobing in the parking lot. If Hal had told me about it, I would have denied the possibility of its occurrence. But, having witnessed the event, I have to say that it was just like her to do something like that. And now, because I think it was so typical, I can't twist the whole affair, and the fact that she was departing for the weekend with Bevins, into something it wasn't. If they had just come down the stairs and driven away, I'd have convinced myself by now that nothing really happened, that he had merely dropped her off at the library. Instead, what I remember is worse than what really happened. Unfortunately, a bad memory is not like bread dough, where the more you knead it, the better the loaf.

And you can't just wash away a memory with soap and water, I think as I walk to the bathroom. In the shower, I close my eyes and let the hot water run over my face. After a few moments my face is numb and my skin is tight. Then the whole sensation rubs away with the towel. Wouldn't it be something if I could do the same thing with my problems? I mean, I could soften them up with some hot water and rub them away with a towel. It would make my life a lot easier.

The phone rings as I'm coming back down the hall. But when I pick up the receiver, there's not a speck of a voice in my throat. I'm like a guppy with my lips flapping at the tank glass.

"Hello, Larry?" asks a voice that is not Millie's, not that I thought it would be. "Is this Larry Brown's residence?"

"Hi Carla," I say, sounding like a frog.

"Larry, are you still sleeping?"

"No, Carla. I just got out of the shower."

"Oh."

We're silent for a few moments. Carla does this sometimes when she calls. I don't know why.

"What's up?" I ask, finally.

"Are you coming over or not? Mom wants to know."

There's some talking in the background that I can't distinguish because Carla covers up her mouthpiece. In a couple of seconds she's breathing into the phone. That means she's ready to continue. With little sisters you have to know the code.

"So what's the occasion?" I ask her, haplessly.

"You know. Today's their party."

She holds the receiver away and yells, "He forgot."

"Carla!" I exclaim, blood rushing to my face.

"What's the matter?" she asks innocently.

"Nothing, nothing," I say, irritably.

"Well?"

"Well what?"

"Are you coming or not?"

"Sure I'm coming."

"Good. We can throw the ball when you get here," she says, excitement rising in her voice.

I was a passive child. When my father said to me, "Let's go to Fenway this afternoon," I knew he meant to stop by the BU library and that his well-intentioned quick stop would take five innings. Carla learned quickly not to accept his saying, "We'll just be a minute." She has him to their seats in time for batting practice.

"But what about the party, Carla?" I ask, deciding that my passive acquiescence to her statement now will turn into hard commitment by the time I get there.

"Who cares about a stupid party!" she squeals.

"Oh, it's not that bad," I say in a big-brotherly voice.

"Mom wants me to wear a dress," she says loudly, mostly for my mother's benefit, I suspect.

"Well that's what girls wear to parties," I say.

"Larry, where do you come from—Mars?"

"What?"

"I'm not wearing a dress!" she yells. "I'll sit in the garage the whole afternoon."

"Carla. Calm down, why don't you," I say, firmly.

"No!" she insists. "I won't."

I let a few moments pass, while she breathes angrily into the phone. Then I quietly suggest to her that sitting in the garage would be no fun and that the likelihood of my playing catch with her would be increased by her accommodating our mother for the party. She acquiesces, and I'm feeling smug until she demands that I get over there right away. I had planned to stop by Millie's house to prove, hopefully, that she had not spent the night out in Rockport after all. Carla was having none of it.

"I'm bored," she cries. "Everybody's running around with dishes."

"So, help them."

"They won't let me."

"Why not?"

"Because I dropped some stupid plate. It wasn't my fault. It was slippery. Dad told me to go outside and play in the traffic."

"He did not."

"He did so."

"He was kidding," I say, laughing at her ingenuity.

"So what. Is that a thing to tell your baby daughter!"

"Oh, brother."

I remind her that I have to take the bus and won't be arriving instantly. After I get dressed, I walk down the hill to Winthrop Street to catch the bus to Medford Square, where there's no one around. While waiting for the bus to Winchester, I get up on the back of a bench and traverse it a few times, arms outstretched, one foot in front of the other. My mind works on making my legs move and my body balance. Self-analysis is perilous under these circumstances.

The bus driver blows his horn at me just before the bus gets to the bench, and I jump down on the seat. I had my back to him and didn't see him coming. A bus horn always sounds so small and tinny, like it should be in a compact car, not in a big, huge bus. The driver looks at me skeptically when I hand him my wrinkled transfer slip, then he bangs the doors closed and pulls out onto the road. His face is stern and unapproachable.

The bus ride to Winchester goes quickly because there are so few riders. Carla is sitting on the front porch with her baseball glove and ball, and she jumps to her feet when she sees me coming up the sidewalk. She has on her red "Sox" hat, through a hole in the back of which protrudes her ponytail. Last summer Betsy cut a slit in the back of the hat and then mended the material so the intrusion looked like a giant buttonhole.

Besides the hat, Carla has on a flowery dress with a bow on the back, white tights and her baseball shoes with the rubber cleats.

"Carla, you look super," I exclaim, using all the enthusiasm I can muster without breaking into a laugh.

"Don't remind me," she says.

"What's the matter?"

"Mom made me wear this, and you tricked me."

"Was it the dress or the cleats that she made you put on?"

"Ha, ha. Very funny, Larry."

"Okay, okay. So, who's here already?"

"Everybody," she sighs. "Who cares!"

I hear a blur of voices from inside, and some slightly louder conversation, although still unintelligible, from a group on the side porch. Over Carla's shoulder I see a crowd of people through one of the living room windows.

"They're the same ones who always come, Larry," she cries. "You know, the ones who talk all the time."

Then she demands we throw the ball around, and it takes a few minutes for me to convince her that we should be going into the party and being polite. Actually, I don't convince her; I resort to the bribery routine again.

"Come on, Carla. We'll throw the ball after the party."

"Promise?"

"Promise. That's the deal."

"Oh, all right, but I'm not going to talk to anyone."

"Okay by me."

The air is warm and stuffy inside, and the din from all the talking makes me feel like I have water in my ear and that I should lean over and hit the side of my head with the butt of my palm. My mother is wearing her bright red and blue plaid dress. Although her hair is streaked with gray, she wears it like a college girl's, shoulder length and pulled back on the sides with two blue barrettes. For a long time her hair was short, in a style I always thought was generic mother and middle age, although I don't mean that in a pejorative sense. In the family album there were many pictures of her with long, elegant hair when she was much younger. The sudden cropping took place when I was about Carla's age, which would have been right about the time

Carla was born. So I've always thought the short hair was her badge of courage for the fifth child. Or maybe it was her scarlet letter.

She squeezes my hand.

"Oh, thanks for coming Larry," she says warmly.

"Are you kidding? Would I miss this?"

"Oh, brother. I can't stand this," Carla says and rolls her eyes, just before she walks off toward the kitchen.

"My sentiments, also, Larry," my mother says. "I'm grateful enough that you came. No feigned enthusiasm is required."

"Well, it looks like everyone is having a good time," I say.

"I think so."

"And you look great."

"Your father says the backside of life is smooth. That must account for my good looks recently."

"I don't understand."

"No. You're too young yet."

"If you guys want to have your secrets, it's fine by me," I say, shaking my head.

"We don't have any secrets," she says, quizzically.

"I was kidding."

"Oh?"

We stand near the front door, which is a couple of yards from the living room. It's not that far away from the guests, but it makes me feel detached, as if we are watching all these people through a glass, like they're fish in an aquarium.

Not far away, Professor Wright stands with five students whom he engages in an excited conversation. He makes long sweeping motions with his hands and arms. And the students' heads gently sway with his gesticulations. Their movements are so subtle, and his are so dramatic. The other guests are clustered into smaller batches beyond Professor Wright's group. They're far more abstract when quickly observed, an odd assortment of geometric forms and colors.

I close my eyes and recreate the scene in my mind. What I see is an impressionistic snapshot that captures the enthusiasm of the moment but not the detail. That's what an experience is, I think, as I stand there amidst the sea of voices and the scent of my mother's perfume. An experience is a collection of perceptions, all of which combine contemporaneously. It's all very abstract, and becomes even more perplexing if you consider the relationship of experience to thinking. There's a vast difference between the spatial attributes of experience and thought. An experience expands or contracts geometrically depending upon the collection of perceptions involved, and your mind will often discern its entire corpus in a single moment, regardless of when the perceptions occur. In fact, an experience could be composed of perceptions that occur years apart. A thought process, on the other hand, is linear; it occurs as time passes, maybe not so slowly as communication or physical activity, but at a noticeable pace, nevertheless. I smile behind my curtain of thought, suddenly perceiving myself as an Aquinas disciple.

"Larry," my mother says, most likely detecting my inner smile. "Earth to Larry. Come in please."

"I'm here, I'm here," I say, quickly.

"Daydreaming, were you?"

"No. Just thinking."

"A penny for your thoughts, then."

"I was thinking about how things often look one way from a distance, and then, when you get close, they turn out different. Do you know what I'm saying?"

"I don't know," she says, giving me an odd look. "Do you mean actually or figuratively?"

"What?"

"Well," she says, "often you can have a first impression of a person that, when you get to know him, turns out to be incorrect. The same is true with a place, or a job. For example, has teaching turned out to be what you thought it was?"

"Oh," I say, "I wasn't thinking so abstractly. What I was thinking about was something like two parallel lines that look like they converge in the distance. You give me too much credit."

"Nonsense," she scowls. "I always underestimate you, and I don't believe you were thinking about two parallel lines. And, by the way, my question about teaching wasn't a rhetorical one."

"Well, perhaps not lines, but things physical, nevertheless," I say, shrugging.

"If it's physics you want to discuss," she says, a little perturbed, "I'm going to pass you off to Sally's father."

"Oh, boy," I laugh. "I give up. What do you want to know?"

Before she can pursue me, however, we are interrupted by a person whom Carla has just let in the door. And then there is a stream of new arrivals, each ringing the doorbell and each being greeted by Carla, wearing her cleats, and escorted to us. To the fifth couple we hear Carla remark that they don't have to ring the doorbell. Can't they see that there's a party inside? My mother laughs.

"Oh, dear," she says. "I'd better take over this job for a while."

And she's off to the doorway with her "Hello, I'm the other Professor Brown" greeting, which makes me laugh. We had a childhood full of Professor Brown jokes. At dinner, after they'd been discussing some obscure topic, one of us would say, "Would the real Professor Brown please stand up?" Or we'd answer the phone and call out, "Professor Brown, it's for you." Betsy loved to run upstairs before they could say "Which one?"

But my mother and father were different in many ways. I came to appreciate that as I got older. On the one hand, my mother would never have a party like this for her students. She hates big groups of people. She doesn't teach freshman classes, where you have to lecture in a big room. Most of her classes are seminars. She likes to have personal relationships with her students. My father, on the other hand, just wants to know as many students as he can. That's why he teaches big classes with current themes. The topics my mother comes up with always amaze me. They're things like "The reasons for the prevalence of ecumenicalism in turn-of-the-century French colonies while the citizens at home were taking their first existential steps toward agnosticism." Now that's a topic.

I remember one Sunday family dinner when my mother and Betsy had an argument over my mother's choice of seminar topics.

"Mom, why do you teach such obscure topics?" Betsy asked her.

"Why, they're not obscure at all. They just sound that way to you because you don't know the area," my mother responded.

"But they have no zing, and they don't sound like they're relevant at all," Betsy said.

"Relevant? Relevant to what?" my mother asked defensively.

"To now. To what's going on in the world today. You know, like the poster in Dad's office that says 'Literature is alive and well.'"

And then, to our surprise, my mother suddenly got angry.

"If history were alive and well, it wouldn't be history, would it? Has the world gone crazy with this 'relevance' stuff?" she said curtly.

"What?" Betsy stammered, trying to think of what she had said.

And my mother continued angrily, "It's the battle cry of your egocentric generation, this term 'relevance.' I suppose I could be a 'pop historian' and uncover all those relevant people of the past who had the vision to seek what you think today is important. But that's not history, that's fiction for narcissists."

Then she stormed off. Poor Betsy didn't know what to do. Finally, she turned to the rest of us at the table and, in a meek attempt to vindicate herself, said, "I didn't mean to start an argument. I just thought she could make her topics sound a little more interesting."

While I was thinking, I must have been wandering between the guests because I am startled when one of my father's professor friends slaps me on the back of the shoulder as I walk by him. The slap on the back is one of those stupid things men do to each other. Women hug each other, and a man and a woman will kiss each other on the cheek. But men slap each other on the back. I've often thought that a simple nod of the head would accomplish the same thing and be a lot less trouble. Of course, if one is lost in thought in the middle of a room full of people, one is not likely to notice the nod. So, there may be a point to the backslapping after all.

My father puts his arm out for me as I approach him. All the while he keeps talking to a pretty brown-haired girl who looks familiar. She's just on the fringe of my memory. I've seen her recently, but I can't remember where. And then I remember that she works in the Medford Library and helped me find a volume of Roethke's poems last week. I was looking for the poem "In a Dark Time."

"Are you smiling, Larry, because you heard our conversation from across the room or because I have the remnants of an hors d'oeuvre on my chin?"

"Hi Dad. Were you telling a joke?"

"Oh, I don't tell jokes," he says, seriously.

"I didn't think so," I say.

"I was talking about Auden," he says to me and then returns his attention to the girl, raising an eyebrow. "There's the smile again. He did hear us. And he's thinking to himself, 'Oh, no. Not that old crusty Auden again. Every year I come to this party and he talks about Auden.'"

"Not so, Dad," I say, indignantly.

The girl stands there with her hands together in front of her, looking at the two of us.

"Hi," I say. "I'm Larry Brown, the only son of this gentlemen you've been talking to."

"No, no!" my father exclaims. "Let me do the honors. How rude of me. Jennifer, this is the one and only Larry Brown, as he says. Larry, this is Jennifer Barrows, one of my new students."

"Jenny," she says, looking at me. "The one and only Jenny."

"Oh, that's good," my father laughs. "Now that we have the family trees pruned, let's get Larry into this conversation. We were talking about 'Musee¢ des Beaux Arts,' Larry. You remember the poem, don't you?"

"Just read it again yesterday," I say.

"That a boy! So what about Auden," my father says. "Is he photographer or commentator? Jenny says photographer, I think."

"Well, not entirely," she says. "I looked up a picture of the Breughel painting. The poem seemed so comprehensive in its description, but I'm not sure all Auden was doing was writing a description of the painting."

"They're not mutually exclusive," I say. "A photograph can make a comment. Where would *Time* magazine be otherwise?"

"So the poem works on two levels?" my father asks, rubbing his chin.

"Maybe three," Jenny says. "Two for the painting and another for the poem."

"How's that?"

"Well, the painting presents a picture, which the poem describes. That's one. Then the painting, by the manner of its presentation, makes a comment on the picture it presents, and the poem conveys the comment. That's two. And then the poem comments on the picture and its comment. That's three."

"That is very thoughtful," my father says.

"So what's the comment?" I say.

"Larry, you're always so quick to get to the substance," my father says. "Sometimes the best part of literature is in the mechanics."

"Don't you like puzzles?" Jenny asks.

"Only when I can look at the picture on the cover of the box before I start," I say.

"You can't just skip over the technique," my father says.

"Don't talk to me about technique! I teach grammar. Remember? And basic grammar at that."

"Larry's a teacher at a public school in Medford," my father explains.

"Really!" Jenny exclaims. "What grade?"

"Seventh."

"Seventh. And you only teach grammar?"

"Well, there's spelling and vocabulary."

"I always loved the poetry and stories when I was in seventh grade."

"We do a little of that."

"There's a lesson in Auden for them, anyway," my father says.

"Wait a minute, Dad. Let me get it. Don't fly too close to the sun or your wings will melt and you'll drown."

"Well, that's getting right to the substance, isn't it?"

"I don't know," Jenny says. "I think the sun melting the wax is only ancillary. Isn't the main action, at least in Auden's view, on the boat? Isn't he saying that we're so self-involved that we skip by tragedy or failure as an everyday occurrence?"

"I'm not sure of that," my father says. "I've always thought that the poem typifies the Platonic paradox."

"Platonic paradox?" she asks, wrinkling her nose, as if the concept made her think of an old sandwich.

"You remember, Larry! Don't you?" my father says excitedly. "It's Plato's proposition that art is nothing more than a copy of life."

"I thought that was Shakespeare," I say. "That art holds the mirror up."

"No, no, no," he shakes his head violently. "You're all mixed up again. And Shakespeare was nothing more than who came before him."

"Well, he was pretty good at telling old stories, if you ask me," I say, grinning at Jenny.

"But that's another topic," my father says quickly, looking at Jenny in an effort to get her attention back on what he is saying. "Look at what Auden does. He weaves into his poem several paintings. *Landscape with the Fall of Icarus* is just one of them. All of them depict 'suffering.' He uses that word in the first line. Remember? That's the Auden technique. He immediately throws out his principal image, and then he slowly puts it in context. And look how he does it. He doesn't just say that people are casual about other people's suffering. He writes the poem in a casual style, as if he were standing in the museum in front of the paintings and speaking in an off-handed manner."

"So we should picture him standing in the museum scribbling some thoughts on a notepad," I say.

"You could look at it that way. Yes."

"I saw Auden read his poetry when I was in college," I say, giving Jenny another grin. "He didn't seem like the sort who would scribble notes in a museum. He was more the type who lined his books up perfectly on the shelves and had his tea at exactly three every afternoon."

"The poem's all the more impressive then," my father says. "To you, that is, after you've seen the poet."

"I know you're setting me up, Dad."

"Oh?"

"We're back to the importance of technique, aren't we? That aspect of literature I'm so inclined to skip over."

"Are we?"

"Oh, come on."

"So we are."

"I'm confused," Jenny says.

My father and I laugh. I can't help it. She's probably taking it wrong. It's not she. It's that to me we suddenly sound like a couple of old farts discussing the theater, like you hear sometimes when you're standing around the lobby during intermission waiting for your date to come out of the bathroom.

"Sorry," she says.

"Oh, no," my father says. "It's a continuing debate Larry and I have."

"Jenny," I say, "Professor Brown believes that in life there are only a small number of truths, all of which were reduced to writing by Homer and Plato."

"And a few others," he says, with some annoyance. "There are the myths, and don't forget the Old Testament. Whatever the Greeks and the Romans missed, the Christians picked up."

"Anyway," I interrupt him, "as for its substance, all modern literature does is rework these few truths. So, it's technique and style that carry the day."

"Larry, you should have been a lawyer or a journalist," he says, disgustedly. "You have slanted my premise in an incredible fashion."

"Wait a second," Jenny says. "Every spring I see the same flowers, but each time I see them differently. Icarus fell into the sea and drowned, right before his father's eyes. Children skate on a pond. A man stands in a museum in front of a wall of paintings. So what if there's a derivative truth. In the moment of occurrence, there's something new."

Her hand glides up and brushes the hair back behind her ear, making her blouse open at the collar and expose her collarbone. She's quite a pretty picture, standing there with her face flushed and her hair still moving from the flip of her fingers.

"Dad," Carla yells across the room.

She leans nonchalantly against the door to the kitchen, even though her voice sounded urgent.

"Is the cheese dip supposed to be smoking?" she asks.

Behind her a cloud of smoke billows. She takes a bite of an apple and shrugs her shoulders before she looks back into the kitchen.

"Excuse me," my father says. "You two carry on."

He runs toward the kitchen.

"Carla," he yells. "Open a window, why don't you."

"Sure. Anything you say," she says, as she walks across the room looking up at the ceiling in an exaggerated fashion.

Jenny laughs.

"Happens all the time," I say to her.

"Really?"

"Last year the punch bowl went over."

"Do you come to this party every year?"

"For as long as I can remember."

"And you talk about Auden every time?"

"No. Not always. I was just kidding around, actually. But I like the poem. I hope it didn't sound like I didn't."

My mother laughs in the kitchen. Jenny looks in that direction and moves her hands to the small of her back. Then she stretches by pushing her elbows out behind her. That makes the blue material of her blouse pull tight across her chest. I can't help looking.

"So, should we talk about Auden some more?" she asks, as she relaxes her stretch.

"Oh, let's not, and say we did," I say.

But I can't unfasten my eyes from her chest. To avert my gaze I rub my temples. The palm of my hand is like a visor on a cap pulled down low on my head, which makes me look at the floor. It makes me look at our feet pointing at each other.

"Are you okay?" she asks, probably dumbfounded at my curious stance.

"Just a headache," I say, quickly.

"I've got some aspirin," she offers.

And I muddle my way out of accepting her aspirin with a fib that I'm allergic to aspirin. She asks, of course, what I do when I have a headache. The hole gets deeper as I frantically try to think of an answer that won't just give rise to another question. Then, it occurs to me that a good cure for a headache would be meditation, although I have no scientific evidence to prove that. I do know something about meditation, however, and I steer the conversation in that direction, from describing my own attempts to how Bradley was deeply involved in it.

"My cousin Bradley was very serious about it. Is very serious, I should say. I think he still meditates."

"But did he buy a book or what?"

"Oh no. He learned it from a guru named Maharishi Mahesh Yogi, who he met in California. They have meetings, I guess. They probably have them at Medford."

"He's the guy with the Beatles," she exclaims.

"That's the one," I say. "Anyway, Bradley went to meetings once or twice a week, and meditated twice a day, morning and evening."

My father is back, suddenly.

"So, I expect by now you have Auden boiled down to his essence," he says, looking at both our faces for a clue.

"Oh, you bet," Jenny laughs. "And you?"

"One less pot to wash tonight."

"Oh, too bad."

"My regret is that I've missed your analysis of the poem," he says. "Give me a synopsis."

There's a thin, chest-level cloud of cheese dip smoke spread across the room, hanging in the air like a summer fog over a swamp. My mother opens a few more windows. Jenny starts right in on Auden again, as if we had been talking about him the entire time my father was gone.

The truth be told, Bradley really came to meditation by way of drugs. They were serious drugs Bradley was doing. I discovered this one summer, when we all gathered at the Narrows in August. Bradley showed me how to meditate then. And he told me about the drugs. What Bradley was doing was acid and the other hallucinogens. For him they were an avocation, not a form of entertainment. He did acid to discover what he thought were new levels of consciousness. He was dropping into a world of self-fulfillment, what he called a journey into the divine, where one came together with all things around him. He was after the peak experience. He was trying to find himself. These were the things Bradley described to me at the Narrows.

My cousin Sally and I weren't babes in the woods. Although not with Bradley's intensity, we had experimented in college as well. We were caught up in the "consciousness explosion" set off by Timothy Leary and Abraham Maslow. And we also searched for the peak experience, although, perhaps, with a bit more parent-instilled trepidation than did Bradley.

In those years, everything was a "high" and everybody was optimistic. We were all going to save the goddamn world. Then the cloud of smoke rose over Hanoi, and, after some symbolic shouting, we walked away. Just like that, we walked away. Our entire generation changed its attitude in one afternoon. By 1972 it was all self-aggrandizement.

What happened to Bradley was that his experimenting with acid got reckless. On each trip he'd try to go a little farther, to get a little closer to what he thought was the perfect state of bliss. And he would never quite get there. So the next trip would be longer until he was staying in a semi-delusional state for days at a time. Then, lucky for him, someone he knew from that group that worked with the migrant workers found him and introduced him to transcendental meditation.

Of course, Bradley pushed TM to the limit, just like he did everything else. I remember how one summer at the Narrows, when we were kids, Bradley and I built a raft and floated it off our small Pleasant Bay strip of beach. We had sawed and painted for weeks, so I was content to swim out to it and spend the day dangling my legs in the water and watching the sailboats tack across Pleasant Bay. Not Bradley. When he wasn't finding imperfections in our work, he was pushing himself to make longer dives by running across the raft diagonally, for that was its longest space, and flinging himself toward shore.

The same thing happened with TM. Bradley saw the technique as the runway from which he could fling himself into cosmic consciousness. As I understand it, when you do TM you sit cross-legged in a quiet corner, imagining a pool of water. The strain of your everyday life ripples the water and prevents you from seeing the bottom of the pool. With a great deal of concentration you supposedly can make the surface of the water calm so you can see the bottom, at which time the secret of life, or some revelation of that genre, will be revealed to you.

One year later, Bradley left the yogi's group to join the Divine Light Mission. He became dissatisfied with them the following year and returned to the migrant workers health organization. He has been with them since then, mainly, I suspect, on account of the coddling by a couple of his coworkers. I received a post-card from him. It had a picture of some bluffs overlooking the ocean on the Northern California coast, and he had scribbled on the back: "Life is good. I have found a small group of brothers and sisters who believe, as I do, that there is a second world all around us, the world of the everlasting soul, that at our choosing we all may be one with. I will come to you one day to show you. In the meantime, peace. Bradley."

My recollection is interrupted when Carla suddenly appears in the periphery of our threesome.

"Dad," she says. "Mom wants you."

She nods her head in the direction of the door, where my mother stands with an older, well-dressed couple.

"Who's that?" I ask.

"That is the new Dean of Fletcher."

"He doesn't look like a dean," I say, looking at him again. "He looks like a lawyer."

"Well, surely he is, wouldn't you think?"

"Whatever he is," Carla says, "he's leaving."

"Sorry, Jenny, but I have to run off again," my father says, before he departs.

Jenny laughs, genuinely, and shakes her head at me as he departs. Carla looks at her through narrow eyes. I start an introduction, but before I get two words out of my mouth, Carla says, "We've met." Then she turns and strolls toward the kitchen.

"So we were talking about meditation before, and your cousin," Jenny says after a moment. "What's his name?"

"Bradley."

"Right. Bradley. He's following the Maharishi."

"Oh, no. Not anymore. He's fallen in with some other group on the West Coast. Same type of thing, it sounds like."

"He's not a preemie, is he?" she asks, her face darkening.

"What's a preemie?"

"Preemies are members of this religious sect called the Path. They have a guru named Misha."

"Misha. Why does that sound familiar?"

"I hope it doesn't. If that's who Bradley is hooked up with, you should talk to him. If he'll even listen to you, that is."

"What do you mean?"

"My brother is a preemie. He gave up everything in his life to join the sect. It's awful."

"What's his name?" I ask, not knowing how to respond to the consternation I see on her face.

"Josh."

"He's older than you?"

"A couple of years."

"Well, was he always the religious type?"

She shrugs her shoulders and looks across the room, at nothing really.

"No. I wouldn't say so," she says, quietly, and avoids eye contact, as we let some moments slide by.

"So, where did you guys come out on Auden?" I ask, putting as much enthusiasm in my voice as I can muster. "Tell me quickly, before he comes back, so he won't discover later that I wasn't listening carefully."

"You weren't listening!" she exclaims, brightly.

"I admit it. And I'm not sorry about it either."

"Oh, that's terrible," she laughs.

"At least, I don't think I am."

"Listen," she says, becoming serious. "We don't have to change the topic."

"It's okay," I say, shrugging my shoulders. "It's a party."

"Really," she says. "About a year ago Josh came back from San Francisco and told my father that he was no longer his son, that he was a child of Misha and would be giving all of his worldly goods to the Path. The look on my father's face broke my heart.

And to his calm inquiries as to what this was all about, Josh kept smiling and saying 'I have seen his light,' or 'Misha has given me knowledge.' That was all he would say, how Misha wished him to do this. My father finally lost his composure and told Josh to get out and not come back until he returned to his senses. I ran after him, out to the front sidewalk, where a bunch of his friends from the Path were waiting in a van. 'How can you do this to him?' I asked. His face showed no emotion, just a stupid blissful smile. It really bugged me. 'That's not my father,' he said to me. 'That was the devil trying to keep me from the Path.' Just like that, he called our father the devil. I couldn't believe it. I wanted to smack him across the face to see if maybe he was hypnotized or something, and I could snap him out of it, you know, like in one of those old zombie movies. That's what he reminded me of. But I didn't, and he just turned around, got in the van and left."

She looks at her shoes for a moment, and then shrugs her shoulders again. Her voice doesn't sound distraught, but I can tell she is, because she keeps shrugging her shoulders. She shrugs them three times in a row.

"So that's it," she says.

"When did this happen?"

"Last year."

"And you haven't heard from him since then?"

"Oh yes," she sighs, shrugging her shoulders again. "Unfortunately we have. A couple of months ago, just before school started my father reconsidered his position and decided to find Josh. So he hired a private detective, and when the detective located Josh, my father went to see him to try to talk some sense into him. But he had no luck. Then he threatened Misha, or someone he thought was Misha. Evidently, it's hard to tell who Misha is. Anyway, my father said he was going to the police, and that he would go to court to have Josh declared mentally incompetent, if necessary. Can you really do that?"

"I don't know."

"Well, it doesn't matter because a couple of days later a lawyer representing the Path—that's what they call themselves. Did I tell you that?

"Yes."

"Anyway this lawyer wrote my father a letter saying that the Path was prepared to contest any legal action that my father brought and that they had hired a psychiatrist who had evaluated Josh and was willing to testify as to his competence."

"That's amazing," I say, shaking my head in disbelief.

"Isn't it? They're very well organized."

"So that's it?" I ask. "There's nothing more to be done."

"Not really. My father talked to his lawyer, and they decided that at the end of the day there wasn't much of a chance, and that it would be an awful process. I guess they even talked to the police down on the Cape. That's where the ashram is. Did I tell you that?"

"No."

"I can't keep track. Anyway, evidently we're not the only ones with this problem. The police told my father that several other parents had tried similar tactics unsuccessfully. The police say they've investigated, and it doesn't appear that anyone is being held in the ashram against his will."

"And you've not heard from him since?"

"No. I mean yes. Oh, whatever," she says, laughing, her eyes sparkling. "I often have this problem with double negatives, Larry."

"That's because you had a bad English teacher in the seventh grade," I say, wryly.

"That could be. Anyway, I've seen him recently. About a week before school started he sent me a postcard. It had this wonderful picture of the moon coming up in a night sky over a desert. It reminded me of one of those big landscape photographs. Oh, you know the photographer, I'm sure. They're black and white, and they're taken in Arizona or New Mexico or someplace like that."

"Ansel Adams?"

"That's right. I'm terrible about remembering things like that. I'll forget Auden's name by tomorrow. Don't tell your father that."

"I won't. But I'm surprised there was an Ansel Adams photograph on a postcard. Did it have a gallery name on the back? Sometimes galleries make postcards for a show."

"Oh, no. On the back it had the ashram's name and address, beautifully printed. 'The Path to God' it said, and gave the address. I'll bring it with me and show you next time I see you. It may not really be an Ansel Adams photograph."

"Okay."

"Anyway Josh wrote on the postcard that life was wonderful, of course, and the rest of that stuff, and then he asked me if I wouldn't visit him for a weekend."

"So, just out of the blue, he sent you the postcard?"

"That's what my father asked. He was suspicious that they were trying to lure me into the ashram and that they would keep me there. He's convinced that Josh has been brainwashed somehow."

"You weren't afraid to go?"

"Well, at first I was, particularly after my father kept going on about Korea, and how they brainwash prisoners. He's been reading about the Moonies and he thinks, I think, that all gurus are in some way linked to Korea. But my mother kept saying, 'He feels bad about leaving. He's feeling guilty. This is just his way of wanting to mend his fences, by contacting Jenny.'"

"So you went?"

"I went."

"And was he mending fences?"

"No. At least I don't think so. We completely avoided talking about our parents. Actually, we never talked about anything serious. We just joked around like we used to, and sometimes he talked about how great it was to be alive, and so on. He had duties around the ashram. I don't know what they were, but he'd be gone for hours at a time. And one of his friends would always come around and visit when he was gone, or take me for a walk. What a beautiful place they have. It's almost like a summer camp. They have their facilities spread out through this wooded area looking out on Nantucket Sound. There's an old big house, so it must have been an old estate. I can't remember whether it's Harwich or Chatham. The postcard said Chatham, but it was only a post office box. I think its Harwich."

"Did they do religious things?"

"Oh, all the time. But it always seemed so low-key and they never pressured me about them. For example, every night they would gather for 'satsang,' which was a time for the older, more experienced followers to impart Knowledge to the others. That's with a capital 'K.' They have all these words that are displayed on posters with a picture from nature, like the postcard picture. And when they say them you can always tell they mean them with a capital letter, like Knowledge, and Truth and so on. Anyway, at the satsang almost everyone had an experience to tell about his or her journey down the Path. Capital 'P.'"

"So you were Impressed? With a capital 'I.'"

She laughs and tosses her head to one side. Then her hand comes over and briefly touches my sleeve.

"Yes, I was impressed!" she exclaims and her eyes twinkle for a moment before she goes on. "Saturday was such a nice day, and the satsang was so inspiring, that Saturday night, when I lay down, I had this unbelievably peaceful feeling, and I slept better than I'd slept in a year."

"And they didn't try to make you stay? Josh didn't even suggest it?"

"Oh, no. Not Josh. But on Sunday morning, when Josh went off for his duties, one of his friends came around and took me down to the beach. It was such a beautiful day, and he was such an interesting guy. He wasn't at all like the others, who all seemed to be so wrapped up in the whole Path thing. At the time I thought he was Misha, because he acted so casually, and everyone who passed us bowed to him. But now, I'm not sure. When he talked he didn't use any of the words with the capital letters, and he knew about so many things. Anyway, after a while he said, 'Many of the others think you would be a fine candidate for the Path.' I told him I didn't think so. He looked at me for a long time, until I became frightened. Then he said, 'I think you're right.'"

She shifts her weight, and looks off into the distance for a second, as if she were suddenly back at the ashram, and the events had just occurred. For a time I'm caught up in her intricate features, and the waves of emotion that emanate from her.

"So that's it? He didn't say any more?" I ask, finally, interrupting her recollection.

"No," she says quickly, but struggling to make her eyes focus.

"Nothing?"

"Well, not about joining the Path," she says as she focuses on my face again. "On the way back from the beach he talked about how big a problem the poison ivy was in the summer, and how the ashram had to buy calamine lotion by the case."

"And Josh didn't ask you to stay either?" I ask, feeling, suddenly, from all my questions, like Dick Cavett.

"No. And that's just it. I think that's what made me suspicious. It was as if they told him not to ask me. The whole thing had this air of being rehearsed, except for that one walk on Sunday with guy I thought was Misha. He didn't even tell me his

123

name. I'm sure he didn't. Anyway, I had a wonderful time, but I also left with this twinge of mistrust."

Out of the blue, I remember the two goons at George's, and the kid clamped onto the table who didn't want to leave with them. Then, as I'm about to exclaim to her that I remember where I've heard Misha's name before, I hear "Larry Brown, my boy," called out behind me, after which I receive a slap on the back delivered with such force that I trundle forward into Jenny, like a sack of potatoes falling off the back of a truck. My father and the perpetrator are laughing like a couple of madmen, and I'm flustered and embarrassed.

"This is Professor O'Neill, Jenny, in case you haven't been introduced," my father says as I untangle myself.

"Good god, man," O'Neill says to me after he shakes her hand. "A wind could blow you over. Don't you eat nowadays or is teaching your only passion."

"Just too busy to eat," I say, struggling to be good-natured.

My father continues to be amused by the mishap. He rocks from heels to toes with a silly grin on his face until he notices my imperfectly concealed consternation. Jenny straightens her blouse.

"Well, we didn't mean to interrupt, and we'll be on our way," O'Neill says, looking at the two of us, but not really making any move to leave.

"Nonsense," my father says, putting a hand on my shoulder in a manner I believe to be apologetic. "They were just talking about Auden."

"Good lord," O'Neill says. "Not that crusty old fart."

"That's the guy," I say, watching for the pained look to come across my father's face.

"But better," O'Neill goes on, "than that old British pervert you were talking about last year. Summers Somebody, or something like that."

"Somerset Maugham," I volunteer, glancing at my father in a manner suggesting ambivalence over his apology.

"That's him," O'Neill bellows.

"That's he," I mutter, drawing a quizzical look from O'Neill and a cross look from my father.

"Somerset Maugham!" Jenny exclaims.

"Oh, don't listen to him," my father says to her. "He's nothing but an Irish rumormonger sometimes."

"The Kingdom's fields have been sown with pansies, I tell you," O'Neill mutters.

"So say your friends from the north," my father says.

"So they do," says O'Neill, gloomily. "So says my friend Lenny Bloom, the poor bastard, and that tart to whom he has the sad misfortune to be married. Moll?"

"Molly Bloom," I volunteer again, not to be helpful but to claim some small amount of retribution for my father's amusement over my earlier discomfort.

"That's it. Molly Bloom," says O'Neill in a hushed voice, as if Joyce's character were standing in the next room. "Now there's a wicked woman for you. You have to watch out for the stage performers, laddie. They'll diddle you every time."

He winks at me, and before I can object, Carla walks up and hands him a plate of hors d'oeuvres.

"Oh, you're such a sweet child, Carla," he croons.

"Oh, brother," she says, looking down at her feet.

"Professor Brown, you've done justice to the saying 'Practice makes perfect,'" he says, looking from me to Carla. "She's as close as they come."

"Well, bye," Carla says, and walks away, as O'Neill turns his attention in Jenny's direction.

"And what connection have you, young lady, with this rogue?" O'Neill asks, nodding his head in my direction.

"Oh, we just met," Jenny says. "I'm a student in one of Professor Brown's classes."

"Then perhaps I've come to your rescue," O'Neill says.

On his plate are a tiny hot dog, a stuffed mushroom and two Ritz crackers with an orange and purple swirled substance on them. I imagine Carla slopping the stuff onto the crackers, like she was spreading glue on a piece of construction paper. "Oh, they're going to love this!" she'd exclaim in her sarcastic way, shaking her head from side to side and curling her lip. O'Neill picks one up.

"Delicious looking. Want to try one, laddie? We need to fatten you up," he asks, glancing at me before he pops it into his mouth.

I shake my head and he chews for a moment.

"Well, then, Mr. Brown," he says, finally, "since you're not eating, tell us all what matter of import you were about to impart when we walked up."

"Matter of import?" I ask, in as innocent a manner as I can muster.

O'Neill is a psychiatrist by training and he is cagey in the use of his populous manner. He never forgets what you say, and he always comes around to probe a little deeper about what you said earlier. When your defenses are down, he surprises you with a question out of the blue. And then, before you know it, you're chatting away about things you swore you would never talk about. Suddenly, you're a monkey performing for a banana.

"Yes, laddie, the matter that had your attention so captured when I arrived," he says, raising his eyebrows.

"We were talking about my brother joining a cult," Jenny says.

"Which one?" he asks, mercifully directing his inquisition away from me.

"The Path to God," she says.

"Ah, the Path. Misha's flock."

"You've heard of it!" Jenny exclaims.

"Definitely. The Path is a notorious, charismatic cult. It's very popular nowadays."

"And you know something about it?"

"I know a little," he says. "Cults are popular in psychiatry circles. From an academic perspective, of course."

"No. I mean the Path."

"Yes. Them too. But most of the cults that are so popular today are very much the same. Oh, they differ on the surface in their ideologies, or they put a different face on it, but they all have many attributes in common. You're interested in cults because of your brother, are you?"

"Yes. I've looked for some books in the library, but I haven't found much," Jenny says, seriously.

"Oh, no," O'Neill laughs. "You wouldn't find a book about the new cults. But I've seen an article in a psychology journal. I know I have. Take a look in the Guide. And I know some graduate students who are writing papers on the topic, if you're really interested. There will be a book out before long."

"Oh," Jenny says in a defeated manner, as if she had expected to find a book that would provide her with a cure for her brother's absence.

"Let's see," says O'Neill, sensing her disappointment. "Maybe I can come up with a few of the common attributes?"

"Oh, good."

"Let's see if I can get them all."

He lifts his hand and looks at it intensely, with this theatrical look of concentration on his face. He's about to count on his fingers. To hide my disbelief, I extend my focus from his hand out to the room beyond, where, through a space in the crowd, I see Carla trying to get my attention. She holds up her baseball glove and points at it. My eyes snap back to O'Neill when he rotates his wrist and grabs a finger with his other hand for emphasis. He launches into his presentation on cults.

As he drones on about a cult creating its own little social system, I look around the room. The inhabitants have all divided into small groups like ours, many of them centered around a professor, who, like O'Neill, is doing most of the talking. After a statement by O'Neill about cult members being highly suspicious of people from the outside world, Jenny's eyes widen.

"That doesn't sound right," she interrupts. "I visited my brother recently and I felt so welcome. Everyone at his ashram seemed to accept me immediately, and I wasn't ever recruited."

"You were in their ashram?" O'Neill asks in a surprised tone. "That's a little unusual, because they're usually closed to the outside world. Even in the case of a recruit, by the time he gets there they've spent quite a bit of time indoctrinating him. Anyway, in your case you may have simply been taken in by the cult's recruitment technique."

Jenny looks puzzled. O'Neill grabs two of his fingers and continues on his discourse. When he works in a reference to Freud's work on crowd behavior, my attention shifts to Jenny. I observe that on her round face, her eyes and mouth compete. I can't recall having ever seen a face with two notable features like hers. After some careful scrutiny, I decide that Jenny's mouth has the commanding position. I don't know if its the fullness of her lips or the width between their corners, but her mouth seems to me to be so prominent that she is unable to conceal even a fleeting thought. The curve of her lips bends as O'Neill talks. Are they displaying concern for her brother, brought to the surface by O'Neill's words? Or is this curve only an unconscious body movement caused by some unconnected stimulus in the room, such as the acrid smell from the kitchen of the burned cheese dip?

She looks over at me briefly, and her lips bend slightly in the other direction, before she moves her eyes back to O'Neill. And I feel, suddenly, that I missed something, that by watching her mouth I missed what her eyes were saying. It's as if she asked me a question that I didn't quite hear.

"I wish I knew whether it's what he really wants," she interrupts O'Neill again. "I just don't know. He says he's happy, but something seemed so—so wrong."

"It could be that something is wrong," O'Neill says, taking a deep breath in preparation for a launch into the remaining portion of his lecture, and then exhaling, suddenly, when he notices, as I do, the frightened expression that falls upon Jenny's face. "Oh, no," he says in a reassuring tone, "I don't mean wrong in the sense that someone is perpetrating some evil on your brother or is trying to do him physical harm. No. I mean wrong in the sense that his personality has somehow become out of whack."

"Did you say, 'out of whack,'" I say with a forced grin, trying to change the somber direction the conversation seems to be traveling.

"It isn't a very scientific term, is it," he mutters.

"It's as if he's become a different person," Jenny says, her eyes unfocused by her thoughts.

"Sudden personality change," O'Neill exclaims. "All at once a person is someone else, as if their identity were suddenly transformed into the cult's identity."

"How can that happen?" I ask. "Is it some type of hypnosis or brainwashing?"

"Sudden personality change is not hypnosis, because it's not a temporary state that can disappear with the snap of one's fingers," O'Neill says, and snaps his fingers for effect. "Brainwashing is probably closer to what I'm talking about, but it's been used in such a negative connotation lately, you know, in connection with that whole Korean episode with that ship. What was it?"

"The Pueblo," I say.

"That's right. In any case, I think a better term would be 'altered consciousness.' It's a term accepted from a clinical perspective, and it has been used for a long time, as far back as William James, and maybe farther," O'Neill says, as he wrinkles his forehead and stares into the distance, demonstrating a batch of stereotypical scholarly affectations.

"I don't understand," I say. "How can someone's consciousness be 'altered'?"

"Oh, well, let's see" he says, pulling himself out of his distraction. "First we need to understand 'consciousness', don't we?"

He revs up to launch back into the subject, but Jenny is too quick.

"I'm not sure I see how this is relevant to the Path," she says. "I agree that my brother is really into what he's doing, but I wouldn't say he was in a trance or anything."

"Oh, no, it's not so noticeable as a trance," O'Neill says. "Let me ask you. What is it that your brother is 'into'?"

"Finding peace and harmony is what I guess he would say. Or, wait. I remember now. He talked about getting free of negative emotions, and how good he felt, how free, how full of energy afterward."

"Being enlightened," I say, remembering that Bradley told me once that he escaped from his negative emotions with his meditation.

"You're replaying the message," O'Neill chuckles. "It's the message from all of these cults, that if one transcends all of the ugliness in the world, one will come to peace with it and reach that wonderful state of 'cosmic bliss,' or, in the radical Christian sects, the state of being 'saved.' In the case of the Path, the state is induced through four stages of meditation at the end of which there is an intense bright light. The light, of course, represents God and you travel down the path, that is, go through the stages, to reach him. Hence, the name, the Path to God. Everything about the world glows after that experience, that is, after you reach the light, because it radiates through you and you become a part of it."

"But it's as if we no longer exist," Jenny says, her voice unsteady. "Josh has totally and completely turned us off. And for that? For a bright light?"

O'Neill doesn't see her distress this time.

"I've heard this altered state referred to as an impenetrable wall of self-proclaimed joy," he says, looking around as if he is speaking to a lecture hall and not just the three of us. "From a clinical standpoint, it's extremely interesting, and I'm hoping to see some studies done shortly. In fact, I have a graduate student ..."

His voice trails off when he notices the tears, which I had watched well up in her eyes, stream down Jenny's cheeks. He shuffles his feet, not knowing what to do. My father steps around me, and puts his arm around her shoulders.

"Surely we can find another topic," he says. "Even Auden wasn't this bad."

"I'm okay," Jenny says.

"I've had a little personal experience with altered, I mean, personality changes in cult members," O'Neill says slowly, "and I know it can be a frustrating experience for family members."

"Oh," Jenny says, "you mean someone in your family has gone through this?"

"No, no, not so personal as that," O'Neill says. "I recently met the parents of two Yale students who hired a man to bring them back from the Path's ashram."

"What do you mean 'bring them back'?" I ask.

"Well, he kidnapped them, actually."

"Kidnapped them?" Jenny asks, incredulously.

"Yes," O'Neill says, seriously. "It was in all the headlines a few months ago. The two Yale students had dropped out of school to join the Path, and their parents, after they had tried everything else, hired this man—his name is Sam Henry—to get them back. Mr. Henry has evidently developed quite a reputation for this kind of thing. A couple of years ago his son was almost carried off by a cult in California, and he was so appalled by what he learned when getting his son back that he quit his job, a very good job too, I think, being an urban planner or something like that, and took up what he calls "deprogramming" cult members. I saw him testify at his trial, and he is quite an impressive man."

"He was on trial?"

"Yes. Mr. Henry was being prosecuted for kidnapping and assault."

"But that's preposterous," Jenny says.

"Oh. It was quite a show," O'Neill says. "Didn't you read about it in the papers? Even the media seems to be against him. They took up the district attorney's claim that he was impinging upon the students' rights to freedom of speech and religion."

"Why were you there?"

"Actually, I was testifying as an expert witness, a psychiatrist, in support of Mr. Henry. Interestingly enough, Mr. Henry's defense was being provided by a group from Yale, and I was appearing at their request. Yale is my alma mater, you see, and . . ."

"Dad," Carla, who tugs on my father's sleeve, interrupts. "Mr. Levine was looking for you."

She nods her head to the right and he looks behind her.

"Jack," he says. "I thought you were going to be a no-show."

"Better late than never," he says, looking uncomfortable on account of the sudden attention the four of us pay him. "My god, I hope I haven't stopped anything at a critical time."

"Oh, not at all," my father says, amiably. "In fact, you're just in time. We're just into your field. Joe was about to tell us about a trial at which he testified."

Jack Levine dated my sister Betsy when he was in law school. They were a complete mismatch, as it turned out, because both of them were so opinionated. Jack would come over for dinner and they'd spend the entire meal picking at each other. If he said something was black, Betsy would say it was white. No matter how trivial the topic was, they'd treat it like it was the death penalty issue. Even when they broke up, they bickered over the reasons why they were breaking up.

"Well, proceed, please," Jack says.

"We were having a fascinating discussion about cults," my father says.

"Interesting," Jack says in a manner that leads me to think that we may be in for an entertaining confrontation between a psychiatrist and a lawyer.

"Joe was about to tell us about the trial in New York of a man accused of kidnapping a couple of cult members," my father says.

"Black Lightning," Jack says. "You're talking about Black Lightning."

"That's right," O'Neill says.

"Black lightning?" I ask. "What's that?"

"That's how the members of that religious sect refer to the kidnapper," Jack says.

"That's what they call Mr. Henry," O'Neill says.

"What was the name of that sect?" Jack asks.

"The Path to God," O'Neill says.

"Right. The Path. And the judge threw the book at him, too. Didn't he? The guy deserved it."

"Well, I don't know about that," O'Neill says.

"What do you mean, Jack?" I ask. "It sounded to me like he was rescuing those two Yale guys."

"Bullshit," Jack says.

"There were equities on both sides," O'Neill says, defensively.

"Nonsense. This guy was attempting to prevent them from expressing their beliefs. You know, the First Amendment. You've heard of it," he says looking at O'Neill, with the tight-lipped smile that I remember seeing across our family dinner table when he and Betsy were debating.

"There was an issue of mental competence," O'Neill says.

"Only an academic one," Jack says, raising his eyebrows. "That must have been your testimony regarding altered states of consciousness."

"Well, yes, and I think the phenomena deserves study," O'Neill says, curtly.

"Sounds like science fiction to me," Jack says, smiling now at Jenny.

"You can make fun of it, Jack," O'Neill says, "but a joke is never a cogent response and usually only betrays the inclination to avoid an issue."

"Oh, Shakespeare," my father says, which draws a puzzled expression from O'Neill.

"You're right. I apologize," Levine says. "But the psychiatrist who testified on behalf of the Path administered a battery of psychological tests and stated that he found the boys' mental competency to be unquestionable. Under those circumstances I cannot see how this forced 'deprogramming,' as it was called, is anything more than an interference with their rights to practice the religion of their choice."

"Well, forced deprogramming was an unfortunate characterization," O'Neill begins.

"Wait a minute," I interrupt, unable to stop myself. "You've made a giant leap of faith, Jack. You said the 'religion of their choice.' It could be that the Path is as coercive as you accuse the deprogrammers of being."

"The boys testified themselves, Larry," Jack says, "that they were members of the Path under their own free will."

"So, what if they'd been programmed to say that," I respond, feeling a little unsure of myself. "Maybe they even believe it, but not really, in a free sense."

"Oh, come on, Larry. You mean they were being tricked into believing something?"

"Brainwashed," I blurt out, hoping that O'Neill will come to my aid. "Like in Korea."

"We already determined that they were mentally competent," Jack says. "Are you disagreeing with that?"

"No," I say, worrying that I am going to paint myself into a corner. "But I think that there's something you're ignoring. I think you can be brainwashed and still be perfectly competent to make your way through life. You can still say things with conviction. Look at the crew of the Pueblo."

"Actually," O'Neill says, coming to life, "that was exactly the point of my testimony, Larry, although I don't like referring to it as 'brainwashed.' The state of consciousness of an individual can be altered in such a manner that his freedom to choose is taken away. In fact, there are documented cases of prisoners of war who, when liberated, didn't want to leave their captors."

"It's a distinction without a difference," Jack says.

"No it's not," I say. "I think there is a fundamental right to freedom of thought that supersedes the right of free speech. There must be. The right to free speech is meaningless without freedom of thought. And it could be that the freedom of thought was being robbed from these individuals and we failed to discern the theft."

"Sounds like a good argument, Larry, but I'll tell you why it's not. You can't determine it, this thing you call 'freedom of thought.' Even if I were to agree with you that a person could be robbed, as you say, of his freedom of thought, which I seriously question, I don't see how you could set any kind of standard that one had been so deprived."

"Well, who cares about some crummy standards," I say, emotionally. "Is a wrong a right just because you can't make up a lousy standard?"

Jack laughs at my ineloquence, but I'm worked up enough that it doesn't bother me. I can feel my heart beating in my throat. For an instant I remember the altercation at George's where I was so calm. The contrast is a bit unnerving, but I recover.

"Larry," he says, "your wrong may be someone else's right. We don't live in a vacuum."

"But it's clear from the way the Path works, isn't it? If those guys were really free, they wouldn't be so confined, so—I can't think of the word."

"So indoctrinated," Jenny says.

"Right."

Jack looks at us for a moment, and then shakes his head.

"You're making a value judgment, aren't you Larry?" Jack asks.

"How's that?"

"You're confusing your distaste for the Path's religious practices with whether they should have the freedom to conduct those practices."

"I don't know. I don't know if I really find their practices distasteful. But so what? Suppose one of their practices was to sacrifice a co-ed at each full moon. Do they have freedom to do that?"

"That's a bad example, isn't it? Nothing about the Path's practices is violating a law. They don't hold anyone against their will."

"Maybe not physically," I say.

"Maybe not any way," he retorts. "The police investigated. They conducted interviews at the ashram. In front of their own parents the boys said they wanted to go back to the ashram."

"You can't tell just by asking," I say.

"Oh, come on, Larry. How do you tell then? Should we administer a polygraph? Do you think they're lying about their own freedom? And, let me ask you this. If they were all being held against their will, and there are no armed guards or barbed wire, why is it necessary for Black Lightning to kidnap them? Why don't they just pack up and walk out?"

"I already said why," I say, uncertainly. "Because they don't realize they're captives. They don't know any better."

"You say that," Jack says, "but it defies logic. Should the law step in and prosecute the parent of the adult child who is too insecure to leave home?"

"It's not the same thing," I say, looking at O'Neill for help.

"It isn't?" Jack asks. "How is it different?"

"Well, it stinks," I say, unable to think of anything better.

"Spoken like a true barrister," Jack laughs.

"I not sure it's all that funny," I say, which removes the smile from Jack's face. He probably remembers that I rarely became involved in any of the arguments around our family dinner table. I left that to Betsy. I continue, "Those two guys from Yale could easily have been friends of yours or mine, Jack."

"I share your empathy, Larry," he says in a compromising manner. "But, even if they were friends of ours, are they in mortal danger? Does society have some duty to protect them? I know that you rail against my insistence on standards. But we need some basis for determination of when an individual must be protected."

"I don't know. But suppose for a minute I'm right, and there is some form of psychic coercion that holds them in the Path. What's to keep this power from some more nefarious use?"

"Larry," he says. "Perhaps you're blowing this out of proportion. They're just a bunch of kids chanting and selling flowers in airports, or whatever they do. It won't last. They'll grow up, and pretty soon the ashrams will fall apart. They'll fade away just like most of the sixties flower children have faded away."

"I don't know," I say, unwilling to back down, although unsure about whether my passion grows from any logic. "What if Misha is some crazy guy who tells them all to drink Kool-Aid laced with cyanide, and they do it? We'll all be responsible."

"Larry, don't you think you're getting a little carried away?" my father says, as O'Neill slips away toward the food table.

"Actually, as I said before, to some extent I share your sentiments, Larry," Jack says. "But how can you permit a kidnapping on account of sentiment? If you determine justice by sentiment, you wind up with chaos."

When I look over at Jenny she has a perplexed look on her face, so I shrug my shoulders, unwilling to continue my failing argument. In fact, I'm not sure why I'm steamed up over the topic; this was about Jenny's brother. And it pisses me off that O'Neill just abandoned me to Jack's clutches.

"God. Did you hear me?" Jack says and slaps his forehead with a theatrical flourish. "I sound like the voice of the establishment. After all those years of berating it, I've turned into it."

That draws some polite laughter from Jenny and my father, who I am sure are relieved to find an expeditious end to the discussion. They move toward the food table. Jack puts his arms around my shoulders.

"So, how's the teaching going this year, Larry," he says with a friendly deference.

"Oh, not bad," I say. "The kids are good. The administration stinks."

"That's the name of the game, unfortunately," he sighs. "And how about you?" he asks Carla, who is standing next to us, wearing her baseball cap now.

"School stinks," she says to him, and then turns to me.

"Are you ready yet?" she asks me, as she pounds the ball into her mitt.

"This looks serious," Jack says.

"It is," Carla says. "You want to come? There's an extra glove in the garage."

"No. I'm going to find the food," he says.

"It figures," she says.

"What do you mean?"

"When you're not talking, you're eating," she says. "Parties are stupid."

"You know what. I think you're right," he laughs and pulls the cap down over her eyes.

"You do!" she exclaims as she pushes the brim up.

"I'm afraid so," he sighs.

"Then why do you do it?"

"Because I'm hungry," he grins. "That's what happens when you get older. All these things get more important."

"Oh," she frowns. "I'm never going to get old."

"I hope you're right," he laughs.

"I am right."

"Anyway, I'm too hungry to talk about it anymore," he says, grinning at me as she tosses him a look of disgust.

"Take it easy, Larry," he says and, after winking at Carla, who sticks out her tongue at him, he walks over to the now-crowded food table.

"How stupid," Carla says, and then looks at me. "Well, are you ready or not?"

"Oh, I don't know, Carla," I say.

"Come on! Now what's the matter?"

"I'm kind of bummed out."

"What do you expect?" she almost shouts. "Standing around in there with all those toad brains."

"Keep it down," I say, looking around. "What's a toad brain anyway?"

"Look at them, lots of brains, maybe, but they all look like toads hopping around in there," she says, her voice rising again.

"Not so loud, Carla. Anyway, you don't give them a chance. They're not so bad. Besides, the expression should be 'brainy toads.'"

"Stop talking like my smart big brother," she cries.

"I'm not talking like that," I say, indignantly.

"You are too. And you're a toad brain yourself. So there," she yells at me before she stomps off to the kitchen.

I wander to the front door, ignoring the people who are casually looking at me on account of my little altercation with Carla. Jenny and my mother are shaking hands.

"Leaving so soon?" I ask.

"I'm afraid so," she says, pleasantly. "I have my roommate's car and she needs it at five."

"Well, we're glad you came," my mother says and opens the door.

My mother's action stirs a memory in me. A few years ago I met Millie at one of these mixers, and my mother did the exact same thing. She opened the door for her right after saying, "We're glad you came." The memory distracts me and I awkwardly try to walk out the door at the same time as Jenny.

"Maybe you could give me a ride back to campus," I say when the three of us are finally on the porch.

"Sure I can," Jenny says.

But I had not seen Carla sitting on the lawn. She's tossing the ball back and forth between her hand and her glove, and she won't look at me.

"Toad brain," she yells as I start to walk down the sidewalk with Jenny.

"Carla, come on inside," my mother says.

Carla stands up and walks by me. The sun has turned the treetops in our front yard orange. Jenny's blouse is filled up with the breeze.

"Thanks anyway," I say to Jenny at the end of the walk. "I'm going to stick around a little while longer after all."

As I go back up the walk, Carla comes out on the porch with an old baseball glove of mine. It's as if she knew all the time that I wouldn't leave.

"I found this in the garage," she says.

"You knew I wouldn't leave," I say to her.

"Of course. You'd feel too guilty. That's how big brothers are."

"But, I'm not a toad brain anymore?"

"So what if you are," she says and throws the ball to me.

6

A FEW HOURS AGO I went to sleep with the phone on my chest. It's not something I ordinarily do, but I was convinced that Millie had tried to call me just as I was arriving home from my parents' party. I heard the phone ringing when I was on the porch downstairs, about to unlock the door, but I didn't reach it in time because I dropped the keys several times and tripped on the stairs. When I pushed through the door into my bedroom, I knew I'd heard the last ring. So, I didn't even bother to pick up the receiver.

I'm sometimes a crepe hanger. Betsy used to call me "Old Cassandra Larry." She thought she was so smart when she was in college, coming home with all these sayings she'd use just to show how well read she was. I now know that she was only trying to impress my father. And she was jealous of me because I was the boy. Penis envy is what it's called. Betsy had a late case of it. Most girls get over it by the time they're five.

I'm not such a pessimist that I didn't expect Millie to call back, although I feared I would fall asleep and not answer in time again. So, when I turned off the light, I put the phone on my chest and waited for her call. But I eventually fell asleep. That's why the phone's first ring about five rings ago scared the breath out of me, rendering me incapable of picking up the receiver until now.

"Hello," I say quickly.

"What took you so goddamn long?" Hal growls.

"What?"

"Never mind, never mind," Hal says anxiously. "Did you see the paper? Go find it. You have to see it."

I just want to go back to sleep, not to hear about something in the newspaper, which, knowing Hal, probably has something to do with sports. I know I'm not going to get rid of him unless I listen to him, so I put the phone down and go to look for the paper. I can hear his shouting from the receiver, even from across the room. The paper is on the floor next to the kitchen table, where I threw it earlier, before I went to my parents. Millie began my newspaper subscription last summer when she stayed with me for a few weeks while she was taking a dance workshop.

I don't remember Millie's summer visit with a great deal of fondness. She was supposed to be staying with Hannah in the house that she and Hannah now live in, and every other day her mother would call her at Hannah's number. Hannah would make an excuse about Millie's whereabouts, and then call here so Millie could tear over there to call her mother back. It was like a long-distance bed check. When Millie would call back, she'd call collect so that her mother would see Hannah's number when she got the bill.

I was going to cancel my subscription until I saw the delivery boy. He's very conscientious. If he throws the paper wrong so it doesn't land on the porch under the overhang, where it won't get wet, he turns around, gets off his bike and moves the paper.

Hal is right. I had to see it. The picture on the front page is startling. It's that kid from George's Place in what looks like a school graduation picture. The headline says, "Boy Drowns in the Charles." The line below it in smaller letters says, "Police Suspect Suicide."

"I don't believe it," I gasp.

"That's the guy from George's Place," Hal says. "Right?"

"Yeah," I say. "But I don't believe it."

"Hey. Look at the picture. It's the spittin' image."

"No, no," I say, trying to read the article and talk at the same time. "It's he all right. I was there when they pulled him out of the river. I saw the body. I just don't believe it was suicide."

"Wait a minute," Hal gasps. "You saw the body? You were there?"

I tell him the story of chasing the cat behind the police lines and seeing the corpse. He can't believe I didn't call him immediately, and he raves for a couple of minutes, which gives me a chance to read the rest of the article that's on the front page. Then he can't believe that I didn't mention to the police that I had seen the kid the night before in George's Place. It all happened so fast, I explain to him.

"Oh, it wouldn't have mattered anyway," Hal says. "If someone really wants to kill himself, there's nothing anyone can do."

"I don't believe it was a suicide," I say. "I don't know why. I just don't believe it."

"He was full of heroin," Hal says, yawning. "The article says so. He probably flipped out and jumped into the river."

"Does he look like a junkie to you?"

"That's a graduation picture or something," he says. "Even a junkie doesn't look like a junkie in his graduation picture."

"Yeah, but when we saw him at George's Place, would you have thought he was a junkie?"

"No. But those are the ones who always fool you. They look straight as arrows, and it turns out they're rapists or drug fiends or something."

"Come on," I say, a little irritated at him suddenly for being so quick to dismiss the whole thing.

"Well, who knows? Anyway, what's to debate? He had drugs in his body."

"Drugs don't make you jump in the Charles."

"He had emotional problems, the article says."

"It's sad," I say, deciding to let it go. "He looks like a nice kid."

When I turn to the remainder of the article a few pages into the paper, I discover that it mentions Misha. It says that the boy had for a time been a follower of the Path to God. There's a quote from a 'spokesman' for the Path. "He was a good boy," the quote says, "but the problems of the world were too heavy on his shoulders. We tried to help him, but he refused us."

"I'm tired," Hal yawns into the phone. "What a weekend. You should have come."

"Yeah."

"Okay. I'm going to go to bed. Jesus, Larry, it's the middle of the night. Don't call me so late next time," he says, just before he hangs up.

I'm staring at the newspaper picture and thinking about how much the whole matter is going to disturb Jenny, when the phone rings again. I pick up the receiver in a flash.

"What now?" I ask, thinking that Hal has called back to grace me with one more stupid comment.

"Larry?"

"Oh, Millie," I stammer, the blood rushing to my face. "I thought you were Hal."

"Oh, what would he want?" she asks, the tone of her voice cool.

Millie doesn't like Hal because he dropped out of Harvard, which has caused her to assume that he's low class. Her brother went to Princeton, and, of course, he graduated summa cum laude, went on to Harvard Law and now practices law with a prominent firm in New York. His name is Gerald, but you can't ever call him Gerry. He gets pissed off if you call him anything but Gerald, even though Gerald isn't even his first name. He signs his name "C. Gerald Doeton." The "C" stands for Clinton.

He confided to me once that he thought the name Clint Doeton sounded like a jock's name, and he didn't want to be thought of as a jock, although he is one. Herrick went to Princeton also. But he is definitely not a jock. I wanted to ask Gerald if he knew Herrick when he was there, but I decided against it because I didn't want to hear him say that Herrick was odd.

The irony in Millie's feelings about Hal is that she has grievously misclassified him. The first day of college Hal walked into our room with a lacrosse stick in his hand and said, "Good to meet you old chap. I'm your roommate. Harold R. Green, but you can call me Hal." He comes from a family that made a fortune in the munitions business. His father threatened to disown him when he dropped out of Harvard. Of course, Hal didn't really drop out of Harvard. He flunked out, although the Dean said he should treat it only as a sabbatical. After all, no one with a family fortune really has to leave Harvard. But Hal did, and I suppose he left his inheritance behind also.

"Nothing," I say to Millie. "We were just talking shop."

"Oh," she says. "Well, I just called to see what you were up to."

"Not too much. I went to my parents' house today for their annual mixer. What have you been doing?"

"Nothing," she says quickly. "How was your parents' mixer?"

"Fine, fine. Same old thing. Just like every year," I say, debating whether to ask her again.

"That's nice," she says.

"And the weather was great today. Wasn't it?" I ask, thinking I should probably just leave it alone.

"Yes, it was," she says.

"Too bad we didn't go to the shore today, what with this nice weather and all," I say, pushing harder.

"You're probably right," she says in a tone that makes me think she is suspicious.

"And this was probably the last good weekend this year," I continue.

"Larry, what's wrong with you," she asks, irritably. "Do you have some fixation with the weather suddenly or what. I didn't call to talk about the weather."

"I'm sorry," I say quickly, suddenly regretting my impudence.

"And besides, I couldn't go away this weekend, anyway," she continues. "I spent most of my time in the library getting ready for midterms. So I don't want to hear about how great the weather was."

"Okay, okay. Skip it," I say.

"I didn't see you Saturday night," she says in a conciliatory way, after a moment or two.

"Saturday night?"

"You know, silly, at the closing night for the show," she coos. "I was expecting you to come by and wish me luck."

"I didn't know," I say in a monotone.

"I thought I told you it was the last night."

"No. I mean I didn't know I should come by."

"Oh, Larry," she says in an exasperated way. "You shouldn't be so timid."

"I guess not," I say, timidly.

We're quiet for a few more moments.

"Well, I just called to remind you about this Friday," she says, finally.

"Friday?" I ask, my mind for some reason as blank as a just-washed blackboard.

"Larry, you should write yourself notes," she scolds. "My parents are coming in on Thursday. We're going to dinner with them on Friday. Remember?"

"Oh yes. I have it written down on my calendar at school. I wouldn't have forgotten."

"And Thursday—you remember Thursday?"

"Thursday?"

"Yes, Thursday," she says, exasperated again. "Thursday night we're going with them to the Parents Reception at Dean Howell's."

"I remember," I say, not convinced myself that I really do remember.

"Larry," she says, sternly. "We waited for you at Anthony's last spring for thirty minutes. I don't want that to happen again."

"It was a mistake," I say, feeling defensive suddenly, and irritated that she can't forget one small incident that happened months ago.

"A mistake!" she cries. "How can you make a mistake about being somewhere at a certain time?"

"I went to the wrong restaurant, that's all," I say, stiffly.

"Or you had the wrong day," she goes on. "You did that to us once also."

"I won't make a mistake this time, okay?" I say, raising my voice a level, feeling like my next action will be to throw the phone on the floor.

"You don't have to get defensive about it, Larry," she says, quietly.

"I'm not being defensive!" I shout.

"Well, you sound defensive. And you're shouting."

"Well, I'm not," I whisper loudly, for the effect.

She never lets the old wounds heal. My mind races through indignation and rage. I've been trying like a madman all day to blot out the image burned into my brain of her bare back in the parking lot. And in our first encounter after that incident, she harps on my past tardiness as if I were a felon. But her aggressiveness shuts me down. In the few quiet moments that transpire, while I wait for her next salvo, tears brim in my eyes.

"I think you should wear your brown suit coat," she says, referring to what I and the rest of the world call a blazer.

"Okay, Millie," I say, somewhat emotionally, my voice cracking a bit, as I carry the phone across the room to the armoire. "I'll wear my brown blazer. Here it is. I'm taking it out of my closet right now, so I don't forget. And while I'm at it, what pants should I wear with it?"

"Is there something wrong?" she asks after she listens a few moments to the sounds of my pushing the clothes around my armoire and banging the door closed. "You're being so testy tonight, Larry."

"Testy. I'm not being testy," I sputter with anger. "I'm just getting out my suit coat like you asked."

"Look, if you don't want to go, fine."

"I didn't say that. Did I say that?"

"Then why are you acting so obnoxious?"

"I'm not obnoxious."

"You sound obnoxious."

"Well, I can help the way I sound. What about the yellow pants?

"I don't like the yellow pants. You know I don't like the yellow pants."

"I didn't know that."

A moment passes. The back of my neck and the tops of my shoulders throb, as if I have a sunburn. But my knees are weak and my stomach's a knot. So I sit down on the bed.

"I have to go, Larry," she says, in a quiet, but matter-of-fact voice. "It's late."

"Okay. Fine," I say, refusing to do what I've always done before in such circumstances, which is beg her not to hang up.

"Well I won't see you till Thursday then," she says, quickly. "I'm going to be studying for midterms."

"Fine," I say. "I'll see you on Thursday then."

And, she hangs up. Click. Just like that.

I feel both exhilarated and miserable, in a crazed sort of way. After I turn the light off, I can't close my eyes. On the ceiling, dimly lit by the street lamp outside the house, I suddenly see projected an image of myself naked and supine in the middle of the parking lot behind the Medford College Theater. But I'm smiling. In fact, I'm smiling so much my face appears blissful. A few feet away stand the two goons from George's Place, extending their arms to me, beckoning me to a captivity that will free me from Millie's tyranny, transforming me into an Alan Bates standing at the gates of the asylum, holding his birdcage.

7

I'M MAKING MY WAY ACROSS the Hillside toward Dean Howell's house on Thursday night in a mood that can only be described as no better than fractious, when into my head pops an image of a man walking rapidly toward a cliff so high that off its precipice is nothing but a huge blanket of clouds. My view of the man is panoramic, for I must be situated upon some venue higher than the cliff toward which the man strides, and I observe that over the next rise in his path his doom awaits. The mind, if given full rein, can perform the most extraordinary feats, and mine now gallops to a realization that I am the man approaching the cliff. Yet, I do not stop my climb. My gait is purposeful, and my considered intention is, in fact, to hurl my body and soul into the white uncertainty that stretches before me when I reach the precipice. It is with this vision in my head that I turn and march up the walk to Dean Howell's door.

My ominous arrival at the Howells, and my unsettled state of mind, may be attributed to my disconcerting discovery yesterday evening upon my return home from school of a postcard wedged in the door. On its picture side was a scene of the moon rising over the desert, one of those Ansel Adams images, like Jenny described her brother sent her. And sure enough, when I turned it over, there was printed at the top "THE PATH TO GOD." I walked up the stairs thinking how sorry I was that I missed her. I thought she had grown tired of waiting for me to come to the library to look at her postcard, as I had promised, and decided to come knock on my door.

When I couldn't remember telling her where I lived, I looked at the card again and discovered, with heart-stopping amazement, that the card was addressed to me. It was a card from Bradley, and it had no stamp. "Larry," it said, "I came by to see you. I've been remiss in telling you that I've moved back East, and I wanted to see you in person to explain. I've been living on the Cape, not far from the Narrows, with a group of very wonderful people. We're doing community service work this afternoon at the Community Center in Melrose. We'll be there until 8:00. Come by if you can. Peace. Bradley."

I looked at my watch. I could make it if I had a car and could leave immediately. And that's where Millie got involved, or, I should say, where she got in the way. I knew when I dialed their number that with my luck, she, and not Hannah, would pick up the phone. Hannah would have asked no questions. Millie, however, was indifferent about my urgency. She started telling me about her stupid Kafka class, as if that had been the purpose of my call. My haste gave way to impertinence, I can see now, and I said, "Give me a break, Mill, and tell me about the lousy Kafka class when I get back." She retaliated. She put down the phone, counted to twenty, loud enough for me to hear, and then told me in a sarcastically polite voice that she was sorry but Hannah was not at home.

I ran over there, even though there really wasn't much of a chance I was going to make it to Melrose by eight. I had counted on Hannah bringing the car to me. Of course, Millie was waiting for me on the porch.

"Why, Larry," she said in her sweetest voice. "Come in and have some tea."

"I can't, Millie," I said, gasping for breath, not so much from physical exertion but from the anxiety of speaking to her. "You know I'm in a hurry."

"Well, Bradley can wait a minute, can't he?"

"I don't know," I said meekly.

"You've got plenty of time," she said as she walked back into the house.

"Only for a minute, Millie," I said, mustering some resolve.

But once I was in the kitchen, Millie went on and on, and I kept looking at my watch, until my desperation overwhelmed my cowardice. When she turned her back, I looked at Hannah and she nodded, so I grabbed the keys and ran out the door, yelling "See you later" as the door closed behind me.

I didn't go far as it turned out. I had forgotten, in my haste, what Hannah had warned me about so many times before. Because the car is a convertible, Hannah attaches an anti-theft device to the steering wheel and brake pedal. So, when I put the car in reverse, the horn blared and, as hard as my leg pumped at the brake, the car would not stop moving backward. I watched the red car parked across the street from the drive-way loom in the rear-view mirror. Just before I hit it, I popped the gear lever into drive, which propelled me forward. But the brake still wasn't working and the horn was still blaring, and now the garage loomed in front of me. Hannah yelled something I couldn't hear. I did the gear lever trick again before the garage, and then again before the red car. It was Bevins's car, it occurred to me in the midst of my panic. The red car I was being so careful to avoid was Bevins's car. I flipped the gearshift again. I had to stop somehow. It was his car or the garage.

I intended to ram that beautiful red machine, as distraught as I was that Millie's antics had probably caused me to miss Bradley. But at that moment Bevins came flying out of the house, hurdled over the porch banister like some goddamn track star, flung open the door next to me, reached in and turned off the ignition. I hadn't thought of that.

"Nice going, Champ," he said as he dropped the keys into Hannah's hand and walked back up the porch stairs.

"I'm sorry," she said to me. "I tried to tell you."

"Boy, was that stupid," I said.

"No. How would you know? It was my fault."

"It wasn't your fault. I was in a hurry," I said, looking around for Millie, who was nowhere in sight.

"Well, go on, then. He might still be there."

I didn't make it, of course. The custodian at the Melrose Community Center told me they left about ten minutes before I got there. When I brought the car back, I tried to avoid any incremental embarrassment by dropping the keys through the mail slot. But Millie knew that I'd do that, and she left me a note taped to the front of the door. "Don't forget the Dean's Reception tomorrow night," it said.

So, here I am. There are beds of marigolds lining the walk up to the front door of the Dean's house. The cool night air increases their aroma. Some people hate marigolds because they have such a pungent scent, as compared to the subtle fragrance of a rose bush. Millie's mother has a rose garden.

The Dean's front door is wide open. I could be any drunk, wandering in off the street. Mrs. Howell, the Dean's wife, suddenly comes around the corner.

"Oh, Larry. What a surprise!"

She pinches my cheek. I hate it when she does that. She's been doing that since I was ten. And she's drunk, like she usually is, like she's been for as long as I can remember.

"Good evening, Mrs. Howell," I say politely.

"Well, I'm so confused, Larry," she says, her eyes rolling around in her head. "I thought you had graduated already."

"I have, Mrs. Howell. I'm here with the Doetons."

"The Doetons?"

"Millie Doeton is a senior."

"The Doetons? I don't believe I've met the Doetons."

"Oh no?"

"No. I don't believe the Doetons are here yet, Larry."

"That's unusual. They're always on time. No, there they are. Over there," I say, pointing across the room.

"Oh, yes," she croons. "That rather tall lady. I remember. She grows roses, she was telling me. I've never liked roses myself. They have such a sweet, sticky odor. I much prefer marigolds. Did you notice my marigolds on the way in? Aren't they fantastic?"

"Yes, Mrs. Howell," I say sympathetically. "They're wonderful."

"And they smell so good this time of year. Oh, is that Professor Simpson? He has a yard full of marigolds."

"Yes," I say, eagerly.

"Robert! Robert Simpson!" she calls to him and stumbles away.

By the end of the evening her eyes will be glazed over and the Dean will be propping her up at the door. Her first name is Heidi. Heidi Howell. She could have kept her maiden name. I remember Jake criticizing Brett for changing her name. Jake saw everything with clarity and certainty.

The Doetons are standing together in a clump, like radishes in a garden. Mrs. Doeton has a stupid smile plastered on her face, while Millie gazes around the room pretending she hasn't noticed that I've arrived and ignoring some anecdote that her father has just delivered.

Mrs. Doeton is a tall, thin woman with very short blond hair, cut in the fashion you see in pictures from the Roaring Twenties. Her height overwhelms any figure her body possesses, and occasionally she holds herself with her neck slightly outstretched in a manner that makes her look like a giraffe. The shape of her nose reminds me of a photograph of Virginia Woolf. Mr. Doeton has very few distinguishing characteristics. His face is slightly flat, and its flatness makes describing him difficult. He has jet-black hair that he wears in a crewcut, which I guess is an unusual feature today. His posture is forward leaning and his shoulders bend inward, probably from so many years of working at a desk.

I approach them in as casual manner as I can, as if I had been around the corner talking to the Dean for the last fifteen minutes.

"You're late," Millie says, and then looks away at the rest of the party.

"Oh, Millie. He's only a minute late," Mrs. Doeton says, looking at me and smiling. "Isn't this a lovely party? And this house is so beautiful. Look at that vase on the mantle. It's priceless."

"Well, that just goes to show that priceless things can be bought," Mr. Doeton says.

"Perhaps you should have become a professor, dear," she says to him, ignoring his tidbit of wisdom. "We struggled over that decision, didn't we?"

"Don't remember that," he says, still staring at the vase.

"Oh, it would have been an exciting life," she exclaims.

"No doubt, but I wonder if it would have been the best choice," he muses. "You know you test your choice of vocation by your love of the drudgery it requires."

"Maybe so," she says, "but my guess is that we would have been quite happy on a university campus."

"Ah, a woman's guess is more accurate than a man's certainty," he says, winking at me.

I try not to react, because I feel Millie's gaze upon me. But I can't help myself.

"Kipling," I say.

"What?"

"That saying was written by Rudyard Kipling."

"Oh. Well I'm sure I read it someplace."

"Alex is an avid reader," Mrs. Doeton says.

"That's right, he'll read anything," Millie says.

"Although, sometimes I wish he didn't remember what he read quite so well," Mrs. Doeton sighs.

"But it's a gift, to remember everything you read," I say.

"Not when he repeats it ten times," Millie says.

"Dear Millie," Mr. Doeton says, grimacing. "Don't you know that a thought can be original even though uttered a hundred times before? It's all in the context."

"You're incorrigible, Alex," Mrs. Doeton exclaims as Millie shakes her head and looks away.

"Thank you, Dot," he says, tilting his head toward her slightly.

Mrs. Doeton puts her hand on the top of her chest, just at the base of her neck, a posture she often adopts when she is anxious. I look desperately for someone with whom I can dilute our unstable mixture. I see Jack Levine.

"Jack!" I call to him, waving frantically.

"Larry Brown," he says, laughing as he walks over to us. "You must be on the party circuit this week."

"Party circuit?" Millie asks, looking from him to me.

"Sunday, I saw him at a cocktail party for freshmen," he says to her. "And this evening, here he is at a reception for seniors. Do you think he hit the other classes in between?"

"Cocktail party for freshmen?" Millie asks, staring at me.

"That was my father's party for his new students," I explain.

While Millie continues for a moment to examine my face, I notice her mother's eyes widen upon her discernment of Jack's garb. He wears a brown tweed coat over a sweater, no tie, corduroy pants so old that the cloth over the knees has lost its ridges, and tennis shoes.

"How are you, Jack?" I ask, deciding to suspend the introductions for a moment and to leave Mrs. Doeton in suspense. "How's the sailboat coming?"

"Oh, not too fast," he says, shaking his head. "I'm taking it apart faster than I'm putting it together."

"Is it in a bottle?" Mr. Doeton asks.

"Oh, no," Jack laughs. "It's in my garage."

"Jack," I say quickly, pretending that I've only just come to the realization that they haven't met before. "This is Millie Doeton and her parents, Dorothy and Alex." And then I add, "Jack is a law professor at Fletcher."

"Very pleased to meet you," he says, slightly nodding his head to Millie and her mother, who smile in return.

"Likewise," Mrs. Doeton says.

"So it's a real sailboat you're building?" Mr. Doeton asks.

"Absolutely!" he exclaims. "The real thing. Nothing elaborate though. It will have only one mast. It's my first try."

They don't get it. They're from Hartford. They don't know anything about sailing.

"The attempt can often be more satisfying than the completion," Mr. Doeton says.

"I don't know," Jack says. "I've never finished anything."

Millie and her mother furl their brows, in unison, as if rehearsed. Mr. Doeton laughs, at least. He has a remarkably good disposition, all things considered.

"So you must be the lucky senior," Jack says to Millie. "I'll bet you're happy that you'll soon be through."

"Oh, yes," she says maturely. "Actually, I'm really looking forward to getting out into the world to apply what I've learned."

If Mrs. Doeton wasn't watching me, I would roll my eyes. Jack maintains his composure, but his face appears strained.

"Well, that's nice," he says. "And Dorothy. I'm sorry. It's Dorothy, isn't it?"

She nods, apprehensively. I can see she is too intimidated to say her usual, "Oh, you can call me Dot. Everyone does."

"What will you do, Dorothy, now that you don't have Millie to worry about?" he asks, a slight smile tugging at the corner of his mouth.

Millie glares at me as if it were I who asked the question.

"Oh, I haven't worried about Millie for years," she laughs nervously. "Have I dear?"

"She sleeps like a baby. Not a care in the world," Mr. Doeton says.

Jack laughs graciously, which reminds me that my father once told me that he thought that underneath the rough-and-tumble exterior Jack was a kitten. That's probably why my father secretly wishes Betsy had married him.

"Then you have no other children at home?" Jack asks Mr. Doeton, giving Mrs. Doeton a change to relax her face muscles.

"No," Alex says. "We have a son who is older than Millie. He's about Larry's age. Graduated in '66 from Princeton. Went to Harvard Law. Now he's working at a firm in New York."

Mr. Doeton forgets to mention the Order of the Coif, or how old Clint was varsity track, or how proud old Clint was of his varsity letter that was plastered on the jacket with the leather sleeves – the jacket that he wore over his madras shirt and khaki pants every day, until he decided he no longer wished to be viewed as a jock. But I don't bring it up.

Bradley's brother Herrick and Clint are the same age, but they're nothing alike. What Herrick cares about most in life is his clarinet. When I think of Herrick, I picture him sitting on the old easy chair at the Narrows wearing his cap backwards and playing his clarinet with his eyes closed. Herrick is actually a very talented clarinetist, and in high school he once played in a big recital at Symphony Hall. The problem was that he was required to wear a tuxedo, which he detested. So, at the last

minute he put on his cap, which is how he came out on stage—
in his tuxedo and his cap. And that's how he played the Brahms
Concerto. He played it so well that the accompanists stood up
and bowed to him.

"Well, you must be proud of him," Jack says to Mr. Doeton.

"Oh, we certainly are," Mrs. Doeton says.

"And are you a lawyer also, Alex?"

"Oh, no," Mr. Doeton laughs. "I'm an accountant."

"The question wasn't as random as you think," Jack says in
response to the perplexed look on Millie's face. "I can't tell you
how many of my law school classmates were becoming lawyers
because their fathers were lawyers."

"Then your father was a lawyer?" Mrs. Doeton asks.

"No, he wasn't, actually," Jack says, looking across the room
in a distracted manner.

It's ironic, it occurs to me suddenly, that Jack's father was
an accountant also. He worked for an international oil company.
But I'm sure he won't tell them, because of the accident.

"But Dorothy," Jack says, turning to her enthusiastically, as
if a switch inside of him had suddenly been tripped, "we must
certainly ask you as well? Are you a lawyer?"

"Oh, no. Not me," she laughs.

"Well, why not? In this day and age, certainly a son could
aspire to be like his mother. Don't you think?"

"Oh, not Clint," she says, her face turning slightly crimson.
"Particularly in my case, since I'm a secretarial science teacher."

"But that's great," Jack exclaims with a sincerity that even
I believe. "Teaching is certainly an admirable profession. Larry
and I think so. Don't we, Larry?"

"Millie is thinking about teaching also," I say, trying to
deflect the attention away from both Mrs. Doeton and me.

"But it's just secretarial science that I teach," Mrs. Doeton says, not seeing, or unwilling to go along with, my tactic. "That's nothing like law or English."

"Oh, the topic is irrelevant, I've always thought," Jack says. "What's most challenging is to inspire your students to think."

"Exactly," says Mr. Doeton enthusiastically. "It takes more time to understand a thought than to conceive it."

That stops us all for an awkward moment. Finally, Jack nods his head and smiles.

"Dorothy," he says, "is it a public school you teach in?"

"Yes, it is. It's a high school."

"Well, you might be interested in this very lively debate I had last week with the students in my Politics of Education seminar."

"Politics of Education? Is there politics in education?" Mr. Doeton asks.

"Alex, there's politics in everything. Haven't you heard?"

"I guess not."

"Whenever words are spoken, there's politics," Jack says, maintaining a serious composure. "You've heard the saying, 'Men more frequently must be reminded rather than informed'?"

"Oh, yes. I see what you mean."

"Jack," I say, looking at him skeptically, "I think the more correct observation is 'When a politician speaks, the facts are lost forever.'"

"You've got that one a little wrong, Larry," Jack laughs. "I think the saying is that once a newspaper prints a story, the facts are lost forever. But it's close. If there were not politics, I doubt there would be newspapers."

"You make it sound like gossip," Millie says.

"Maybe that's why I like it so much," Jack quips.

But Millie doesn't laugh, like the rest of us, at Jack's quick wit. She's off balance, and her demeanor is cool.

"But we fell off the topic, didn't we," Jack says, returning his attention to Mrs. Doeton. "That happens so often when education is the topic. Everybody's been to school, but people aren't used to talking about schooling as if it were a science, like poly sci, for instance, or biology. But it is a science isn't it? There are principles, and theories, and studies and whatnot. Don't you agree?"

"Well, I suppose so. Yes," Mrs. Doeton says, although from the look on her face I'm skeptical that she has the slightest idea what Jack is talking about.

"Okay. Well, here's what we were talking about in my seminar. Does your school divide students into classes by ability?"

"Let's see," Mrs. Doeton says, her face showing her struggle to answer the question. We have honors classes, if that's what you mean. They're classes for the very smart children."

"And everyone else is treated the same?" Jack asks.

"No," Millie says, leaping into the conversation in response to Mrs. Doeton's nod. "We had different levels, Mom. Besides honors, there was the college level, which is where you were if you intended to go to college. Then there was the regular level. And there was also a trade school level. That's the level you probably have in secretarial science."

"And there's something wrong with that?" Jack asks Millie quickly, his face animated with the look of a hunter whose prey has suddenly stumbled into view.

"I didn't say that," Millie retorts weakly, confusion showing on her face.

"To me it sounded like you put them on the bottom."

"Well, they aren't as academically inclined."

"Ah, I see," Jack says dramatically. "So it's something called 'academic inclination' that causes you to divide students into these separate classes."

"Well, they're divided by grade also," Mrs. Doeton says.

"Yes, but I mean within a grade," Jack says, refusing to shift his gaze away from Millie.

"'Tracking' is what you're talking about. Right, Mill? 'Tracking' is what its called," I hear myself say, knowing even before the glare she throws at me that I am striking the match that will ignite the conflagration.

"The term 'tracking' has a pejorative connotation," she says coolly, almost in a growl. "It sounds like you're dividing cattle by size and sex."

"Okay, so let's call it something else," Jack says. "Whatever you like."

"I've heard it called 'achievement classification,'" Millie says.

"Fine," Jack says quickly. "Then we'll call it 'achievement classification.' And you determine a student's achievement classification by his 'academic inclination.' Is that it?"

"Well, yes, basically," Millie says, her voice showing her surprise that Jack had obviously read the literature.

"And how is it that you determine academic inclination?"

"That's what a guidance counselor does," Mrs. Doeton says.

"Okay," Jack chuckles, "but I don't think Millie would agree if Larry characterized guidance counselors as ranch hands sitting up on the fence looking for size and sex. Is it a subjective determination?"

"It certainly isn't. It's done with testing," Millie says.

"Like a blood test?" Jack asks, opening his eyes wide.

"Like an intelligence test," Millie says.

"I see," Jack says, nodding his head. "A student sits down and takes a test. You add up his score, and if he gets over a certain number he goes in the honor class, and if he gets below another number he goes with the trade group. Is that it?"

"It's not so simple as that," Millie says irritably. "There are exceptions to the rule."

"There are?" Jack asks, acting as if what Millie said had never occurred to him.

"Certainly. Guidance counselors exercise discretion. And nothing's perfect. There may be some misclassifications occasionally, but overall the benefits are worth it, certainly."

"The benefits?" Jack asks, maintaining the look of amazement on his face.

"Yes, the smarter students don't get bored, and the slower ones get more help."

"So the smarter you are, the more academic inclination you have. Is that it?" Jack asks, now looking innocent.

Millie's back is as straight as a rod and her chin juts out contentiously. Jack stands informally, one hand in his pocket and the other holding a wine glass in which he whirls a tiny amount of wine. If she takes a swing at him, it'll knock him off his feet, just as certain as I'm standing here.

"I didn't mean it that way," she says, pursing her lips.

"Yes. But what you meant isn't the point," Jack says, unable to contain his opinions any longer. "What matters is what the real result is, and the real result, in my opinion anyway, is that tracking, or however you characterize it, is, more often than not, inaccurate and inherently unfair. But that's not what disturbs me the most about it. There are plenty of inequities in life. Some of us have to endure more of them than others, and children are particularly resilient to our meddling with their development. What bothers me about tracking is that it's the progeny of racism. As simple as that."

"Why, that's preposterous," Millie says.

"Oh, it's not, Millie," Jack says, emphatically. "And it's not even subtle. It's no different than putting a person on the back of the bus on account of the color of his skin. Do you know what makes racism so bad? It's that it works so well. Believe it or not, it's very easy for a person to believe he's inferior, particularly when all the messages start to come across when he's a child. That's what tracking does to all but a select few. Putting a student in an inferior track is a self-fulfilling prophecy. The lessons that are taught and the way a student learns to behave are all affected by the track you place him in."

"But of course he is placed with others of his same ability," Mrs. Doeton says cautiously.

"Bullshit!" Jack says, so assertively that Mrs. Doeton takes a step backward. "Based on what?"

"It's based on objective standards, and the testing is fairly administered," Millie says.

Jack's face is a little flushed, both from the argument and, I suspect, from the wine. He lifts a new glass of wine from a girl passing with a tray full of them.

"Okay. Let's explore that, Millie," Jack says, after taking a sip. "You're talking about intelligence tests. Is that right?"

"That's right," she says curtly.

Most people defer to Millie's opinions, or at least politely accommodate them, by this point in an argument, giving her the same respect one gives a snake that slides across one's path. Of course, Jack, being a lawyer, is comfortable with snakes.

"Who invented the intelligence test?" Jack asks.

"This sounds like a midterm," Mr. Doeton quips, reminding me suddenly of good old Mr. Cleaver.

"Oh, I didn't mean it that way. I'm sorry," Jack says, looking at Mr. Doeton sincerely. "Sometimes I get carried away."

"Oh, please continue," Mrs. Doeton interjects quickly. "Besides, I know the answer. Binet."

"Binet is right. I bet you even know the year he designed the first intelligence test," he says to Mrs. Doeton, who is momentarily distracted by the astonished look on Millie's face.

"A historical context is always essential," Mr. Doeton says, always ready with an aphorism.

"I don't remember the exact year, but it was around 1900," Mrs. Doeton says.

"The turn of the century," Mr. Doeton says.

"Exactly," Jack says.

"So what does Binet have to do with achievement classification?" Millie asks.

"Do you think there's such a thing as innate intelligence?" Jack asks, turning to her but ignoring her question.

"That's a hotly debated issue right now," Millie says.

"But you didn't answer the question," he says to her in a friendly manner.

"I do believe there's such a thing," she says.

"So on day one, either you have it or you don't."

"Day one? Have it?" Mrs. Doeton asks, looking confused, as Millie fails to hide her impatience.

"Brand-new baby. Right out of the womb, and either you can put a Harvard cap on him or you can't."

"Oh, I see," she says, hesitantly.

"If you could find a way to measure it," Jack says, then laughs. "I don't mean the cap, of course."

"There's more to it than that," Millie says ignoring his levity. "You know that."

"I don't know," Jack says, becoming serious again. "Benet's test didn't purport to measure innate intelligence. At least, that's not my understanding of what he was doing. He was using his test as a diagnostic tool, trying to determine whether students needed special education. But the IQ tests today are prognostic. They assign you a number on a scale that almost assigns you a role in life."

"That's overstating it," Millie says. "It doesn't assign you a role, it merely evaluates your ability to achieve."

"And do you think that's right? That, in fact, innate intelligence can be so accurately measured?"

"Well, perhaps it's not an exact science, but it appears to be a good indicator."

"Something like predicting the weather," Mr. Doeton says.

Jack laughs. He laughs so hard, he slops a few drops of wine onto his coat sleeve. It blends right in with the weave, and the other stains. Mr. Doeton chuckles also, although I suspect he is not quite sure why what he said was funny.

"Now there's an exact science," Jack says.

"It's better than that," Millie says coldly.

"I don't think it is. I really don't. In fact, I don't think that you can measure innate intelligence at all, or if you can, that the measurement should be used in the manner educators are currently trying to use it. Did you know that the early proponents of measuring innate intelligence were descendants of those who determined that white Anglo-Saxons were more intelligent than other cultures by measuring their skulls."

"That's an unfair characterization," Millie says. "A great deal of study has gone into the preparation of intelligence tests."

"Do you have a high IQ, Millie?" Jack asks.

"Does she ever!" Old Mr. Cleaver exclaims.

"That has nothing to do with it," Millie says indignantly.

"I'm sorry, Millie," Jack says. "I know that sounded like an accusation. And if it was, I'm guilty also of the crime alleged, so I always try to bring it up in conversations like this, although I could have used a little more tact. All of us tend to be prejudiced to a degree by what we are, whether it's the color of our skin or number of our IQ."

"Oh, no offense taken, I'm sure," Mrs. Doeton finally says when it's clear to all of us that Millie has been overcome by her hostility and is not going to respond.

"Okay. Good," Jack says, cheerfully turning back to Millie's parents. "So let's continue with our line of thought, and see what we turn up. I'll ask some questions to get us going. Were either of your parents immigrants?"

"Dorothy's father immigrated here as a very young child," Mr. Doeton volunteers. "Didn't he, Dorothy? It was around the turn of the century."

"That's right," Mrs. Doeton says.

"Well, Millie," Jack asks, observing, as I have, that the hard lines around her mouth had subsided. "Would you say your grandfather was an intelligent man?"

"He was a schoolteacher," Dorothy says quickly before Millie can speak. "He graduated from college."

"What does my grandfather have to do with this?" Millie asks coldly.

"Well, intelligence testing on young men entering the service just before World War I showed that most immigrants who were born outside of the United States were 'retarded.'"

"You're kidding," Mr. Doeton says.

"No kidding," Jack says. "It's an interesting statistic, isn't it? I suppose it's one we'll all choose to ignore if we believe in the accuracy of the tests. The same is true for my grandfather."

"I don't see what all this proves," Millie says. "The early tests were inaccurate. So what?"

"It's a valid point you're making, Millie. The level of sophistication of the tests has certainly improved since World War I. But it wasn't the accuracy of the tests that I was so much attacking as I was the ability of society to use them to preserve a status quo. In the case of my example, the tests turned out to be a confirmation of a popular prejudice of the time."

"So, you use the example as an indictment of the tests generally. That's unfair. Their use today is not the same."

"You really think it isn't? You really think that such a powerful thing as testing can be totally objective?"

"Certainly it isn't so abused that it finds all immigrants are retarded."

"On behalf of their ancestors, I hope not," Mr. Doeton quips.

"Well, Millie," Jack says quickly to keep Mr. Doeton's remark from destroying his focus. "Can you give me the statistics on how blacks score on intelligence tests as compared to whites."

"No."

"Would it surprise you to find out that almost all blacks score as far down the scale today as our ancestors did in 1910? Although, we no longer continue to include the retarded classification. We only just assign numbers."

"So they do," Millie says. "Many whites score in the same lower percentiles."

"But should we not be suspicious about a test when you have results like that? An entire race with only a few exceptions score at the bottom of the scale."

"It doesn't prove the test inaccurate," she says shrugging her shoulders.

"Perhaps we should look at the exceptions," Mr. Doeton says.

"Not inaccurate," Jack says, ignoring him. "I think it proves them invalid."

"How?"

"What are we trying to test?" Jack asks.

"Intelligence," Mrs. Doeton says.

"No! Innate intelligence. Can innate intelligence possibly be so clearly divided along racial parameters?"

"I hadn't thought of it in that way," Mr. Doeton says.

"We may have taken the signs off buses and restroom doors," Jack says assertively, "but we're really continuing the practice in an identical fashion with intelligence tests."

"Oh, that isn't so," Mrs. Doeton objects. "We don't have segregation at our schools. We mix all the children together."

"Do you really? I thought you divided them into groups?"

"What?"

"I think Jack is talking about tracking again," I say.

"We can all see that," Millie snaps.

"But Larry is right," Jack says, looking back at Millie. "Tracking is just dividing students into groups based on ability. And how does the school determine ability? It looks at a student's IQ."

"It's not so simple as that," Millie says.

"I think it is," Jack says. "But you can look around and decide for yourself, Dorothy, the next time you're at school. On a statistical basis I'll bet you find all your black students in the lower tracks."

"So what will that prove?" Millie ask, the agitation rising in her voice. "If you put them in the upper tracks, they won't be able to keep up."

"And there will be chaos," Mrs. Doeton says. "Believe me. And then the able students will not get the education they deserve."

"So the tracking is to protect the able students?" Jack asks, raising his eyebrows. "And by that I mean the white students. There was a similar argument used in the South by proponents of segregated rest rooms."

"It's not the same," Millie says. "We aren't talking about a demeaning thing. We talking about putting them in an ability-matched classroom, so they can get the attention they need."

"Really!" Jack exclaims. "Not demeaning, you say? I keep coming back to the innate intelligence concept. You've given them a test. And on the basis of that test you've stamped across their record a low IQ. Then you put them in their own classroom for their own good. Come on, Millie. You might as well have stamped 'INFERIOR' across their foreheads."

"Well there's good and bad in everything," Mrs. Doeton says. "And maybe we're overlooking the good. Tracking allows the school to cater to a student's strengths and weaknesses. Even if there is an appearance of segregation, as you say, isn't it out-weighed by the good?"

"I don't see the good," I say.

"You wouldn't," Millie says.

"Oh, Millie," Mrs. Doeton says. "The good, Larry, is that you give the slower students a better chance to develop. If they were in classrooms with the faster students, they'd be overlooked."

"That may sound good in theory, but I'm not sure it works that way," I say. "Frankly, my upper-track students could use a little bit of the spontaneity and freshness of the students from the lower tracks. And the reverse is true for the academics. I'm not sure tracking isn't just taking the easy way out. And I'm not sure there's only one kind of intelligence that predicts a student's ability to be successful in an academic setting."

"But Larry, don't you see," Jack says in a mocking tone. "Tracking is efficient, and this is, after all, a world of efficiency. By the time these students get to junior high, you can sort them out into taxi drivers, secretaries, astronomers, and what have you."

"Well, that sounds promising," Mr. Doeton says, playing along with Jack's sarcasm. "No more identity crises. No more difficult career choices."

"It's the Great Society, isn't it?" Jack laughs.

"Our worst enemy in life may be anarchy," Mr. Doeton says, chuckling, "but our second worse is efficiency."

A girl comes by with a tray of tiny slabs of pink fish on little circles of dark brown bread. There's a dab of translucent sauce on top of each of them, and green specks peppered over that. I suddenly imagine that Carla is in the kitchen taking a pinch of the herb, whatever it is, and tossing it playfully above the tray. It's how you spread them out, she would tell me officiously.

"Hey, we're just throwing around some ideas," Jack says while he's chewing one of the delicacies. "That's the best part of cocktail parties, isn't it?"

"Just like throwing a baseball around," Mr. Doeton says. "A little exercise is good for the soul."

"Oh, you're so right, Alex," Jack says. "Sometimes a good argument can be cathartic, can't it? But I always go away after talking about racism with this terrible empty feeling. We've spent so much social time and effort on desegregation, and where has it really brought us? I just don't know. What worries me is that racism breeds in the staging areas of social inter-action, where the class status skirmishes occur. If you look at tracked students, its uncanny how often you can guess their track simply from their social status or their color."

"Well, there certainly are complicated issues involved," Mrs. Doeton says, brightly.

"Tiring issues, if you ask me," Millie grumbles, looking away.

"Oh, no, dear," Mr. Doeton says. "Private passions grow tired and go out, but political passions are never extinguished."

"You should take my class, Millie," Jack says, grinning. "I'm teaching it again in the spring. You won't find the issues tiring."

"What's it called?" Millie asks with a politeness that sur-prises me.

"Politics of Education," he says. "But it's not a course for the weak-hearted or the thin-skinned."

"Good education must be rubbed into us like an ointment, and with rough hands," Mr. Doeton says.

"I've never heard it said better, Alex," Jack says.

"Why, thank you, Jack."

"Will you excuse me," Jack says, holding out his hand first to Mr. Doeton, and then to Mrs. Doeton. "It's been a pleasure talking to you."

"Oh, likewise," the Doeton's say in unison.

Millie nods her head. Jack looks at her a moment, then winks at me, with the right eye, so she doesn't see him do it.

"Take care," he says, and moves off into the crowd.

"Well, he certainly is an opinionated person," Millie sputters after he's out of earshot.

"There's an old saying," Mr. Doeton says, "that every word we speak awakens its opposite."

"Isn't that true," I say, grinning until I notice the squint of Millie's eyes and the purse of her lips. "But it's just Jack's delivery. He loves to argue. You shouldn't take it personally."

"I'm not taking anything personally," Millie snaps. "Why would you say that?"

I shrug my shoulders, unwilling to expose myself any further by saying more.

"The man is a conceited bore," she says.

"Oh, Millie. He was just a little argumentative," her mother says calmly. "And he certainly knows his subject matter."

"He only knows his version," Millie spits.

"The most controversial issues are those as to which no clear evidence exists for either side," Mr. Doeton says.

"Well, from listening to him, you'd think all the evidence was on his side."

"Then listening did us some good," Mr. Doeton says, "because he who knows only his own side of an issue knows little of it."

"Oh, bunk, Daddy. Don't you have anything to say except old sayings?"

"Oh, Millie," Mrs. Doeton says, slightly alarmed at Millie's petulance.

"The hardest task of a daughter's life is to prove to her father that her intentions are serious," Mr. Doeton says quietly, unperturbed.

"What?"

"I'm not going to repeat it, dear," he says. "It's just an old saying. You can look it up. It's from a book called *Reflections of a Bachelor Girl*. I can't remember the author, but it's good reading, if you ask me."

Without my being conscious of it, Mr. Doeton, while speaking to Millie, has casually led us to the front door, where we and the Dean and his wife exchange adieus. And, suddenly, the night air seems so cold that I think the little beads of sweat on my forehead are going to freeze up. I think I see my breath, a phenomenon that brings me comfort, like discovering five fingers when I hold up my hand.

"Can we give you a lift, Larry?" Mr. Doeton asks.

"No, thanks," I say quickly. "I just live over the hill."

"Are you sure? It's bitter cold, and you don't even have a coat," Mrs. Doeton says.

"It's really not far," I say. It wasn't bitter cold, only the chill of fall. "And I get warm climbing the hill. Really."

"Well, thanks for joining us," Mr. Doeton says. "And I understand we'll see you for dinner tomorrow."

"Yes, Larry. Don't forget about dinner tomorrow night," Millie says quickly, as she leans over and kisses me on the cheek.

"Brrr. It's cold. Let's get the heat on, Alex," Mrs. Doeton says as she gets in the car.

After another admonishment from Millie about tomorrow night's dinner, they drive off and I walk up the hill and around the corner. I rub the cold part of my cheek where Millie kissed me. That failing to dispel the numb sensation in the area, I put my hands in my pockets and hunch my shoulders against the cold wind that blows toward me during the rest of the journey home.

8

ACROSS THE COMMON, IN THE dim early morning light, I can
see Jenny in a bright red parka, walking around her car and looking at her watch. Above her is a huge white setting moon, glitter-
ing in a cloudless sky just turning blue. The air is sharply cold,
and so dry that the small white clouds forming from my labored
breathing—the result of my having just run up the stairs behind
the library—appear to dissipate noisily into the atmosphere the
way that a glass loses its form at the moment of its impact with
the floor, exploding into a million flashing fragments.

I'm not going to dine with the Doetons tonight, as it turns
out, which accounts for my feeling discombobulated as I stroll
toward Jenny, still trying to calm my breathing, its rapidity
being as much the result of my confrontation with Millie only
moments ago as the steep climb to the Common. Events of the
last eight hours have intoxicated me in a sense, dampening
my enthusiasm for even doing so much as taking another step.
I'm not an ebullient drunk, either actually or figuratively. But I
manage to keep my feet moving in Jenny's direction.

Jenny sat on my steps last night when I returned home from
my skirmish at the Dean's reception. It was hard to make out
her demeanor as I approached her because the porch light was
behind her. Without more than a tacit acknowledgement of my
return, she turned toward the door as I dug in my pocket for my
key, and we proceeded up the stairs single file.

"I hope you haven't been waiting long," I said, after I threw our coats on the coat rack with a strained casualness meant to conceal the curiosity in me sparked by her presence.

"No. Really, I just got here," she said, looking at me expectantly, as if it had been I who had directed this rendezvous. "Your father gave me your address."

"Oh, good," I said skeptically, while motioning for her to sit down.

Very often when I say, "I just got here," I have in fact been waiting for so long that I have just decided to go home. And sitting on my couch last night, waiting politely for Jenny to disclose the reason for her unexpected visit, it occurred to me that my using the phrase with Millie, as often as I do, may confirm in her mind the belief that I am the one who is unremorsefully tardy. In other words, she accepts without question my polite expostulation as my admission rather than her excuse. She may have actually adopted a strategy of coming late herself in order to compensate for my supposed incompetence.

My ruminations upon Millie's manipulation of my unfortunate choice of an idiom were quickly interrupted by Jenny's blurting out, "I think your friend Bradley is living in Misha's ashram." Her complete distraction with the matter—and her conviction that such news would be of such great import to me being so pressing that she had waited on my doorstep—caused me to delay disclosure to her of my card from Bradley while she for several minutes unfolded for me, with a great amount of detail that in several instances included what appeared to be a verbatim rendition of dialogue, her brother's phone call to her father for the purpose of obtaining some dental records. In response to the father's inquiries, Josh reported that a member of the ashram who was familiar with the Cape had referred him to a local dentist. Josh had evidently also mentioned that this same ashram member had previous worked with the migrant workers in California.

As she spoke, her eyes betrayed a turmoil that I thought raged uncontrolled inside her, and although I did not until later comprehend the reason why she should be feeling so desperate, I finally snatched the first opportunity, while she was heaving a sob over the degree of distress the call had caused her father, to interject that I already knew of Bradley's proximity on account of the card he had left on my doorstep. The disclosure did not have the desired effect of quieting any concern she had over how I would receive the news, which I believed was in part the fuel that fed her anxiety.

"Oh, he was right here in Melrose," she cried, after I had retrieved the postcard for her review. "And was Josh with him?"

"I didn't have the opportunity to find out," I replied, and then offered an abridged explanation of my inability to get to Melrose in time.

"But I have access to a car," she said bitterly. "You knew that, and you didn't think to call me."

I gave her no response, although I have since thought in my defense that my acquaintance with her was not of such tenure that in my impatience after I received Bradley's card I should be expected to have considered the possibility that she might have provided the transportation to Lexington. In any event, I could only gaze across the room at her disconsolation and think to myself that the affinity that I had felt toward her upon our earlier meeting at my father's party was suddenly but a fleeting memory. It was as if we had been floating together on two inner tubes that were tied together and the rope broke, so that now we were drifting in the same vicinity, yet disconnected, cognizant of the risk that a breeze would separate us, but neither of us making an effort to reestablish the former propinquity.

When at last she broke the silence, I learned the real cause of her distress. She informed me that she intended the next day to go to the Cape where, using the ruse of delivering to Josh his dental records, she intended to kidnap him. This had recently been planned by her father, she informed me, and all that had been lacking was an opportunity, the present one being all the more advantageous because it was presented at Josh's instigation. Although she was determined to go through with her father's plan, I guessed that my failure to disclose to her that Josh was in Lexington, if he had in fact been with Bradley, had deprived her of one last chance to talk some sense into Josh before her father implemented his desperate scheme.

"Oh, come on. Kidnap him!" I exclaimed in disbelief. "How are you going to do that? Are you going to tie him up and throw him in the trunk?"

"If that's what it takes," she said, sullenly.

"It's impossible," I said, shaking my head. "You couldn't possibly overpower him. And you can't hit him over the head with a pipe or something. You can't. And even if you were willing to hit him, the chances are that he'll have someone with him. It could even be Bradley who goes with him."

"I think Bradley is going to be with him," she says, calmly. "He told me that the person who told him about the dentist is going with him."

"Well, you see," I cried, putting out my hands in an expression of futility.

"But, I thought you would help," she said, quietly.

"Me!" I exclaimed, almost laughing at the absurdity of her proposal. "You can't be serious. And, supposing for a minute I agree to help, do you really think I'm going to overpower either one of them?"

"We're going to have help," she said defiantly, refusing to be put off by my attitude.

"What kind of help?" I asked her, skeptically.

"Sam Henry is going to help us."

"Sam Henry," I said in amazement. "You mean the deprogrammer who was on trial in New York. That guy we were talking about last week."

"That's him."

"You're joking."

"I'm not. My father has hired him. He's on his way to the Cape right now."

"But why?" I asked after we had sat for a few minutes in silence, the magnitude of the situation suddenly striking me.

"My father is very determined about this," she said, quietly.

"No," I said, shaking my head. "I mean, why are you getting involved? I thought you liked the people at the ashram."

"I no longer believe that they are as harmless as they appear," she said. "Did you see the report in the paper last week about the boy who drowned himself in the Charles?"

"You don't know if he really drowned himself. He could have just fallen off the bridge," I said, finding it ironic to be taking a position contrary to the one I had only recently expostulated to Hal.

"The incident really scared my father," she said, ignoring my explanation. "I mean, that could easily have been Josh. "

"So why doesn't your father go down there with Sam Henry," I proposed.

"Josh doesn't trust my father. He's worried that my father would do just what we're planning to do. But he trusts me."

"And you think it's the right thing to do? To just drag him away from the ashram and his friends against his will?"

"I don't know what's right," she said, her voice cracking. "One minute I'm positive we should kidnap him, and the next minute I'm skeptical."

"Shouldn't he have the freedom to choose for himself?"

"He's not free to choose now. Misha, or whoever, has chosen for him."

"He's free to walk out, isn't he," I postulated. "There's no barbed wire, is there? You were there yourself."

"If Misha has taken away his ability to choose, then it doesn't matter whether he's free to walk out, does it."

"You mean his mental ability to choose," I retorted.

"Why am I explaining this to you," she cried, suddenly. "These were your arguments the other day. Weren't they?"

I looked away from her then, not only because her indictment of me was so sharp, but also because a comical image of her plan suddenly came upon me. I pictured us pouncing on Josh, throwing a burlap sack over his head and throwing him in the trunk of their car before we sped away to some hidden rendezvous with her father. At that moment I determined that I would go with her, if only to see how such an event would actually occur.

"What will I be required to do?" I asked, my question serving as my tacit consent to her request that I help her.

"Mr. Henry has a plan," she said, smiling her appreciation.

What followed was an agreement to meet at six the next morning in the Common, where I now see Jenny impatiently waiting, my escapade at Millie's house having made me late, and a long discussion concerning the length of time it would take to drive to the Cape, the location of a restaurant called the Clam Shack, which I assured her I knew well, and various other admonitions she delivered to me on Mr. Henry's behalf concerning the care I was to take in guarding my planned whereabouts for the next two days. It became clear to me that she considered my participation in the scheme a necessity, if for nothing else than for its ratification of her resolve to carry out the plan, and I wondered for a time what would have been the result of my refusal to participate.

When Jenny departed at midnight, I sat down to compose a note to Millie that would meet with Henry's requirement that I keep my activity a secret yet offer a credulous excuse for my missing dinner with her parents. My attempts to create an explanation, however, resulted only in raising doubts about the whole affair. The thought that Bradley has been brainwashed by a guru named Misha was preposterous to me, and continues to be so even as I approach Jenny and her getaway car. Bradley is a person who is skeptical about everything. Eventually, his skepticism gets the best of him. I've seen it happen a million times. There must be another explanation for his presence at the ashram.

It was at that inopportune moment that Hal called to tell me that I would have another chance to accompany him to the Cape after school the next day, and, without giving the matter much thought, I expanded the small breach of the rule I was about to break with my note to Millie to a full-blown disregard of the confidentiality of the undertaking in which I had determined I would take part. To recount Hal's raving about the lunacy of our plan would be superfluous at this point because he ultimately not only relented to my decision to accompany Jenny and Mr. Henry, but also insisted that he join us. Nothing I said would dissuade him, and, having already told him of our meeting place and knowing of his plan to go to the Cape in any case, I determined that it was prudent to consent to his involvement, particularly in light of his statements that he would show up whether I consented or not. How I am going to deliver this news to Jenny and Mr. Henry, I have chosen to determine at the last moment.

After Hal's call, I abandoned the composition of my note to Millie, thinking that my head would be clearer in the morning. But I couldn't sleep. Either the anticipation of seeing Bradley the next day or simply being on the Cape, close by the Narrows, caused me to remember a summer night we camped out on the beach up along the National Seashore near the Nauset Light. I was just a couple of years older than Carla is now, and I remembered vividly the bright full moon and the crashing and hissing of the surf. Bradley, Sally and I talked in low tones. Bradley was going through his boarding school phase. He was positive he was going to go, although my aunt and uncle told me last year that they had never given it any consideration. At the time, however, Bradley had us convinced.

"You're crazy," Sally said to him, in her peculiar defiant manner that always made Bradley upset.

"No, I'm not," Bradley insisted vehemently. "It's going to be fantastic."

"It's not," Sally asserted, shaking her head. "You're going to be homesick."

"I'm not," he cried. "I'm not going to be homesick a bit. I won't have to listen to Herrick play his stupid clarinet anymore, and I won't have to put up with all the other phony stuff that goes on around here."

"Oh, so, you think this is phony, do you," she yelled at him. "Wait till you get to a phony boarding school with all those rich kids walking around with their lacrosse sticks. Then you'll see what phony is."

"You don't know what you're talking about," he said defensively.

"Yes, I do, Bradley," she stated, confidently. "Boarding schools are phony. And they're full of kids who are so phony, nobody else wants them. Which one are you going to, anyway?"

"I don't know yet. It depends," he said, reluctant to say any more to her for fear of her retort.

"Well, you're stupid to go. You're stupid just to want to go," she said, looking away from him.

"You two think there's nothing else in the world but this place," he declared emotionally after a moment, glaring at both of us. "That's what you think. Well, there's this whole world out there full of things, and you're going to miss them all. But I'm not."

Sally and I were so surprised at his sudden rancor that we didn't speak. Neither of us knew what to say.

"Why don't you guys go to sleep," my sister Betsy said, finally. "You're keeping the whole beach awake."

"What if I can't sleep," Bradley said in an obnoxious whine.

"Then go jump in the ocean," Herrick chimed in suddenly. "Boarding school, for christsake. He wants to go to boarding school. He'll keep his whole goddamn dorm up all night long."

"Just shut up, Herrick!" Bradley shouted.

"Oh, go jump in the ocean, Bradley," Herrick said with a yawn. "I'm going to sleep. Mom and Dad aren't going to send you to any lousy boarding school anyway."

"You don't know anything, big shot," Bradley sputtered, and then, before any of us could do or say another thing, he got up and ran into the waves, throwing his clothes off to either side of him as he went.

When I slept, the memory of that summer night crept into a dream that began with an aerial image of our group on the beach, huddled together against the cold ocean air. The scene zoomed in suddenly, as if viewed through a telescope. I could distinguish the white cold cream spread across Sally's face and the seams of Bradley's shirt that he had put on inside-out after he had emerged from the ocean. The churning waves were luminescent. The moonlight was brilliant. And the shadows from the tall grasses growing on the dunes behind us lengthened as the moon moved. What happened that night, as I watched in my dream state, was that the moon sneaked over us, and time sneaked past and took away from us, without our realizing it, a wonderful part of our lives. We were such good friends.

When I awoke, I had a hard time extracting myself from the dream. Nothing so practical as meeting Jenny on time seemed of any consequence. In fact, as I washed my face I wondered whether the whole scheme had merely popped out of my sleeping mind. But I saw the note I had written to myself to call Miss Hanrahan about my absence, and the time and purpose for which I had awakened so early took hold of my senses. Time has no respect for what befalls you, I thought as I walked toward Millie's with my hastily written note clutched in my pocket. You can sail your life's course with the smoothest of tacks, until one day you'll awaken and before the day is over your dog will die, your sister will get hit by a car and there will be a coup in Chile. There's no sense in it. It's as if all these occurrences were discrete little segments delivered to you in those compact little boxes that take-out Chinese food comes in.

My plan had been to push my note surreptitiously through the mail slot at Millie's house and then make a hasty retreat to the Common to meet Jenny. As I stepped onto the porch, however, the door swung open, and there stood Millie, looking as stern as I looked surprised.

"I thought that was you coming up the walk," she said, looking behind me as if she suspected I had an accomplice with me.

"I was just dropping off this note," I stammered, pulling my hand out of my pocket and holding up the wrinkled paper to prove my assertion.

"Brrr!" she said, dramatically. "Come on in out of the cold."

"I really have to get going," I replied quickly, but to no effect, because she had already turned inside the house with the complete confidence that I would follow her, which I did.

"I was making tea," she said when we reached the kitchen, "when I looked out the window and saw a man, I didn't know then that he was you, running in the strangest manner up the street. So I watched him—you, that is—until you turned the corner."

"I wasn't running, really."

"Oh, no?" she said, raising her eyebrows and looking amused.

"I was just walking fast."

"Well, you looked like a penguin," she said, and then proceeded to do what she thought was a fair imitation of my approach to the house.

"I just had my hands in my pockets," I said, pressing my lips together.

"Anyway, it was the funniest run," she continued, after she came over to me and turned down the collar of my coat. "I thought the penguin was you, but I couldn't tell for sure because you were hiding behind your coat flaps."

"I wasn't hiding."

"Well, you looked rather stealthy anyway," she said merrily.

"It's cold," I said with enough indignation to make her study my face for a moment. "I was trying to keep the wind off my neck."

"Oh, well," she said, finally. "Have some tea, then. It will warm you up."

"No, really," I said, a little more assertively than before. "I don't have time."

"Oh, Larry. That's silly," she laughed. "It's only six in the morning."

"I know what time it is," I said in an even more hostile manner.

"You're so intense," she said seriously. "You don't have to get to school so early every day."

"I am not intense."

"Have some tea," she ordered. "I can't get over how strange you looked coming up the street."

She handed me a cup of tea and walked into the living room, where she sat on the couch next to Hannah, to whom I nodded.

"But I said to Hannah," she continued after she was settled. "'Why, I think that's Larry running by.' And she said 'No, it can't be, it's too early.' But I was sure by that time, so I went to the door to call to you when you went past the front of the house. And there you were. What a surprise!"

"I was just dropping off a note," I said.

"If I knew it would be this exciting," she laughed. "I'd get up this early every morning."

"Oh, right," Hannah said.

"Well, you just don't need as much sleep as the rest of us, Hannah," she said.

"I really have to get going," I repeated, wondering to myself why I felt like I needed permission to go.

"Oh, sit down, Larry," Millie said, perturbed, "and warm up for a minute."

"I can only stay a minute," I said, hesitantly, glancing at my watch for effect.

"I have this huge Kafka test today," she said after I sat down on the edge of a chair. "Isn't that absurd?"

"I don't know," I said. "I give tests."

"Well, for seventh graders I suppose it's fine. You have to test them to make sure they're doing the work. But to give a test to a bunch of college seniors in a seminar is ridiculous."

"I suppose it's rather Kafkaesque to give a test," I said.

"What are you talking about?"

"I mean, if a person can turn into a bug, what's so absurd about giving a test to college seniors."

"I'm not sure I follow," she says cautiously.

"That's how it seems to me, anyway."

"You have such strange notions sometimes, Larry."

Hannah suddenly giggled.

"What's so funny?" Millie asked, the ends of her mouth turning down.

"It rhymes," Hannah said, as her eyes sparkled mischievously.

"What?"

"What Larry said. It rhymes. It's Kafkaesque to give a test."

"Pretty good, wasn't it?" I quipped.

"I didn't think it was so good," Millie said.

"I like tests, myself," Hannah said, trying to look serious and deflect what appeared to be a touch of ill humor arising in Millie.

"You do?"

"They make me learn the material. I'd never memorize all this stuff if there wasn't a test."

"But that's microbiology. That's different."

"Millie, I'm late," I interrupt. "I have to go."

"Oh, Larry, relax. School doesn't start for a couple of hours."

"I'm not going to school today, actually. I'm going to the Cape."

"What?" she asked as her face became severe.

She looked at Hannah, as if Hannah knew what I was about to say. Hannah shrugged her shoulders.

"I'm going to the Cape to rescue Bradley," I said, as I stood up.

"What in the world are you talking about, Larry?"

"I wrote you this note," I said as I handed her my missive.

"What's an ashram?" she asked as soon as she had finished reading.

"It's like a commune where all the cult members live."

"So, did he just get there?"

"No. I mean I don't know. I think he's been there for a while."

"So what difference will one day make? You're taking off school for this? It's Friday. You can go tomorrow."

"I'm going with some other people who are going to help."

"Who?"

"Just Hal and some others. You don't know them."

"You got Hal into this?"

"He volunteered."

"We have plans for tonight, Larry," she cried, her voice rising with her anger. "I made the plans a whole month ago."

"I'm sorry, Mill. I really am," I said, sounding as apologetic as I could. "This just came up. I didn't know."

"So what am I going to tell my parents? That you had to run down to the Cape to rescue your fucked-up friend from this band of holy rollers?"

"I'm sorry, Mill," I said, determinedly. "I really am. But this is something I've got to do."

"Well, isn't that fine, Sir Lancelot," she spit the words at me. "Go ahead. But don't go bringing your sword around here any more."

And then a moment of impropriety overcame me. Into my head flashed an image of myself dragging around a huge sword and, try as I did, I was unable to prevent a grin from momentarily passing across my lips. That ever so slight movement of my facial expression turned out to be the spark that ignited the explosion, for she promptly picked up a magazine from the coffee table and flung it against my chest. Then she dashed up the stairs.

"Wow," Hannah said, as we both looked from the stairs to the magazine on the floor.

"I'm sorry. I really am," I stammered.

"It's nothing you did, Larry. It's what she just did. That was really something."

"She's just disappointed."

"She's really mad."

"Still."

"You need to do what you think is right, Larry. Everything else will work out."

"Hannah," Millie yelled from the top of the stairs. "You shut up."

"Mill, please try to understand," I yelled up to her.

"I understand perfectly," she said coldly, and then slammed the door to her room.

There followed my sprint up the library stairs to bring me to my present position in the middle of the Common. Jenny leans casually against the car as I approach, my chest still feeling the impact of the magazine and the physical exertion of the climb. Explaining what has just occurred is impractical, I decide, and I resolve to tell her I overslept if she presses me about my tardiness. When I'm next to the car, her eyes, the tops of which are hidden by her bangs, study me, but she doesn't say anything.

"I overslept," I say, quickly. "And I had to drop off a note. Sorry."

"Don't worry about it," she says, brushing her bangs to the side so that her eyes seem suddenly bigger.

When we get past the city and turn east, the sun shines through the windshield and I close my eyes. When I next open them we're just approaching the Sagamore Bridge.

"You've been sleeping," Jenny says pleasantly, smiling in a way that says she doesn't expect me to respond.

When Bradley and I were kids, crossing the Cape Cod Canal was a big event. On the bridge the atmosphere inside the car would suddenly become giddy, full of exhortations that we were never going back to the city, or to school, or to any of those things that we were made to do. For many years Sally and I, and sometimes Bradley, whenever he wasn't sullen, were convinced that we would one day move to the Cape forever, and we would always exclaim while on the bridge that one day we would cross its span without plan to return. But Herrick each summer had the classic line. He would hold his cap over his heart and say in a solemn voice, "The worst year of my life is dead. May it rest in peace."

9

THE CLAM SHACK DOES NOT live down to its name; it is actually a pleasing structure on Orleans Bay, immediately across, and with an excellent view of, the Orleans marina. Many years ago Elmo's Bait occupied the site where the Clam Shack now sits. Elmo's Bait was a shack from which Elmo sold bait during the day and plastic buckets of fresh clams in the late afternoon. For this reason many people called the place "Elmo's Clam Shack." That's why the new owners, after they bought the land from Elmo and tore down his shack, called their new structure the Clam Shack. Elmo didn't care that they dropped his name. With the money he made from the sale, he bought a new house up on the bluffs at Truro, and one rarely sees him in town anymore.

We were late arriving in Orleans on account of my mishap with Millie, and Sam Henry was sitting at a table near the restaurant's big windows facing the bay. Jenny didn't see him at first because he was reading a newspaper, his back facing the windows and the newspaper obscuring his face. I, of course, had no idea what he looked like and was relying completely on Jenny, but I would never have guessed the man she finally leads me to is he, not only because his back is to the view of the bay, which is how only the locals sit, but also because he is a burly black man in overalls, looking like someone I would have picked for the driver of the wrecker that we parked next to.

"Larry, this is Patrick Henry," Jenny says as he stands to greet us, and to my astonished expression he replies, "I ask people to call me Sam, which is my middle name, because I can't stand the Patrick Henry jokes." His broad grin, and the way he holds my hand for an extra moment while he looks directly into my eyes, convinces me that he is a sincere, affable man.

He has a soft but strong voice, like you hear from an announcer on a radio station that plays classical music. And all his features are rounded, which gives his countenance an unthreatening demureness. He moves around the table with a gliding motion in order to hold Jenny's chair. It's an unusual show of grace for a place like the Clam Shack, and for a man wearing overalls instead of a blue suit with a handkerchief protruding from the breast pocket. I can hardly take my eyes off him. He is Black Lightning. He is the man who, the cults claim, beats their members into submission during his deprogramming attempts.

"There is a problem," he says, immediately after we are all seated.

"Already!" Jenny exclaims.

"It is not serious," he says in a manner that defuses Jenny's alarm. "The problem that we have is that the dentist has canceled all of his appointments for the day."

"What?" Jenny says, her lips stretched with disappointment. "How do you know?"

"I spoke with your father this morning."

"Well, maybe we can get them out another way," I say. "What if Jenny and I just go over there and say we want to take them for a drive, or something like that?"

"Sure," Jenny says. "We can say that we had already planned to take off the day so we came anyway."

He studies both of our faces. Then he beckons the waitress by elevating his coffee cup. After she leaves, he folds both his hands on the table, like he's about to say grace. I assume from his failure to answer that he isn't enamored with my suggestion.

"When did you last see Bradley?" he asks quietly.

"Summer before last."

"When you see your friend again, the chances are that you will not know him," he says slowly. "Oh, you will think you know him, because his physical character will not have changed that dramatically, but you will not know him. And he will not know you. Perhaps he will not even recognize you."

"What do you mean?" I ask, some disquiet rising in my voice.

"Your friend's mind will be snapped shut by the joyous peace and harmony bestowed upon him by Misha. It will be invisible, but a wall of armor will go up between the two of you, because all that you represent to him will be a threat to his peace and harmony. You will represent all that he has been indoctrinated to see as evil. All that is in you, and that was between you, has been destroyed in him."

"Come on," I say, nervously. "That's ridiculous."

"It is what happens in these situations."

"It sounds like what happens in one of those movies where the aliens turn a whole town into zombies," I say, trying to convince myself that he is overstating the case.

"You will see for yourself," he says. "Bradley will be very much like a zombie. He will show no desires, no emotions, no pain, nothing. Incredible. Yes. There is nothing so incredible as a person's mind locked in bliss."

"But how?" asks Jenny.

"The ways of the cult are complex, and perhaps later we can speak in more detail. For now it is sufficient to tell you that by clever and deceitful ways Misha hooks his followers into completely rejecting the world as we know it. Through techniques based on fear and doubt, a person is stripped of his ability to think and choose until the only course he follows is Misha's course, a course that involves no choices, that requires complete and total passivity."

"Who is this Misha?"

"A person like you, I suspect," he says, while raising his eyebrows, "although I have never seen him."

"But from India or Korea or something like that," Jenny says.

"Would that make a difference? I don't know that he's not from Brookline," he says.

"Really!" I remark in a way that causes him to look into my eyes for so long that I have to look away to the view of the marina.

"You don't believe what I say about your friend," he says in a low tone.

"I guess not," I admit.

"Well, let's hope that I am mistaken and, in any case, that you will have the chance to determine for yourself whether what I say is accurate."

"Do you think they will let us in the ashram?" Jenny asks.

"Even if they would, I would not suggest it," he says.

"Well, how then . . . ," Jenny begins, and then stops when Henry raises both his hands.

"Do you think that Larry's arrival, completely unexpectedly and unannounced, would not arouse suspicion?"

"Well I guess it would," Jenny says.

"Wait a minute," I say. "What's the difference? Even if we were arriving to take them to the dentist, I would be unexpected."

"Larry, I never planned for you to go to the ashram," Henry says. "What I have planned is . . . "

He stops talking suddenly and looks up at something behind me.

"Hi guys," Hal announces as he puts a hand on my shoulder.

"Oh, Hal," I say nervously, as Henry regards him suspiciously and Jenny flashes me a look of panic. "You found us."

"It was a cinch."

Henry stands up and Hal looms over him, like a basketball center standing next to the referee.

"I didn't know you were bringing anyone else," Henry says with a completely blank expression that I suspect masks deep agitation.

"This is Hal Green," I say quickly. "He's a good friend, a fellow teacher, and someone who doesn't accept 'no' as an answer. Sam Henry and Jennifer Barrows."

As small as Henry is next to Hal, his hand wraps around and covers Hal's hand like a vise.

"Hal was with me that night in Boston when we saw that boy from the ashram who later drowned in the Charles," I explain quickly after Sam has sat without speaking for several moments. " We watched these two guys try to convince him to go back to Misha. I told you about this, Jenny?"

She shakes her head no.

"I'm here to help," Hal says sincerely, sensing Sam's discomfort. "You can trust us."

"Oh, it's not a matter of trust," Henry sighs and smiles at Hal. "These things sometimes take on a life of their own when too many people are involved, and the more people, the easier it will be for the ashram to find us, should we be so lucky as to be able to get Josh and Bradley away from them. You have to remember, I've had some serious problems arise in the past, and I may be facing a jail term in New York."

"I understand," Hal says, slowly, "but with all of us we also may increase the chances for success."

"Of course. But, I must be candid with both of you," Sam says. "I had originally intended to take only Josh away from the ashram, not Bradley. Even after Jenny talked to me of the possibility of you helping us, I hoped to think of a way that we would leave Bradley behind. And I am still anxious about taking Bradley. The law is unclear about the abduction of a child in these cases that is brought about and participated in by the child's parents. But there is no question that Bradley's abduction would be kidnapping. So, your participation and the abduction of Bradley bring with it a new element of risk."

"We can't just leave Bradley there," I say emotionally.

"I can see that now," Sam says quickly, looking at Hal and then at me.

"This isn't something we have any experience with, but the risks for Larry and me are the same as the risks for you, and we're willing to go forward," Hal says slowly, as he turns an inquiring look at me to which I nod my assent.

"I can live with that," Sam says to Hal. "And the benefit of having you there will be to increase the chance that we will be able to separate Bradley from Josh without the use of physical force.

"What do you mean?"

"Misha's followers never leave the ashram alone," he says, leaning over the table now and speaking in a low voice. "And I don't believe that Bradley will count as an escort. I expect to pick up three of them tomorrow, maybe even four. There seems to be an inner circle around Misha, almost like a Secret Service. One of them always goes along when a member goes outside of the ashram."

"You remember those guys at George's, don't you, Larry," Hal says. "They were a couple of creeps."

"I still don't understand."

"The preemies have been indoctrinated to believe that we are devils. I know we can be successful in separating Bradley and Josh from their bodyguard by trickery, mostly because they won't be suspecting Jenny of such a thing. But once that happens, the ruse is up. They will know from all they have heard what it is we are doing, and it will be very difficult after that to disengage Josh from Bradley. I am hoping that Bradley's seeing you will disorient him for a few moments and allow us to take Josh away."

"But why separate them?"

"What the hell is a preemie?" Hal asks.

"A junior member of the cult," Jenny says.

"It is impossible to deprogram a preemie with another preemie present. The deprogramming process is intensely personal. Part of the technique is to bombard a preemie with very personal things, statements about his family, events from his past, those kinds of things, as part of an effort to get his thought processes going again, to stimulate his emotions, his sympathies, even his insecurities and fears. As long as another preemie is present, they will prop each other up, reinforce the teachings and keep up that invisible wall that keeps everyone but Misha out."

"And what's to happen to Bradley after we separate him from Josh?"

"I don't know," Henry says sympathetically, shaking his head. "We won't be able to hang on to him very long without deprogramming him, and I should not be doing that without a parental consent. Even if I had a consent, deprogramming two preemies at the same time would be difficult, almost impossible. Unless you can somehow convince him to stay with you, you must expect that he will return to the ashram. In fact, that may be the best thing."

"How can you say that!" I exclaim, astonished at his last statement. "If going back would be good, why are we kidnapping them? Going back would be tragic."

"Not so tragic as staying out without help," Henry says. "Witness the boy who drowned in Boston."

"That sucks," Hal says in a voice so much louder than ours that Sam gives him a scolding look, which causes Hal to lower his voice almost to a whisper. "Sorry. But what are you saying? If you don't want to stay, they knock you off. Is that it?"

I look around the room to see if Hal has drawn any attention to us. Back over Henry's shoulder a waitress unloads clean silverware from a basket into a slotted tray in a drawer. Her body sways as she performs the task, keeping rhythm with a silent tune playing in her head.

"Oh, the Path didn't kill that boy," Henry says, chuckling in a kind way at the emotion Hal has demonstrated. "At least, they didn't kill him in the actual sense. Maybe the amount of dependence he had on the ashram killed him in an approximate sort of way. But, perhaps for several years, the ashram had saved him as well."

"Sorry for being stupid," Hal says, shaking his head, "but I don't understand that at all."

"It isn't intuitive. You're right," Sam says, smiling. "Preemies are mentally conditioned to the point of personal addiction to Misha. It truly is a brainwashing process. Being outside the ashram in an uncontrolled circumstance is traumatic. Whatever insecurities caused a preemie to be easily susceptible to Misha's influence are magnified when he is separated from Misha. The boy who drowned in the Charles had experienced serious psychological problems prior to joining the Path and had a long history of abusing drugs. The Path offered him a retreat from his problems. It allayed his distress by suppressing his personality. If the Path killed him, they killed him by covering up his stress and by keeping him away from counseling or other rehabilitation techniques. At the end, when the Path finally caught up with him, they may also have turned him away as punishment for his frequent flights from the ashram, although I'm sure they ultimately intended to take him back. Rejection, followed by reconciliation, is a technique they sometimes employ. They just misjudged the magnitude of his reaction to their rejection."

"Then you knew that boy?" Jenny gasps.

"I did. I made an unsuccessful attempt to deprogram him. What I do doesn't always work. And even after what appears initially to be a success, there is a long and dangerous period of readjustment that I call a time of floating. During that boy's period of floating, many of his old anxieties manifested themselves. He became seriously despondent and his parents could not bear to see him that way. In a moment of weakness for all of them, they actually took him back to the ashram."

"Incredible," Hal says, after a soft but emphatic whistle and nod of the head. "After all that, they took him back to the ashram."

"You are both teachers," Henry says. "You must know that this is a hard time for a young person to be coming of age in America. Never in our history has society offered so many opportunities, so many things to experience, to feel, to be. But never have young people been offered so little direction. The nation's affluence has eroded the material that ambition is made from. And positivism, optimism, excitement for life—whatever you call that spirit that drove the settling of this country—has escaped us, lost in the desperation of the Vietnam War, in the bullets of the assassins of the Kennedys and King, whisked away like the gasoline vapors rising from the front of the gasoline lines. We are a nation of narcissists, all of us wanting desperately everything we can have before it's too late, before someone drops the bomb, before the black hole of the workforce swallows us. When a young person can never get enough of this experience to satisfy his narcissistic craving, he looks for the ultimate. He sees nature and he seeks to be one with it. He lusts after serenity, and satisfaction, to be whole. And so he turns to the ashram, where everything is one, and everyone is the same, and his cravings and all the other anxieties of life go away. Somewhere along the path of affluence he has developed the misconception that he is entitled to be rid of life's anxieties. And Misha grabs this misconception, fosters it, and ultimately snares him in the promise of a life of serenity."

I look from the focused expression on Jenny's face to the relatively indifferent atmosphere of the Clam Shack's environment and the few patrons scattered around the room holding up newspapers or engaged in what appear to be trivial exchanges of banalities, and I'm struck suddenly by the message of Breughel's *The Fall of Icarus*, which, ironically, Jenny had been discussing with my father when I met her. What Sam is saying is so intense, and the reason for our being in this place so serious, that I expect that all of the patrons should be gathered around our table to listen intently to our discourse. Yet no one pays us the smallest amount of attention.

Our waitress stands by the coffee pots, gazing out the window, She comes out of her daze suddenly, as if an alarm has sounded, and she looks around the tables for coffee cups to refill. Not finding one, she grabs the top of her panty hose through her uniform and tugs it higher up by rising to her toes and wiggling.

"A more immediate problem is that we don't have a safe house," Henry is saying in an anxious tone.

"A safe house?" Jenny asks.

"A place where we can take Josh, and Bradley if necessary, after we separate them from their companions. I had one arranged, but only for tonight and tomorrow night. That won't be long enough if we don't start until tomorrow. Besides, I looked at the place earlier, and it isn't really suitable. It's in a local neighborhood and too close to several other houses that are occupied year round. I'm afraid we'll draw too much attention. The first thing Misha will do is notify the police. We need something more secluded. Then, there's also the question of tonight."

"There's my family's summer house," I volunteer quickly, without considering the consequences.

"Why didn't I think of that!" Hal exclaims.

"It's fairly secluded, also," I say, excitement rising in my voice. "It's down a long sandy road, about three quarters of a mile from the town road."

"Any chance of someone else showing up there?" Henry asks.

"I don't think so," I say, "particularly during the week. The house isn't used much in the winter, except on holidays."

"And it has a great view," Hal blurts out.

"Does this sound like a vacation?" I pose to Hal, after watching Henry grin.

"If I had an alternative, I would not impose," Henry says after a moment.

"It's no imposition," I say. "Really."

"And you're sure no one will be there."

"Yes. But there is one thing," I say, quickly, as the thought occurs to me. "Bradley knows the house. His family owns it with my family. We've spent all our summers there."

"That may not be so bad," Henry says after he gazes into the distance for a few moments. "The familiarity with the place may help us with Bradley. Let's go take a look at it."

Outside the air is crisp and the old clamshells that pave the parking lot crunch under our shoes as we walk toward Jenny's car. I see Hal's car in the next row, and I try to guess which car is Henry's. As Jenny puts her key in the door lock, Henry, to my astonishment, jumps up into the cab of the tow truck parked next to us. On the door is painted "Jimmy's Wrecker Service, Chatham, Massachusetts."

"I follow you," he calls to us after he rolls down the window.

"Ditto," Hal says as he walks in the direction of his car.

"Who the hell is Jimmy!" I exclaim to Jenny as the car moves toward the street.

"Which way?" she asks, ignoring my surprise over the truck, Henry's possession of it not seeming to be the least bit extraordinary to her.

"Left," I say. "Then straight through the traffic light, around the circle and right onto Chatham Road."

"So what do you think of Mr. Henry?" I ask her when we're on Chatham Road.

"He's committed to what's he's doing," she says.

"I guess so," I say. "It seems that way to me, too."

"He started doing this after he nearly lost his own child to a cult in Southern California," she says.

"I didn't know that."

"It's a story he told the other night at my parents' house. Maybe he'll tell it again. It was that experience that made him see how serious these religious organizations had become."

"I see. But it's all so incredible to me. It's like a TV movie almost. Don't you think so?"

"I believe it because I've seen Josh. Maybe you'll have a different impression after you've seen Bradley."

"I suppose so," I say, although I don't really believe I'll have a different impression because I can't imagine Bradley acting in any way that Henry described, in any way other that his own finicky, discontented self.

"Okay," I say, after we've travelled a couple of miles. "Around the curve up ahead there will be a house with a white picket fence. When we get to it, we start counting."

"Counting?" Jenny asks querulously, her lips breaking into a grin that indicates she expects me to tell her we have to count houses or trees in order to determine where to turn next.

"That's how I find the road down to the Narrows," I say as seriously as I can manage. "There's not a sign or anything, and it's hard to see. So at the white fence you close your eyes and count to thirty."

"You want me to close my eyes," she laughs.

"Sure. It's a straight road after that."

"You're really crazy. You know that?"

"I don't know about you, but I don't count evenly if I have my eyes open," I say with a deadpan expression. "I get distracted."

"But how fast should I go while I'm counting?"

"I don't know. I never bothered with those details."

"Oh, great."

"I tell you what. If it bothers you so much, you just keep driving, and I'll count."

"Okay. Fine," she says. "I can do that. You count."

"Here's the fence," I say quickly and close my eyes. "One, two, three—don't slow down."

"I thought you told me you'd didn't bother with how fast you were going."

"Ten, eleven, twelve. Don't distract me."

"Which way am I going to turn?"

"Left. Twenty-one, twenty-two."

"I don't see anything," she says nervously.

"Thirty," I say, opening my eyes. "You slowed down."

"Do you think we missed it?"

"No. It's right up there. Right between the two big old trees with all the ivy growing all over them."

"I thought you said there weren't any landmarks," she exclaims, looking at me with mock disgust.

"You can't see them with your eyes closed," I say.

"This is stupid," she says in an exasperated tone. "I don't see any ivy."

"It's the winter," I say, innocently. "The leaves fall off the ivy in the winter. That's why I count."

10

AT THE NARROWS THE SKY is blue and the air is crisp. Red and yellow leaves, made brilliant by the morning sun, rain down across the lawn beneath the huge tree that grows right up against the south side of the house. This is one of only a few days in the autumn that the leaves fall like this, and, no matter what the outcome of our plan, I decide that my trip to the Narrows is fortuitous.

I came out onto the porch after we arrived because I felt awkward watching the others walk around and remark how spectacular it was that so many generations had occupied the house or how the view of Pleasant Bay was breathtaking. For me the furniture and the views were reminders of safe, comfortable childhood years. I remembered my grandfather Clements sitting in the rocking chair that was placed in the square of sunlight that poured through a window one Easter Sunday morning, with five children sitting on the floor around him as he told for at least the hundredth time about how it had taken his father an entire year to drag by mule the huge fireplace rocks across the sandy roads. Somehow the memory made the hearth a secret possession that my guests were about to discover, as if it were a page from a hidden diary, and I could not bear to hear Henry's remarks about the craftsmanship with which it was constructed. I retreated as unobtrusively as possible.

During the next hour, I watched the clouds move along the horizon but not appear any closer, as if there were an invisible shield out over the Atlantic Ocean that pushed the clouds to the south, around us. The tide is coming in; I know by the direction that the water is travelling through the channel between Pleasant Bay and Little Pleasant Bay. The direction is easy to discern because Little Pleasant Bay is a basin that fills up and empties every time the tide changes, which causes the water to rush through the narrow channel between our peninsula and the little group of islands that cluster next to the National Seashore. It was this narrow channel that inspired my great grandfather to name the place the Narrows, or so family lore has it.

"Swiss or American?" Hal says suddenly from just inside the screen door, startling me into a complaint but nevertheless causing me to follow him, hungrily, back to the kitchen. Hal is whistling and the melody reminds me of the day in our third year of college he came back to our room clutching a letter from the Dean telling him that he would not be allowed to register the next semester on account of his poor academic performance. We knew the letter was coming; Hal had ignored more than the usual number of warnings, which he had been accorded on account of the large sums of money that his father, a prominent alumni, had contributed to the school. Yet, the actual receipt of the letter was for Hal a bucket of cold water in the face. Not only was he expelled from the university, but he would now be unwelcome at home. A tersely written letter from his father had made the consequences of his expulsion perfectly clear.

I was surprised when I read the expulsion letter to discover that the action was depicted only as a probationary one, and that by attending summer classes Hal would be given another opportunity in the fall. I assumed that his disinheritance was likewise provisional. After only a brief deliberation, however, Hal, to his credit, sent by return mail to the Dean with a carbon copy to his father, his decision to withdraw from the university. And a week later, when he left for Paris to find "the meat inside the nut," as he characterized his search, he was no longer the trust fund baby who had walked into our room at the start of our freshman year carrying a lacrosse stick on his shoulder.

Before he left for Paris, Hal begged me to go with him, but I was too conventional. What experience I hungered for I found vicariously in the books I read, in Joyce and Aquinas, to name a couple. I was the son of two professors, and I could not escape their influence. And Hal was back in a year, resuming his education with a new conviction, and hanging around my apartment, telling me how his experience had set him free. And for me, he believed, a similar tonic was needed to get below the surface I thought my studies had only scratched. "Oh, to know from doing," he would say. "Savoir pour l'avoir eprouve. The feeling is exquisite." For my part I politely shared his enthusiasm for my own enlightenment, vigorously inquiring after every moment of his experience, in much the same fashion that I had seen my mother deflect her sister's encouragement, when I was twelve and old enough to survive my father's care, to use the small inheritance from their father for travel as she had done. The next year Carla was born, rendering my aunt's plans for my mother moot.

"Ham, Swiss, mustard, hold the mayo," Hal sings, as he slaps the plate onto the table. "Il n'y a pas de quoi."

His French is impeccable, the product of his years in prep school, followed by his Parisian sabbatical. I stare at him for a moment, an amazed look on my face generated by the prospect that he has been reading my mind. Of course, he has no reason to pay me any regard, and he eats his sandwich unaware that I for a few moments observe the way he compulsively chews each bite twenty-five times.

"It's quiet," I say, looking around at the empty kitchen.

"Jenny's taking a nap," Hal says, "and Henry went to town."

"I don't know what to think about Henry," I say, abandoning the second half of my sandwich by pushing the plate to the side.

"I know what you mean," he says, looking at the plate and then at me. "But I have a good feeling about him, all the same. I suppose that's stupid, to go and kidnap a couple of guys just because you have a good feeling about somebody, when you're not sure whether what you're doing is the right thing and all."

"It sounds stupid when you put it like that," I say. "It sounds like we're acting frivolously."

"Are you going to eat that sandwich, Larry?"

"No. Go ahead," I say, pushing the plate over to him.

"Anyway, that's not true," he says, as he picks up the sandwich. "Sometimes you do things just because you know that you're right. You follow your intuition, if you see what I mean."

"My intuition tells me we don't know what we're getting into," I say.

"Nonsense," he says, pursing his lips and moving his head side to side. "I figure there's not much to worry about. Just like everything else, we've probably made it into a bigger thing than it is. We'll probably just drive them over here instead of to the dentist. It won't be a big deal."

"What I'm worried about is that it's really going to piss off Bradley, tricking him like this. What if he truly believes in this cult? My taking part in this scheme will insult him. He'll think I don't believe he's smart enough to distinguish a holy man from a con artist, or something like that."

"Oh, I wouldn't worry about that."

"You wouldn't?"

"No. If he's your friend, he'll see what you're trying to do, and thank you for it, even if he thinks you're wrong."

"But what if Henry is right, and he's been so indoctrinated that he thinks I'm a devil or something?"

"Then, we're doing the right thing."

"Oh. But then what?"

"Larry, I'm not an expert at this stuff, you know."

"I know. I'm sorry."

"I look at it this way. Once we get them here, what we do next will become apparent."

"That doesn't give me a lot of comfort somehow."

"Hey. What can you do?" he exclaims, shrugging his shoulders.

"I guess you're right. But do you think Henry is on the level? Maybe he has some ax to grind with these people that he's not telling us about."

"No. I don't think so. He's not the type."

"And he hasn't exactly told us much about his plan. I mean, maybe he's out buying weapons right now."

"That's preposterous. Do you really think that? I have such a different impression of the guy."

"Well, the last couple of times he wasn't successful. Maybe he's frustrated."

"You're falling for the cult propaganda."

"Well, this magazine article I read about him says that he beats up kids after he kidnaps them. They said he stripped a girl naked in Oregon and that in California he tied this guy to a chair and doused him with water."

"Oh, come on," he says. "Can you see him doing that? You can't believe everything you read in the goddamn magazines."

"I guess not."

"I think he's okay, but who knows. I've met Henry, so its natural I'd believe him. We haven't talked to any of these cult guys."

"We did meet those guys in the bar."

"True," he says, "but I wouldn't exactly say we talked to them."

"You did all the talking," I quip.

"Those were not nice people, Larry. Religious or not," he says as he stands up and grabs both soda bottles in one hand before he walks to the sink.

"Still, maybe we should just go over to the ashram and talk to them," I say. "This could all be some big misunderstanding."

"What are they going to say with everybody standing around listening?"

"I don't know."

"This way we can get them alone and make our own minds up. If they scream they want to go back, we'll let them go."

"That's not what Henry and Jenny have in mind."

"So, we'll let Bradley go. We can't do anything about Jenny's brother."

"I guess not. But I don't feel good about this. It's not Henry. I don't know what it is," I say, as Hal walks to the window to investigate a noise in the driveway.

"Henry is back," he says quickly. "Just relax. We've had too much time to think about it. That's all."

"Maybe," I say as Henry comes through the door.

While the door is open, I notice that I can hear the wind blowing but I can't hear the waves. That means the wind is blowing offshore, out of the northwest, which usually is an indication that the temperature is about to drop.

"This is a beautiful house, Larry," Henry says, as he puts two heavy shopping bags on the counter. "I'll guess it's been in your family a long time."

"My great-grandfather built it," I say, politely.

"I thought so. The detail in the wood on the fireplace mantle and the balustrades on the stairs made me think it was pretty old, and that it was built by a craftsman."

"It was probably about a hundred years ago," I say, "but my great-grandfather was a merchant in Boston, not a craftsman."

"I would have guessed even earlier. And, if not a craftsman, he was certainly one who appreciated the work of a good craftsman. Regardless, it's a nice thing to have in the family."

"We almost lost it once," I state, not really sure why I'm volunteering this part of my family history. But it seems right, and I continue. "There was a break in ownership in the 1940s. My mother's father sold the house to pay college tuition for his daughters. Just before I was born my mother and her sister put their money together to buy it back."

"That's really something," Henry says, shaking his head and walking into the living room.

"Hey, I didn't know that," Hal says as we follow him.

"I guess I never mentioned it," I say, shrugging, but wondering why I had never told Hal.

Hal flops down on the couch, while Henry strolls around the room. He stops by the wall near the stairs. We have many family pictures hanging on that wall.

"You have three sisters," Henry says, looking at a group of pictures.

He thinks there are only three because he's looking at a photograph of my older sisters and me taken on the Fourth of July in 1962, just before Carla was born. In the photograph my sister Betsy is smiling so broadly that the sun is reflecting off her braces. What's remarkable is that Betsy cried that entire summer on account of those braces, which she was always trying to hide. In the adjoining picture Betsy and Herrick are standing in the ocean with their arms around each other, looking like the best of friends. That is also deceiving, because one minute they'd be best pals, as in the photograph, and the next minute they hated each other. I remember that one day my father had to run out onto the lawn and break up a fight they were having. The conflict wasn't just a verbal one. Herrick had this huge scratch down the side of his face. After my father pulled Betsy off him, he ran upstairs and didn't come down for a week.

"There's a fourth sister, who hadn't been born when those pictures were taken," I explain to him.

"I see," he says. "And these others?"

"Those are my cousins, who also own the house. That's my cousin Herrick with my sister Betsy. And in the next picture are Bradley and Sally."

"So, this is this Bradley?"

"That's Bradley," I say. "There's a later picture of both of us, over on the right."

"It's such a beautiful place. I wouldn't mind spending the summer here," he says as he turns away from the pictures and walks over to the window. He puts his hands in his pockets and sighs. After a few moments, he turns back to look at me and then sits down in a chair across from Hal. I sit on the hearth.

"I usually find neutral ground," he sighs. "I'm afraid we may be about to add an unhappy memory to your collection of good ones," he says, waving his hand toward the wall of photographs. "I'm not very happy about this, even though I don't seem to have an alternative."

"It will be fine. And it's a good place, because nobody comes around here in the winter," I say quickly, not wanting to comment on his mistaken notion that the Narrows has been nothing but idyllic for all of its occupants. And I can't believe that a man as astute as he appears to be actually believes that the photographs on the wall paint the entire picture. His interpretation of the house's contents is to some extent, I think, an act of kindness on his part, a deference shown before what he suspects will be an unfortunate event for me. And from these thoughts a panic grows inside of me, and, as preposterous as it may seem, I begin to think that Henry knows more than he has told us—that his display of empathy is a harbinger of a suffering that is about to befall me with tomorrow's activity.

"Bradley is going to be a problem," Henry says as he rubs his forearms with his hands.

"Why would you think that?" I ask, a bit defensively, "I don't think he'll get in the way."

"That isn't what I'm worried about," he says as he looks into my eyes.

"Well, what then?" I ask quickly and look away.

"It's you I'm worried about, actually," he says softly as he leans toward me, putting his hands on his knees.

"Me?"

"You. To me Bradley and Josh are strangers. I know about them only what words can tell. Of Bradley you know much more. All the years. This place. All that those photographs show. What you will probably see when Bradley comes here will be very traumatic for you. I don't know."

"Is the guy going to be a monster or what?" Hal asks without moving his hands from their position behind his head. He startles me because he had been still for so long, as if he had become a part of the couch and the coffee table that is supporting his feet.

"It could be as bad as that," Henry says. "And then he could seem to be perfectly normal. I've seen it both ways. But I've never seen a preemie walk out of an ashram, back to his former life, without severe emotional distress. I don't want to tell you I'm positive. I'm never positive. But I'm wary. The worse cases are the ones where the preemie says he's fine, where he doesn't object too much, where he appears willing to endure his separation from the cult."

"Bradley has never been satisfied for long with anything," I say, reflecting to myself with a little amusement how Bradley is actually the quintessential malcontent. "I would think by this time, Misha would be happy to be rid of him."

"As counterintuitive as it may sound, the opposite is often true," Henry says seriously. "The cult offers perpetual satisfaction."

"How's that?" Hal asks.

"By taking away personality, basically. Your personality is a conglomeration of thousands of individual traits. Sense of humor, curiosity, frustration level, those kinds of things. Imagine for a minute that your personality is a big jar of water and that you have lined up on a table next to it ten glasses. Each glass represents one of the general elements of your personality. If you distribute the water between the glasses—for example, you pour humor in one glass, dourness in a second, everyone has at least a little of each category—what do you end up with?"

"Ten glasses all with different levels," Hal says.

"That's it," Henry says. "But with a preemie, you have one glass that is full, and all the rest have small amounts that are equal."

"Which one is full?"

"Bliss," he says. "Eternal bliss. In preemie training it is compared to having everything you want, always, forever. If you can believe that such a state is true, can you see why an individual who is chronically dissatisfied might gravitate toward such a doctrine?"

"Even with bliss, Bradley could be dissatisfied," I quip. "Believe me. It wouldn't be perfect, not for him."

"That's the Bradley you know," Henry says.

"So what are you saying?" Hal asks. "Are you saying that Misha has brainwashed all these people?"

"As preposterous as that sounds, yes."

"It's hard to fathom," Hal says.

"Not really. Remember, every preemie starts out willing to believe what Misha tells him. Most are disillusioned, some are disappointed. The immediate cause isn't so important. What's important is that in their minds life has let them down. To many, society is an easy blame. To others, it may be their parents or their friends. In any case, Misha offers a replacement for all those people, and for society generally."

"Still, you'd think after a while they'd get wise," Hal says.

"What you're forgetting," Henry says, "is that by the time they would get wise, as you say, they have lost their ability to think for themselves. Misha has captured their personalities by that time. He has stolen them with a blitz of indoctrination. It's like watching the white lines going by when you're driving down a highway. Soon you lose touch with everything around you."

"Sounds like you're heading for a wreck," Hal says.

"That's how we get them back," Henry says.

"What do you mean?"

"The same as what happens to you when you're mesmerized on the highway. Something comes along, either a loud sound, like a horn, or a flash of bright headlights, or something else, that snaps you back to your senses. You take control of the car again. We do the same thing to deprogram a preemie. We create a disturbance in the stupor Misha has put him in that snaps him back to himself. His personality is still there—it has only been suppressed, the same way a driver's general alertness is suppressed by the mesmerizing effect of the white lines."

"What kind of disturbance?" I ask.

"It depends upon the person. In some cases showing them something as simple as family pictures will start the process. Other times, starting an ideological argument will work because after a while you can usually bring them around to see that Misha's teachings don't stand on a good philosophical base.

The trick is to get their minds working again. Sometimes finding a disturbance is difficult."

"It's Sleeping Beauty," Hal exclaims suddenly, causing Henry and me to turn toward the sound of footsteps on the stairs.

"Oh, thanks a lot," Jenny says, blushing slightly at the attention.

"Well, Jenny. Are you refreshed?" Henry asks.

"Oh, yes. Thank you. I was so tired."

"One of the best things in life, isn't it? A nap."

"I have to admit," Jenny says, "that I take a nap almost every day."

"I wish I could make the time," Henry says. "I always feel better after a nap."

"It doesn't take long. Maybe twenty minutes," she says.

I can't help noting to myself that Jenny's characterization of her napping routine is inaccurate. Anyone who has weighed a cabbage in the grocery knows that a cabbage does not appear to be as heavy as it actually is. The same is true for things like how much one eats or how long a nap one takes. People who say they don't eat much really eat like horses, and people who say they only nap for twenty minutes really snore away for hours. Jenny has in fact been upstairs for several hours.

"If I went to sleep for twenty minutes, I'd feel like shit," Hal says.

"Some people don't nap well," Henry says.

"Besides, where would I go? I'd have to go in the coat closet in the back of the room or something."

"We don't have a society that's designed itself for naps," Henry muses. "In Spain businesses close for a good part of the afternoon, then stay open later. That accommodates the nap."

"I'd rather be done earlier, to tell you the truth," Hal says.

"It's a natural stress reliever," Henry says. "It's like slowing down after you've walked up a hill."

"Stress doesn't bother me," Hal says.

"Maybe not," Henry says.

"I'm just not the napping type," Hal says. "I have too much energy."

"You fall asleep at your desk all the time, Hal," I say in an exasperated manner, feeling that having to tolerate two such preposterous inaccuracies in one day is too much for me to bear.

"You're crazy, Larry. You come in when I'm concentrating like hell, and you think I'm sleeping."

"Oh, come on. Do you always snore when you're deep in concentration? And why do you study the paint on the ceiling."

"And so what if I do nod off once in a while," he says, defensively. "That's not as bad as being caught sitting in the lotus position on top of my desk."

"What are you guys talking about?" Jenny giggles.

"Old Yogi Larry here was leading his class into the realms of mystery a few days ago," Hal says sarcastically.

"You were?"

"He's exaggerating," I say quickly. "It was just a part of a lesson about mystical experiences expressed in literature."

"Oh, William Blake. Then you're teaching William Blake," Henry says.

"Well, I haven't gotten there yet. And I don't know if I will. I'll be happy to get to Whitman, to tell you the truth."

"I love the lines that describe Mercy as having a heart, 'Pity a face.' And what else?"

"'And Peace, the human dress,'" I say, a little surprised that he appears to have retained these images as if he has just read the poem.

"That's right," Henry says with an enthusiasm that makes me forget my former skepticism about him. "That's a great image."

"All I remember," Hal says, "is the one about the tiger eating the lamb."

"That's not what happens at all," Jenny laughs.

"That shows you what I know."

"Or what you don't know," I say.

"Long division. Just ask me about long division. Or logarithms. Do you want to talk logarithms?"

"Don't overexert yourself now," I say.

"Don't worry."

He leans back in the corner of the couch and yawns. All of us are quiet for a few minutes. I think that I should get up and build a fire because the long shadows over the lawn suggest that the warmth in the house will not last much longer. But the four of us sitting so quietly all of a sudden, with the very slight rumble of the waves in the distance, fills me with such an intense serenity, if in fact one can feel serenity strongly, that I cannot muster the motivation to walk outside to the wood box. I determine that I will wait until someone speaks and the moment is broken.

The sound of waves from the National Seashore is so distant that I may be imagining it, or confusing it with the more immediate sound of the north wind. In any case, the sounds make me recall a trip to Maine I took with Millie last summer to visit Skip, a friend of hers from Hartford. Skip had landed a job in a summer dinner theater waiting tables and acting in bit parts in the performances. In the show we saw he played an elderly butler who is murdered in an early scene; he is hit over the head with a fireplace implement. His early demise was necessary so that he could return to his tables to serve dessert.

Everything that I had anticipated about that trip to Maine turned out to be wrong. I had expected that Skip, being an actor, was going to be a tall handsome fellow with blow-dried hair. He turned out to be as skinny as a rake handle with hair like string and eyes that bulged so painfully out of his head that

I suspected he had an untreated thyroid condition. I had also looked forward to hearing the sound of waves as I went to sleep. Skip did not live near the ocean; rather, he lived in town over a cafe that opened for breakfast at 5:30 a.m., at which time the morning cook banged pans around the sink, cursing the evening cook for his failure to wash them.

One positive thing I have to say for Skip is that he did not pretend to be someone he was not. He didn't make excuses for his bit parts or his seedy accommodations, and didn't aspire to someday being either a great actor or a great waiter. In fact, his one aspiration was to find a position at the end of the summer that would be as comfortable as his one at the summer theater. He was truly a free spirit. And that, I believe, is what attracted Millie to him. She thought that being associated with Skip made her in some osmotic way a free spirit also, a status she periodically wished for. The problem for Millie is, however, that a true free spirit is in fact committed to being uncommitted, and that is a state of mind for which Millie is far too conventional, the necessity of hiding her free-spiritedness from her parents being far too arduous a task for any true free spirit to accept.

Hal starts to snore. He has both his legs up on the couch, his head is back and his mouth wide open. The moment of serenity is shattered.

"That's the guy who never takes a nap. What did I tell you!" I exclaim to the others.

"He's dreaming of lambs jumping over tigers, no doubt," Jenny says and laughs.

"It's a comfort just to watch him," Henry says. "I am enjoying his relaxation vicariously. It's been so long since I have been able to put my head down on a pillow without worrying about what was to happen to me when I awoke or without thinking about all the young people in the ashrams who live so regimented an existence that the frivolous nap is unthinkable."

"I can't believe Misha can persuade all these people to continue as they do," I say.

"But it's not so unusual, really," Henry says, his voice rising with a teacher's enthusiasm. "When I worked in a consumer fraud agency in Texas, I saw many things that dishonest people would do to swindle others out of their money or their possessions. You know. You read about them all the time. And the ones you usually hear about are not nearly as bad as the ones you don't. But they're all the same basically. They prey upon a person's ignorance and appeal to his fancy. And I mean ignorance, too. Many very smart, well-educated people are an easy touch for a good con man. You may laugh and think that no one with any sense would buy snake oil, or an elixir promising eternal life. But what's the difference, I ask you, between those things and healing crystals, or exotic vitamins, brown rice, incense or any of the macrobiotic dietary programs?"

"What about laws requiring truth in advertising? I've always assumed there were some controls over these things."

"The good con artist always stays just on the other side of the laws. Read one of those advertisements carefully next time and you'll see what I mean. And, of course, many of these things are sold by word of mouth, and that's harder to police. All the same, every day millions of dollars are swindled from people who hardly have the income to put food on the table for their children."

"So what's the connection?" Jenny asks. "Is Misha selling something?"

"Yes, he is," Henry says emphatically. "He most certainly is. First of all, let me point out to you that, as in all cults, a big part of a preemie's day is to go out raise money for his group. In this case they sell flowers. You've seen them. Those little pink carnations. Oh, they say they'll give them to you for a donation, but that's just a procedure to keep them from having to obtain a permit. The worse part is that they lie. They tell people that their donations will be used for philanthropic purposes. And the use depends upon where they are. On the West Coast, they say that the money will go to an organization concerned with the environment. In Boston, the latest is that the money will be used by an organization that is providing food to Bangladesh. They are lies. Both of them. The preemies I have deprogrammed have told me that Misha teaches that these lies are okay because all those people are Satan, all people who do not follow the Path are Satan, and it is okay to lie to Satan. It is God's work to lie to Satan."

"It is hard for me to accept," I say. "I believe that your convictions are genuine. But it's hard for me to believe that someone as intelligent as Bradley or Jenny's brother could be convinced to go out on the street and lie to people like that. I mean, I can accept most of the other practices like sleeping on the floor and all that kind of stuff. But when you talk about fraud or coercion, I have a hard time."

"I can understand that, and I thank you for your candidness," Henry says sincerely. "Sometimes I worry about how quickly parents believe what I'm saying, because even to my ears after all this time the story occasionally sounds unbelievable. Parents are quick to accept the story often because it offers an explanation for the total rejection they have just experienced from their child, and to say that he or she has been brainwashed helps with their own feelings of guilt over what is happening. One thing I've found about parents is that, whether they express it or not, they are quick to blame themselves for what happens to their child. I do it myself all the time."

"Do you have more than one child?" Jenny asks.

"I have six, and, lord, I've seen them so little in the past few years. And, if the prosecutors in Denver and New York have their way, I may not see them at all for a long time."

"Are there still charges pending?"

"Oh, yes. I'm a defendant in both New York and Colorado."

"It must be hard," Jenny says.

"If there's one thing I learned growing up in the ghetto in Texas, it's that life is only going to be what you make of it. I'm a strongly religious person," Henry says quietly. "I believe in God as much as the next person, if not more. But I also know that God doesn't pass out favors. In this world you make your own way, and while you're doing that you ought to be prepared to help others along."

"Do you really think Josh and Bradley have been brainwashed?" I ask.

"Absolutely," Henry says emphatically. "As sure as I'm sitting here."

"But how?" Jenny asks. "It's so incredible."

"My first encounter with cults was in Santa Cruz, when a group from the Children of God almost ran off with my son. I was disturbed by the look on his face when he came home that evening and recounted what had happened to him. I was working in community affairs at the time, and about a week later a mother filed a report with my agency that her son had run away to a commune run by the same group. So I began an investigation into the cult's activities and soon discovered from reports at crisis centers and other agencies around the county that there were quite a few young people who had been recruited by that cult. Almost all of the reports were the same in their description of the child when he established contact with his parents, that he sounded like a zombie or that he was reading from a script. At first I thought that perhaps the recruiters were using some form of instant hypnosis. If that were the case, and I could establish it, I believed I would be able to have the law enforcement authorities go into the commune and free all of the children being held there on the grounds that hypnosis was a form of imprisonment. But I was up against what I knew would be the cult's claim, that their members had a constitutional right to practice the religion of their choice. And I didn't have enough evidence to support my hypnosis theory and justify obtaining a warrant. So I decided to go and see for myself, and on a subsequent weekend I went to a beach in Monterey where the Children of God had been seen recruiting. I found them and joined up."

"You joined the cult!" Jenny exclaims.

"Sure. What better way to find out what was happening?"

"But you could have been hypnotized yourself."

"Of course, I had thought of that. But I had to take a chance, and in hindsight I was having a hard time believing in my instant hypnosis theory. And unfortunately what I discovered was not so clear cut as hypnosis, because if it had been I could have closed down the operation immediately. What the cults do is like hypnosis only to the extent that the subjects appear to be functioning on a different level of consciousness from normal people. Basically, once the cult gets you to their commune, usually under a pretext of going to a workshop to talk about whatever social or philosophical topic they have interested you in, they begin a subtle but intense indoctrination process. They never leave your side and before you know it, you haven't slept or had anything to eat for a long period of time. Then they really pour it on, hammering away at all your phobias and anxieties, particularly those that are just below the surface in young adults. You know, family problems, sexuality—things like that. Pretty soon you get so weary that your good sense stops functioning and they've got you."

"So what happened to you?"

"They almost got me. I had the advantage of knowing what they were doing, and I also had the advantage of age, meaning that I wasn't as vulnerable to assault on my insecurities.

That was mainly because none of the leaders were trained to program an older person and a lot of the things they were saying were easy for me to see through. But after a while I did feel myself slipping, drifting off into a fog and agreeing with what a leader was preaching to me. I was so tired and hungry that I was ready to agree with anything just to make them stop lecturing me. Then, in a lucid moment, I knew I had to get out fast. But we were in a secure compound and leaders were very vigilant—so I couldn't just walk out. I had witnessed earlier a girl attempt to leave and a swarm of leaders surrounded her by the time she reached the gate. They were chanting and yelling that Satan was outside, and if she left she would be going right into his arms—that her leaving would lead to a catastrophe being inflicted upon her and her family and friends. It was very powerful and her determination to leave broke down. I did not want to put myself into that position. So I told a leader that I had a thousand dollars in a bank account and wanted to give it to the commune. They immediately arranged for two leaders to drive me to the bank so I could withdraw the money. In the city I told them I needed to use a restroom and we stopped at the bus station. When they did not accompany me into the station, I just walked out a side door and left them waiting for me in the car."

"What did you do then?" Jenny asks.

"At first I went through all the normal channels. I filed a report with my agency and with the governor. When that got no results, I helped some parents file a complaint with the county sheriff. We were unsuccessful, because all of the kids claimed that they were members at their own choosing and did not want to leave the compound. The sheriff's deputies were not helpful—they only noted the smiling faces of the kids and wrote down what they said."

"What did you expect them to do?" I ask. "Drag them out kicking and screaming?"

"You're right. My expectations had been too high. Perhaps I should have immediately recognized what I would have to do to rescue these children. I suppose I still believed in the governmental process and needed to exhaust all the tradition avenues before I resorted to an unconventional strategy."

"Unconventional strategy?" Jenny asks.

"The use of force. Pure and simple. Some people say what I'm doing is kidnapping. But it's not, because kidnapping requires the abduction of a person against his will. Once these kids have been programmed by the cults, they no longer have a free will to exercise."

"But it seems like you could have established that with the authorities," I say. "Couldn't you have had a psychological evaluation done, or whatever it is?"

"That would have been absolutely worthless. I don't pretend to understand the field of psychology, I admit that right away. What I do know, however, is that when it comes to dealing with cult members, every psychiatrist that I've met, whether he was brought in by parents or a law enforcement agency, would offer no more than an opinion as to whether a cult member presented a danger to himself or to society. I came to learn that this determination was the basis for whether or not a person should be committed to an institution, and that psychiatrists in a public forum will generally comment no further. In fact, in all the legal actions that have been brought against me the cult has produced a psychiatrist to render an opposing opinion at the trial."

"So, do you expect to have trouble tomorrow?" Hal asks suddenly.

"Oh, god," Jenny shrieks and straightens her back, almost in a spasm. "You scared me. I thought you were asleep."

"Sleeping? I wasn't sleeping," Hal says, looking around at us.

"I always expect trouble," Henry says, unwilling to stop the direction of our conversation. "It's part of the whole business. Whenever I start to think things will be easy, something unexpected pops up. You've got to always keep your edge."

"But what could happen?" Jenny asks.

"Well, the police could arrest all of us for kidnapping, for one."

"But he's my brother. And it's more like rescuing than kidnapping."

"That's why you're here," Henry says. "And that's why you and Hal will be the ones to go in to pick them up."

"Me? I'm going to pick them up?" Hal asks.

"It can't be Larry. It would be too much of a coincidence if Jenny should suddenly walk in with Larry. And it won't be me. That's how we try to avoid the kidnapping charge, by letting the initiation of the action be by a family member. Besides, there's a picture of me on every bulletin board in the ashram."

"But when we tell them that we're coming here instead of the dentist, Josh—I know him—will say he doesn't want to go," Jenny says. "And then what? That's why we're here."

"We're not going to ask him. We're going to trick him until we have him away from the other members of the cult. As for taking him against his will, we are choosing between two evils in order to avoid harm to him. The greater harm is staying in the ashram in a brainwashed state, doing Misha's bidding."

"Bradley doesn't have a sibling here, only a cousin," I say, intent not to let that fact slide by.

"That is why we must let him go the minute he objects," Henry says after a looking at me with some concern.

"But he may object at the very first moment," I complain.

"Then we must leave him with the other members who are with them, or at the next available moment, even if we have to stop and put him out on the sidewalk," Henry states as sympathetically as he can.

"I thought we were going to help Bradley," Jenny gasps, the full import of Henry's words coming to her.

"That's not why I'm here. I'm here to help Josh. I know it sounds callous, but after we use him to get Josh out of the ashram, Bradley jeopardizes the whole operation. For restraining Bradley, we will certainly all face kidnapping charges."

The light has grown very dim, and the shade from the trees stretches all the way down the lawn to the channel. The wind is blowing harder than it was earlier, rattling a window upstairs on the northwest side of the house. We are featureless shadows in the room, each of us waiting for someone to make the offer of compromise that will release us from this awkward moment. I know that I must be the one to do so. I imagine myself rising from the couch and walking toward the door to meet my shadow coming toward me from the deepening shade on the lawn.

"What you're saying makes sense," I say eventually. "But it's hard for me to accept that I may tomorrow be reunited with my cousin, yet be required simply to watch him retreat."

"Perhaps he will stay," Henry says in a soft voice that lacks conviction, but offers me my piece of the bargain.

"If Bradley doesn't object, then he can return here with us?"

"That would be okay," Henry says.

"And some dinner would be okay with me," Hal declares loudly, having determined, I suspect, that my negotiation with Henry is complete.

"Which I am going to prepare," Henry says as he and Hal stand up. "I have the groceries in the truck. I picked them up when I went into town earlier. I figured we should eat in tonight, and not attract any attention to ourselves. There are not many people on the Cape."

Walking out to the wood box, I know, suddenly, that if I push Henry, he'll help me bring Bradley back to the house no matter what. But I also know that is how he got himself into trouble in New York. He ran out onto the sidewalk and helped a father pull his struggling son into a van. They didn't prosecute the father, but they indicted Henry. I resolve that I will not put Henry in that position.

From the wood box I can see into the bright windows of the kitchen. Henry is busy with a knife at the chopping board, while Jenny leans against the far counter, talking in an animated fashion. Hal is rummaging through the cupboard, pulling out items at Henry's commands. The three of them appear to me suddenly as sailboats in a sheltered cove, straining against their anchors on account of a wind that further out to sea blows the tops off the waves rolling toward shore. And I am drawn to the cove, chased by the following sea, the last boat in before the sunlight disappears into the western landmass and the ocean in this dark time rises in a fury.

11

MY BEDROOM WINDOW FACES EAST. A few moments ago I raised the shade to see whether the horizon would tell me the time. I saw a dim pink line and a gray sky overhead. Now, I lie in bed with my hands behind my head, watching the ceiling brighten and hoping an occurrence so real as the sun rising will dissipate the strange sensation left by the dream I was having just before I awoke. In that dream a huge swan had assaulted Jenny.

Last night I made a fire after dinner and the four of us talked some more about Henry's experience with cults, and what had become of those he had deprogrammed. When Hal and Henry went up to bed, Jenny and I remained, sitting quietly for almost an hour as the fire burned down to a mass of glowing coals. Then, in the dark room, Jenny told me about her family life while she and her brother were growing up, suggesting that therein could reside the reason Josh had joined the Path.

"My mother was very strict with us when we were young," she said. "We had absolutely no freedom. After school we came right home and were in our pajamas by six almost every night. We weren't allowed to take part in any after school activities. We didn't go to summer camp. We did none of those things."

"Well I guess you studied a lot, then," I said casually, assuming that to be their motivation for the curfews.

"Oh, my mother didn't care if we studied," Jenny sighed. "She just didn't want to go to any trouble to drive us around anywhere, or put up with all the other things related to extra-curricular activities."

"And what about your father," I asked. "What did he think about that?"

"For as long as I can remember, they didn't speak to each other. So he never objected to anything she did, probably because that would have involved his having to talk to her."

"That sounds horrible."

"It was. The ironic thing is that the month after Josh left for college, my father moved out and filed for divorce. He had been staying with her all that time on our account, but he couldn't stand it for the additional two years until I went away. All that time he stayed, when in fact their being together only made our lives worse. I was relieved, but Josh took it quite badly."

"What did he do?"

"He quit school after his first year and moved to the Haight-Ashbury district in San Francisco, where he got a job in a health food restaurant. They were famous for their macrobiotic soups. My father said they were good. He started to visit him every few months."

"That's odd isn't it? I would think that Josh wouldn't have wanted the visits."

"Well, of course he would tell my father not to bother, but he would never throw him out or anything. In fact, I think he liked the visits. And my father knew just how to handle him. He would put aside his own dislike about what Josh was doing and take a real interest in his life. For example, he would always stay in a little offbeat hotel in the district, when he could have stayed at any of the nice hotels downtown. I think he would have stayed with Josh except that Josh only had a one-room apartment that was so full of books you could hardly get across it."

"And what about your mother?"

"She would talk to him on the phone—she never visited him—and at first they would get into incredible screaming arguments where one of them would hang up on the other. After one of my father's visits, Josh stopped calling her. She got furious, and claimed that my father was intentionally turning Josh against her. But when she started talking to Josh again, she softened her tone, and pretty soon she was making excuses for him—excuses that usually cast my father as the root of all of Josh's problems."

"So she probably blames him for Josh's joining the cult?"

"Actually, I don't think she views it as a bad thing. I don't know that she's taken the time to understand what has happened. My father actually tried to talk to her about it. It was the first time he had talked directly to her since he left her. But she is so vindictive," Jenny said bitterly.

"I'm surprised in a way that your father has engaged Mr. Henry to do this," I said after a minute, wanting to avoid more of the rancor I sensed Jenny was feeling for her mother. "It sounds like he was being very understanding of Josh."

"Actually, it makes a lot of sense. You see, when Josh was in San Francisco at the health food restaurant, he and my father had a relationship. It was a little one-sided, I grant you, because my father always had to go to visit him. But they talked and, I think, respected one another in their own way. Even after Josh first joined the cult my father was okay. I remember him talking about how Josh was doing all of this fine community service. But the blow came that day when Josh came back East and renounced him, when he said he could never have anything to do with him because he was Satan. That's when my father ordered him out of the house. He just lost his cool. It was a horrible time. Anyway, since then there has been a bit of reconciliation between Josh and my father, although I think it's solely on account of my father's tolerance of Josh. Also, you've got to give my father credit. He made a big effort to understand what Josh is doing, and he spent a lot of time trying to understand what he calls 'this alternative religion movement.' That's how he found Mr. Henry."

I was quiet for a few moments because Jenny's voice, as she told me about Josh and her father, was strained and toward the end was at the point of breaking. The thought came to me that she felt herself implicated in the dysfunction in her family, and as unfounded as it sounds, she felt she had failed them all by not coming up with a way in which they could get back together. I read somewhere, probably in a magazine article, that the child left at home in a divorce often thinks she is to blame for her parents' struggles. It is not implausible that in Jenny's mind the saving of Josh from the cult would be tantamount to a first step in the reconciliation of her parents and hence the reconstruction of her family. But that was not a topic I wanted to pursue with her. After an awkward few minutes passed, I tried to divert our conversation from its prior direction by commenting on the fact that the logs had retained their shape even though they were only a fragile, glowing hulk that would disintegrate if touched. She paid no attention to my observation, however.

"I've been having these ambivalent feelings, Larry," she said from the darkness, "that saving Josh from the cult might be a mistake. Even if, as Mr. Henry says, Misha has made Josh into nothing better than a robot, maybe, all things considered, that's the best thing for him."

"I don't know," I said, surprised by her observation in light of my earlier thoughts. "Of course, when you answer that question you're making up Josh's mind for him."

"I suppose that's right, but someone has to, for god's sake, or he'll spend the rest of his life selling soup and blaming everything on how my parents raised him," she said emotionally, and then paused for a moment while she fought to get her voice under control, during which time the embers in the fire, as if prompted, blazed briefly.

"It's really sad," she continued. "He's so mixed up because of what they did to him. And he's completely taken in with all these religious things. I think that all he really wants is for my mother to love him. He's just searching for a substitute, or he's doing something so outlandish that it will make her notice. I think that's why he moved away, actually. Isn't that funny? He moved away to try to pull her closer to him. And it worked with my father, certainly, but that wasn't enough, I guess."

"Why aren't you as bitter?" I asked.

"Oh, I am," she said, laughing. "My god, am I bitter! But I guess I'm just a lot more practical than Josh. I was always the practical one. Good old Jenny. Always had her homework done. Always ate her dinner. And I can't spend my life worrying about what they've done to me. But I am bitter. I am carrying around that baggage, as you can tell by just listening to me. Baggage I'd like to drop off someplace. Somewhere that I never expect to return to."

"I don't want to sound like a know-it-all," I said, "because I can't relate a lot of what you're saying to my personal experiences, but I think that at some point, Josh needs to pack away this family history in his own trunk, to borrow your metaphor, and drop it off."

"Borrow my metaphor!" she exclaimed, laughing. "Larry, you're just like your father in lots of ways."

"No, seriously," I said, trying desperately to overcome my irritation at her comparison. "Don't you think that at some point a person's past shouldn't be held responsible for his present, or his future for that matter? At some point a person has to lift himself up and say 'It's time to go.' It's time to crawl out of the hole he finds himself in, and go off to the foothills."

"Unless the hole is too deep," she said. "Borrowing your metaphor."

"Okay. But you see what I mean."

"Yes. But I worry that there are some things in life that you just can't beat. And some people are stronger than others. Some holes are deeper than others. And I don't know if Josh can get out of his hole. That is what has me feeling ambivalent. Tomorrow, we may save him from Misha. But we can't save him from his past. No matter how hard my father tries now. Years ago they caused the damage."

"You're angry," I said, stating the obvious.

"I am angry, " she cried. "And when I'm not angry, I'm depressed."

"That's anger turned in on yourself," I said quickly, as I stood up and groped in the darkness for the fireplace implements, hoping to stir some light out of the fire because I could no longer bear to continue this conversation with a shadow. I needed desperately to see her face when she talked about herself. And there were things I knew I would not be able to say to her with only words.

"What did you say?" she asked, after we watched the embers crumble into a pile at the end of the poker. "I'm sorry."

"What depression is. It's your anger turned against you," I said, as I placed a new log on the top of the coals.

"That could be."

"Maybe all this turmoil with Josh will have a good effect on your parents," I said, deciding to verbalize my earlier hypothesis concerning her motivation for helping Henry kidnap Josh. "In your father's case, it will. And he's certainly committed. I mean hiring Henry can't be cheap."

"Actually, Mr. Henry only asks for expenses and a contribution at the end. Whatever we want to pay."

"Well, still."

"In my father's case he's no more culpable than an unwilling accomplice. And my mother is having nothing to do with all of this. She's sitting at home doing crossword puzzles. And she doesn't see why anyone's making a big fuss about Josh in the first place. He's just going through a stage, she says. But that's what she always said. During the last two years he lived at home, when all he did was sit in his room with the door closed because he couldn't stand to witness my parents' silence, she never acknowledged that anything was wrong with him. He would walk around opening drawers and closet doors, then banging them shut, with the most sullen look on his face. And she would just sit at the kitchen table, doing crossword puzzles, or propped up on the couch, reading the latest Book of the Month Club selection. 'He's just going through a stage,' she'd say, or 'He just has trouble making friends.' She never once thought to sit him down and ask, 'What's the matter, Josh?' He probably would have spilled his guts. He was just waiting for her to ask."

"Well, what about you?" I ask. "Have you told her any of this?"

"Oh, no. It wouldn't do any good."

"It could do you some good," I said emphatically.

"I think I'm afraid to confront her," she said so softly I could barely hear her. "Not because I think that she'll yell at me, or stop loving me, or anything like that. What I'm afraid of is that she'll ignore me, that she'll just go back to doing her stupid crossword puzzle, and what I say will have no affect on her."

The log was burning intensely and I could see her again. While she talked, her right hand brushed back the hair behind her ear. She tilted her head to the left, just before she brushed the hair back. That made the hair behind her other ear fall free, but she let that side remain loose, as if she suddenly had no sensation in her body, as if the thought of her mother's disregard made her forsake the urge to tidy her appearance.

At that point the phone rang. There was no one on the line when I answered it, only an eerie silence that made me think someone was on the other end, having intentionally called to ascertain whether I was in the house. Unfortunately, when I returned to the fireplace, Jenny was standing at the foot of the stairs, where she announced that despite her desire to talk some more she could not keep her eyes open a minute longer. I sat downstairs for a short time after she retired, wondering whether some nefarious force had caused the phone to ring, the distraction that reminded Jenny of her tiredness. I thought of Millie, of course, but rejected the suspicion promptly as being too far fetched.

I thought of Millie again when I got into bed. Shortly after I met her, I brought her to the Narrows. It was Labor Day and the house was full of my family and cousins, including Bradley. Millie complained constantly—about the poison ivy and the jelly fish and all the other things she could have chosen to ignore if she were really intent on enjoying herself—and she refused to take part in many of the little rituals my cousins and I undertake when we are all at the Narrows together. One such ritual was a late-night beach walk, which Millie declined expecting that I would do the same. I went, even after she coolly retreated to her bedroom, and in the middle of the walk, when Bradley and I had dropped back a few paces from the others, he said to me, "She's the devil, you know." I laughed at him. "Oh, come on, Bradley," I said. "She just feels awkward because you, Sally and I are such good friends." But he just shook his head and said it another time: "She's the devil." And that was it. He never said anything about her again.

My dream was perhaps spawned by that memory of Bradley and Millie just before I fell asleep. In my dream I awoke from the very bed in which I was sleeping and walked down the hall toward voices coming from the room that Jenny occupied. The hall reminded me of a long, dark tunnel, and I was cold because I was naked, which was the state in which I had gone to bed.

I stood before the room's open doorway, watching Jenny brush her hair in front of a mirror across the room. She wore only a large man's shirt with just a few of the buttons done in the middle of her torso. Although I could discern in the mirror my naked self, standing in the doorway, I suffered no apprehension that Jenny would see me. In fact, she on several occasions appeared to look right at me and made no sign of being aware of my presence. Her eyes would close as she ran the brush through her hair and then reopen when the brush pulled free so that she could guide her hand back to a starting point on her head. As her hand reached up to her head, the front of the shirt would open, which allowed me to see her breasts.

Suddenly, the door to the bathroom opened and Bradley emerged, wearing a long white robe, with a hood that fell over his shoulders and sleeves that billowed with material, flaring from elbow to cuff like inverted funnels. As he walked toward Jenny, the white garment moved, the folds of material stretching and compressing, with the rhythm and the sound of a large bird about to alight.

Bradley stopped behind her, and I suddenly saw an image of the three of us—he with his hands on her shoulders and I some distance behind in the open doorway. Jenny's eyes looked into the mirror's reflection of his eyes. The lids demurely slid over their irises, her face softened and she put the brush down on a nightstand. Then she turned and smiled to him, and her head tilted back to compensate for his height as his sweeping white arms surrounded her. Their lips met gently. Their limbs slid around their bodies. They drew together with a gripping force, like the opposite poles of magnets. A passion arose from the meeting of their chests like an orchestral crescendo. Her hands gripped the loose material covering his back, and his moved down to her ass. He pulled her against him, and his lips moved to her neck. Her head fell back. She closed her eyes. The tops of her breasts swelled through the open collar. He buried his face there for a moment, and then turned his head to the side, as if to listen to the beating of her heart.

Then began a slow, sensual dance of her disrobing. Her hand slid a zipper down the front of his robe. She stood back and reached inside the hanging material, resting her hands upon his hips, and he undid the buttons on her shirt. When he brought his hands up to her shoulders, she dropped her arms and the shirt fell into a heap on the floor behind her.

She stood motionless for a moment—her head still tilted back, their eyes locked together—before he gently placed his hands on her shoulders. Then suddenly, she was back against him, her arms inside his robe, her hands moving down his back. He pushed her abdomen to his loins. With a gasp she backed away from him, but, his hands still behind her, he pulled her back to him in a swift, sudden blow of such force that the air moved by the collision caused his robe to billow out behind him. She staggered slightly, but did not really resist, her body heaving with labored breath. When he lifted her up and placed her on the bed, she emitted a small whimper, almost inaudible under the sound of her breathing.

He moved above her on the bed and knelt between her legs, with his hands placed just to the sides of her shoulders, supporting his hovering torso. The hanging white cloth of his robe covered their bodies for a moment until her hands, held out by straight arms, pushed back his falling body. Although her action stopped his fall, the grip of her fingers upon his shoulders was hesitant, and after a moment of pause, during which he looked upon the closed eyelids on her face, he rose up suddenly to dispel the tension of her arms against his shoulder, then reversed his direction quickly, catching her off guard and sliding his great shoulders down the inside of her arms. His arms now free of his own weight, one of his hands placed a strong grip at the base of her back and drew her to him. The rush of their breathing was like the fire's consumption of a log on the grate.

The fingers on her hands were tight fists upon his back when he raised his shoulders and pushed his upper torso up over her. Her hands gripped the hard, tense muscles in his upper arms and turned white with strain as he pushed his body into her, his knees flat upon the mattress, his head thrown back, his face to the ceiling. She closed her eyes and cried out when she heard his roar from above, and when I looked up at him suddenly, I saw, to my astonishment, not Bradley but a great, white swan, his wings pushing frantically against the air for the thrust that held his shuddering body against the captive girl beneath him.

12

SAM HENRY PULLS HIMSELF UP from a slump in the tow truck seat. He has his eyes pointed down Orleans Road. About a quarter of a mile away, a car comes around a bend. There's a glint of sunlight off its windshield. In a few seconds it's distinguishable as a yellow car, which means it's not the one we're waiting for, although Henry continues to watch it until it passes in front of us. Then he turns back to the bend and waits for the next one. The intensity of his watching makes me anxious.

"They have to come this way," I say optimistically. "It's the only road to Orleans from this side of the Cape."

"We've been waiting an hour," he says, almost in desperation. "Something is wrong."

He turns his attention back to the bend in the road. The tow truck is backed into a space near the end of a parking lot for Louise's Restaurant and Guest Cottages. When we got here about a half-hour ago, Henry went in for some coffee. The coffee must have been boiled, because it is so bitter that drinking it is like chewing on a lemon rind.

"Here they come," Henry says with certainty, although the sun's reflection off the car coming toward us makes it look to me like a pinball. We slide down against the back of our seats and watch them pass.

"There were three of them," he says, dejectedly. "They've sent a guard with them."

"They have guards!" I exclaim as Henry starts the engine.

"They're actually called elders. They're a group of very trusted loyalists, like an inner circle. In many cases they act like bodyguards. I'm sure he's along because they became suspicious. Maybe it was the appearance of Hal. Maybe it was the change of the time of the appointment. I don't know. It doesn't matter. We'll have to deal with it."

"He didn't look like a big guy," I say, trying to act positive, despite the fact that I didn't get a real good look at the third person.

"It's determination, not size, that counts," Henry says and looks at me with an amused expression. "Never underestimate your opponent."

"What are we going to do about him?" I ask, although I can see from Henry's face he is not listening to me.

"They may be suspicious because Jenny's father didn't accompany them," he says with an intent look on his face.

"But I thought Josh refused to see his father."

"That's not exactly accurate," he says, matter of factly. "I was afraid Jenny would refuse if she didn't think it was necessary for her to go. Like you, she was somewhat equivocal about the whole thing."

"But why didn't her father just come?"

"Because it's best to save the entrance of a parent until later. After the initial shock of being abducted, a preemie will usually remember what Misha has trained him to do—that is, go into as much of a trance as possible and try to block out everything being said to him. Having a parent walk in during this phase usually causes a disturbance that allows me to get the preemie's attention. Besides, I think there are a lot of good feelings in Josh for his father just below the surface. So I wanted his father to have clean hands, not to be associated with the abduction."

"So Jenny gets the bad association," I say, incredulously.

"Hopefully, it won't matter after Josh gets his head clear," Henry says, distractedly looking at his watch and missing the way in which my voice has risen. "Three more minutes and then we follow them."

"I still don't understand," I say in an insistent tone that makes Henry glance at me for a moment. "Why didn't you just tell Jenny she was the better person to do this?"

"She'll do better thinking that she is doing it for her father. Why? Like I said, she's like you. She's not convinced that we're doing the right thing."

"Well, I don't know about that," I say quickly.

"Precisely," he laughs. "Look, if I had a choice I wouldn't have either of you here. I only have Jenny along to try to stay on the right side of the law, and you to keep Bradley from being a problem. Don't you watch television? Only the thugs take part in the actual kidnapping. The boss stays home. My part is the part of the thug, right?"

"That's just television," I say.

"Hey, man. Where do you think I learned this?" he says sarcastically. "I used to be a social worker. Remember?"

"So what are we going to do about the third guy?" I shout over the noise of the truck's engine as we accelerate down the road.

"He's going to be a problem," Henry says. "I hope Hal and Jenny remember the alternate plan."

I desperately try to recall the alternate plan. We sat around the breakfast table when Henry went through the plans, but I couldn't pay attention. Then only thing I remember is that Hal kept saying "No problem," and that Jenny took notes on this little pad we keep by the phone.

"There they are," Henry says.

About a hundred yards ahead of us, Jenny's car is stopped by the side of the road. The hood is up, and Hal paces along the passenger side. Just as we pass them, Hal waves his arms and shouts.

"Good boy," Henry says.

Henry slams on the brakes about twenty yards past them. He puts his right arm over the seat and backs up quickly, spewing gravel from the road's shoulder, until the truck is stopped immediately in front of them.

"Jesus. I almost went through the windshield," I complain.

"That's how tow truck drivers drive," he says, grinning at me. "I saw it on TV."

Henry has to jump down to the road because the truck is so high and he is so short. Will that guy in the car really fall for this, I wonder. I adjust the mirror so I can watch them and then slide down in the seat.

"Hey," Hal says.

"Hey," Henry says.

"Got some engine trouble," Hal says.

"Uh-huh," Henry says, nonchalantly.

The two of them bend over the exposed engine. A green van goes by us. It has a large flower arrangement painted on the side that says "Orleans Bouquet—Since 1953." For a few moments the noise keeps me from hearing what Hal and Henry are saying.

"Can't fix it," Henry says.

"Just get it going so we can get to Orleans," Hal says.

"Can't do it," Henry says brusquely. "Busted distributor cap. I ain't got one with me."

"How about if we tape it together?"

"Look at this," Henry says with an irritated voice. "It busted into five pieces. Besides, the rotor inside broke, too. See this thing? It's supposed to go around like this. Can't tape that together."

"Shit!"

"Happens all the time when the weather changes like this," Henry says, shaking his head and acting like the broken distributor is Hal's fault. "You build up all this moisture under the cap when it's hot in the summer, and then when the air gets cold and dry, the whole thing gets brittle and falls apart. I must change twenty of these things every fall. All you have to do when it gets cool is take a cloth and wipe it out."

"Crap," Hal says, acting a little insulted. "If it's so common, why don't you bring some extras on the truck?"

"Three or four different sizes," Henry says, shrugging. "If I had one I'd probably have the wrong size."

"Shit," Hal says again, and I worry that he's overdoing it.

"I'll tow you in," Henry says with some feigned compassion. "It's not that far."

"Just a minute," Hal growls. "Let me talk to my friends."

Henry pulls a huge chain out of the back and then rummages around with some tools.

"He's got to tow us," Hal shouts over the noise Henry is making.

I can't hear what is said to Hal, but in a minute he walks back over to Henry.

"What about all of us?" he asks.

"You can stay in the car," Henry says. "I'm not supposed to, but it won't matter."

"We can stay in the car," Hal yells back to the car.

"But you had better stay out and ride in the truck with me," Henry says. "Too much weight."

"I'm going to ride in the truck," Hal yells as Henry comes back to the cab and gets in.

"So far, so good," he says in a low voice as he begins to back the truck up to the car. "But I don't know what we're going to do with the guy in the middle."

"Come on back some more," Hal yells and Henry eases off the break.

"Whoa!" Hal yells.

But Henry doesn't react immediately. He lets the truck roll a little further. Then he slams on the brake, puts the gears in neutral and pulls out the parking brake.

"Day before yesterday," he says to me before he jumps out. "I practiced for an hour."

When the winch motor whines, the truck's engine races, and the truck rocks. The chains bang against the back. Suddenly Hal stands next to my window.

"I don't know what we're going to do with the new guy," he says as the winch motor whines some more and the truck rocks back and forth.

"What's the matter?" Hal yells when Henry swears.

"Too much weight in the car," Henry yells.

"There's too much weight in the car," Hal yells as he walks back to the car. "Someone has to get out."

"They'll be room in the cab," Henry says. "My helper can ride in the back of the truck."

"There's room in the truck," Hal yells. "Jim. How about you? You're the biggest of the group. Jenny, you can get in the back seat."

"I don't mind riding in the truck," Jim, the guy we don't know, says as he gets out of the car. "And Josh can ride in the back of the truck also."

"No," Hal says quickly before Josh can get out of the car. "I'm already out. Josh, you stay in the car with Jenny and Bradley. Jim comes up in the truck with me. We don't want to break the man's truck. Move in the back, Jenny."

This time the car pops off the ground when Henry operates the winch. Henry comes back to the driver's seat and Hal and

Jim come around to my door. I start to get out when Hal opens the door but Henry grabs my arm.

"Hey, buddy," Hal says to Jim. "Thanks for helping out."

"I was happy to help," he says as he looks around Hal at me. He's wondering why I'm not getting out of the truck. The gears grind as Henry struggles to put the truck in gear. Jim looks up at him.

"Black Lightning," he gasps suddenly.

"Get in the truck, Hal," Henry yells as Hal and I look at each other in terror.

But Hal is off balance. Jim surrounds him, pinning Hal's arms to his sides, and pulls him back.

"Oh, damn!" Henry screams. "Push him off. Get in the truck."

"Aieeeeeeee!" Jim chortles. "Black Lightning. Black Lightning."

"Josh, stay here. Please!" I can hear Jenny yelling, even over the truck's motor.

Josh hurls himself at Hal and Jim, but Hal manages to maintain his balance even with the two of them on his back. Jenny runs in a circle around them.

"Larry, do something," Jenny yells as she grabs onto the back of Josh's shirt and starts to pull.

But just as I get out of the door, Henry barks, "You stay here!" He then sprints around the front of the truck, pulls Jenny back, and pushes her in my direction.

"Hold onto her, Larry. Damnit."

"Josh, please," she cries, as she struggles in my arms.

Henry gets his arms around Josh, but can't pry him loose. Hal is struggling now.

"Get off the man's back," Henry yells.

"Black Lightning!" Jim screams.

The veins in Hal's neck bulge. In a giant movement he flips them forward over his head. Josh lands on his back and starts gasping for breath. Jim struggles to his knees. Hal stands over him.

"All right, you little sack of shit," Hal roars.

"Larry," Henry yells as he struggles with Josh's limp body, and I run over and pick up his feet.

"Get him in the car," Henry puffs.

Bradley has been sitting in the car the entire time, staring at the back of the tow truck. When we push Josh in with him, he starts chanting something. Whatever it is, Josh picks it up. They become mercifully serene in their chanting.

"Larry, get in the truck," Henry commands.

Hal pokes his finger into Jim's chest. Jim keeps stumbling as he is pushed backwards.

"We can make this easy or we can make it hard," Hal says.

"You cannot do this," Jim shouts. "This is against the law. We do not wish to go with you."

"That's good," Hal says. "Because we don't wish you to come with us, turd-bucket."

"Your uncouth epithets have no effect with me."

"Oh, no? How about this, then?"

Hal pushes him harder and he falls to the ground, but immediately springs back to his feet.

"I can't let you take them. I can't. How can you do this?"

"Easy. Maybe you should just sit down and relax."

"You cannot take the Vigilant One," he cries desperately.

"You can go home soon as we leave," Hal says roughly. "It's back that way."

"Vigilant One! What should I do?" he shouts at the car.

"Relax, buddy. You're just making this hard on yourself," Hal says.

"You can not take him," he cries, his voice breaking into sobs.

"Just relax, I said," Hal says, poking him in the chest some more.

"Larry, get back in the truck," Henry, who has been standing next to the truck watching Jim, yells. "Hal, pull Bradley out and let's go. That's all that Jim wants."

"Wait a minute," I say, confused. "Bradley's not doing anything."

"Do it," Henry yells and moves around to the driver's side as Hal turns to me looking quizzical and shrugs his shoulders.

"Larry, get in the truck, damnit," Henry yells. "This is taking too damn long."

"Aieeeeeee!" Jim shouts.

He scrambles around to Hal's right, and makes a dash for the car. But Hal grabs him by the shirt and spins him around to the ground

"Look, buddy. Let's have a truce, okay?"

But Jim shouts again and lunges to his feet. This time Hal nails him, right in the solar plexus. He crumbles to the ground.

"I didn't want to do that," Hal says.

"Let's go," Henry yells, exasperatedly.

As I scramble into the truck, there is some commotion in back that I can't see because Henry has moved the rear-view mirror.

"Oh, Jesus," Henry says, looking into the mirror. But before I can turn around, Hal yells, "Go!"

"This was not the smooth operation I envisioned," Henry says as he grinds the truck into gear.

"I'm getting out," I say, although with so little conviction in my voice that I surprise myself.

"Nope," Henry says in a matter-of-fact manner as he pops the clutch, and before I have a chance to get my hands on the door handle, the truck is careening out onto the road.

"Wait a goddamn minute," I yell at him.

248

"You can't stay here," he says. "Sorry."

"The hell I can't," I scream, but when I get the door open, the road is passing by too fast for me to even focus on.

"Sorry," he says again and shifts into third gear.

We ride in silence. I remember fifteen years ago riding down this same stretch of road in the back seat of the Wrights' car. Herrick was next to me. Bradley was in front. Bradley always had to ride in front, and he and Herrick would always fight over where to sit. But that day Herrick was angry about something else. He pounded the top of the clarinet case in his lap.

"Mom," he moaned. "This is a waste of my summer vacation."

She looked at him sympathetically and said, "Oh, Herrick, it's only an hour a week. It won't kill you."

But Bradley corrected her, as he had a habit of doing.

"By the time we drive to Chatham and back," he said, "and wait for the stupid teacher, it's two hours."

That irritated her.

"Bradley, you didn't have to come," she said sternly. "It's not your lesson."

Bradley yawned.

"Well, there's nothing else to do, anyway," he said after shrugging his shoulders and looking out the window.

Herrick yelled at him, "Maybe you should take the stupid clarinet lessons, Bradley."

But Bradley just ignored him and shrugged his shoulders again.

"You'd probably be able to play it perfectly by now, Mister Bradley Perfect," Herrick shouted. "You'd be able to play the upper B flat. You'd never rrrrush the quaaarter rest."

Herrick mimicked his teacher, but he was crying by that time. His mother looked at him through the rear-view mirror.

"Herrick, you play marvelously," she said.

But he just moaned, "Well, I hate it. Hate, hate, hate, hate it."

Then Bradley looked back at Herrick and made a face I'll never forget. It was full of compassion, like he knew how bad it felt to be as frustrated with something as Herrick obviously was with his clarinet. They held each other's gaze for a few moments until Bradley sensed me looking at him. Then he smirked and said, "So quit if you don't like it."

That made Herrick's neck turn red.

"Oh, shut up, Bradley Perfect. I'll show you."

And we didn't talk anymore for the rest of the ride.

He did show us, finally. About five years later I was in the Wrights' living room with my family, about to leave for Symphony Hall. Herrick had been selected to play that night with several members of the Boston Symphony. I remember that my collar was so tight I thought I was going to have to have a tracheotomy at any second. But I wouldn't loosen my tie as Bradley just a few minutes before had done. His tie was so loose that it looked like a dog's leash. My mother had just ironed my shirt and I was afraid it would hurt her feelings if I did the same. And she had remarked about how handsome I looked.

Then Herrick came down the stairs in a black tuxedo. I'll never forget the look on Mrs. Wright's face. Herrick was perfectly put together, except for the Kelly-green "Celtics" hat on his head. She kept her composure while saying, "Oh dear, Herrick, the colors don't match." He waved her away when she went over and tried to grab it. We all thought he'd take it off before the concert, but he wore the hat onstage.

And that's all I can think about now, as we tow Jenny's car down the sandy lane to the Narrows. I can only see Herrick in his green hat, and Bradley in his loose tie, and their mother crying with pride as the audience rose to its feet to applaud Herrick's unconventional rendition of Brahms. For a minute I believe they

will be at the house when we arrive—my mother and my aunt—
and that my aunt will serve chocolate cake to us as she did after
the concert, and that everything after that will be right again.

13

"YOU HAVE A LOYAL FRIEND," Henry says emotionally.

"It was uncanny," Hal says excitedly.

We stand at a window that faces Pleasant Bay. Outside, in front of us, Bradley sits on the Big Rock, with his legs crossed and his back rigid. He faces the spot on the horizon where the sun rises in the morning. The skin on his back has a golden hue from the late-afternoon sun. Josh is locked in a room upstairs.

"I opened the door and told Bradley to get out," Hal says. "And he did, just like that. Then, before I could close the door, Josh made a dash for it. He pulled away from Jenny and came flying out the door just behind Bradley. But before I could get around to grab him, Bradley stopped him. He stopped him just by looking at him. It was incredible. It was like Josh was frozen in place, right in the middle of the damn road. It was unreal, I tell you."

"So then they just got back in the car? Just like that?"

"Yeah. Bradley put his hands on Josh's shoulders, just like this," Hal says, demonstrating the movement on me, "and guided him back into the car. Then, Bradley got in right next to him. What could I say? He wanted to come with us."

"Well, he hasn't done anything all day except pee on the floor of his room and sit out there on that rock, naked," Jenny says irritably.

"He peed in his room!" I exclaim. "When did he do that?"

"While you and Henry were taking back the truck."

"I can't believe he isn't freezing out there, naked like that," Hal says softly. "Maybe you should go out there, Larry."

Jenny studies her fingernails. She's hostile about Bradley's behavior for a reason I cannot determine. When Hal and Henry walk to the kitchen, she sits in a chair. Then, without my saying anything, she starts talking.

"What happened was, I went upstairs to check on Josh, and when I walked by Bradley's room the door was open and there he was standing in the middle of the room peeing. I just kept walking for a second, and then I couldn't help myself. I went back and said, 'Bradley, there's a bathroom right across the hall.' He turned and looked at me, but he didn't stop. He just kept going. It went all over the room. Then he said, 'I have no control over the forces that are upon me,' or something like that. And I said, 'Well move them into the bathroom at least.' And he did. He grabbed himself to stop, hobbled across the hall like that, and finished in the toilet."

The phone rings. Upstairs, Josh screams. The phone rings a second time. Josh screams again, and this time starts to pound on the floor.

"You'd better answer it," Henry calls to me.

When I pick up the receiver I expect to hear the eerie silence that I heard last night, but the caller is Millie, inquiring about the time of my return. We conspire not to mention the circumstances under which she bid me goodbye, and she talks in such a sweet manner, telling me about the nice dinner she had with her parents and the afternoon of shopping, that I am momentarily lulled into missing her, just as I have been on so many similar occasions. When she inquires coyly whether I can return tonight, however, my view of Bradley's naked back across the lawn strengthens my resolve and I tell her it is impossible. To her insistence that I return tomorrow I tell her I cannot promise, and the phone call ends with an icy comment from her that she can't promise that she'll be at home when I do return. I panic momentarily as I put the receiver back on the hook, wondering if I should return to Boston as soon as possible. But I know I cannot, and I feel a flash of smugness as I walk back across the room at the thought of Millie sitting next to her phone perplexed by her inability for the first time to make me do as she pleases. Hal and Henry are back in the living room with Jenny.

"First thing in the morning," Henry says.

"So soon," Hal says.

"They'll find us by noon tomorrow."

"Who will?" I ask.

"Misha," Hal says.

"While you were on the phone," Henry says, "I was saying that we cannot stay here any longer than tomorrow morning."

"But how would they find us?"

"Bradley," Henry says. "Somewhere along the way, they will discover that Bradley's family has a house on the Cape. Maybe we'll be lucky, and he never told anyone about it. But we don't know. And they'll definitely call Bradley's home. Someone there may unsuspectingly mention this house."

"But they don't know anything about this, or even that Bradley has joined this cult," I say. "I'm sure of that."

"That's exactly why they'll volunteer the information," Henry says. "I don't think Bradley told anyone at the ashram about this place or they'd be here by now. They're probably still trying to locate his family in Boston. If we're really lucky they won't even know he's from Boston, but we can't take that chance."

"What will they do to us if they find us?" Jenny asks, a worried tone to her voice.

"Oh, nothing," Henry laughs, and gives her what I think is intended to be a reassuring look. "They're not going to come over here with baseball bats. They'll bring the police, and file a kidnapping and assault complaint. Sometimes I convince the police to go along with what we're doing. You would help with that, since you're Josh's sister. But in this case, it's not so clear, because we have Bradley too. And we roughed-up that boy back on the road. I don't want to explain anything. I just want to get Josh far away, to neutral ground."

"It's actually a good thing we took Bradley," Hal says. "If we had left him, he would have led them right here."

"You're probably right," Henry says. "I hadn't thought of that."

"Maybe he knew that," Jenny says. "Maybe that's why he came with us. So he wouldn't put himself in the position of having to lead them to us."

"I don't know," Henry says. "Josh is behaving like every other preemie I've nabbed. Bradley isn't. It bothers me. It's another reason to go as soon as possible. I wish we could go tonight, but I've got to get Josh settled down or we won't make it through the first town."

"How are you going to do that?" Jenny asks.

"I'm going to go talk to him. I'm going to put a chair in front of him, put my knees against his, and just start talking. I talk about anything that pops into my head. Any chance I get to take a shot at Misha, I will. Sometimes I'm lucky and I'll get one of them to argue with me. They're the easy ones. You just have to get them thinking again, get them using their reason. But mostly, when you start saying things that are contrary to their programming, they just tune you out, like a clamshell closing up. Then you just have to wait them out. But they're easy to move in that state. It's what Misha trains them to do. To tune out the world and become completely compliant. It's Misha's defense against deprogramming, and actually a good one, because fighting takes up energy and after a while breaks you down. That's why right now I'm letting Josh carry on the way he is. In any case, Josh's tuning me out and becoming compliant when I confront him would work to our advantage this time. So either I'll get right through tonight, when I confront him, or he'll clam up. Either way, it should make it easier tomorrow."

"Where are we going?" Jenny asks.

"To a cabin in New Hampshire, just over the state line. We're going to meet your father there."

"What about Bradley?" I ask.

"I'm sorry," Henry says softly. "We can't take him with us."

"What about just as far as Boston?"

Henry shakes his head. He looks out of the window, as if he is thinking it over. But he shakes his head again, quickly. Before he can speak, the phone rings.

"Bradley Wright, please," a stern voice says as soon as I pick up the receiver.

For a moment I am unable to reply because I had assumed the caller was Millie coming around for a second try at my sympathies. Henry sees the expression on my face and walks over in my direction. My mind races.

"Who?" I demand as grumpily as I can manage.

"Bradley Wright. May I please speak to Bradley Wright?"

"You've got the wrong number," I growl.

"Who is this?" the voice insists.

"Who is this?" I demand so indignantly that Henry makes some hand motions for me to tone down.

"I'm a friend of Bradley's," the voice says, "and I'd like to talk to him."

"That's nice," I say sarcastically, "but there's no one by that name here."

"Is this the residence of F. Wright?"

"It is. And there's no Bradley here."

"I'm sorry," the voice says, after a moment. "I must have the wrong number."

"Yes, you do."

"But tell Bradley to call his family," the voice says quickly.

"Listen, buddy, you've got the wrong number," I say gruffly and then quickly hang up the phone in response to Henry moving his finger frantically back and forth in front of his throat.

"They're looking for us," Henry says quickly.

"They don't know he's here," I say. "They're just going through the phone book."

"How do you know?"

"He called this the residence of F. Wright. It's a misprint in the phone book. Bradley's father is a 'T' for Thomas. If he really knew the number, or who Bradley's father was, he wouldn't have made that mistake."

"Maybe," Henry says. "But let's not take any chances. We should move Jenny's car out of sight. Can we put it in the garage?"

"There's a car in there," I explain. "It's an old car we leave here. We can move it out and put Jenny's in. And Hal's car we can put in the boathouse. It's big enough."

"I'm way ahead of you guys," Hal says smugly. "I already put my car in the boathouse. Come with me, Larry, and we'll switch the others."

When we're outside, I look over at Bradley. His hair is blowing around, the wind is so strong. And the air is cold. Even with my sweater on, I'm anxious to go back inside.

My mother used to make fun of Bradley's curly hair. One time I remember she came up to him in the living room when we were just sitting around and ran her hand over his head.

"You have curls like Shirley Temple, Bradley," she said.

"Oh, mom, lay off, will you," I said, because I was worried about Bradley having his feelings hurt. But it didn't bother him a bit, and she continued pulling at his hair.

"Come on, Larry," Hal says. "I'm freezing. Let's get this over with."

The inside of the garage is dark, and I almost impale myself on a rake when I slide along the wall to the car door. The old car smells like summer, not just last summer, but all the summers wrapped up into one. It reminds me of going to the drive-in, suddenly, because it smells like popcorn.

The engine turns over many times before I get it started. It seems like it was only last winter that the car was new and we were driving up to New Hampshire to go skiing. We'd leave so early in the morning that it would still be dark. And it was always dark coming home. I remember one night when the ski rack came off while we were speeding down the highway. We heard the noise and saw a burst of sparks when the rack and the skis hit the road behind us.

"Larry," Hal says when we're back in the house, rubbing our hands in front of the fire to warm them, "You and Bradley can go back to Boston with me, if he'll go with us."

"I hadn't thought of that," I say gratefully. "I guess I should try to talk to him about it. Where's Henry?"

"Upstairs with Josh," Jenny says without glancing up from a magazine.

I pull the old picnic blanket out of the closet and walk out the door toward Bradley. The blanket smells like mustard. The screen door makes a rusted screech as I go out, a noise that Bradley always hated. I look at him quickly, expecting him to wave his arms and say "Arhhhhh! Why doesn't someone oil that door!" But he does not move.

When we were younger, Bradley possessed a power to convince me to do things I wouldn't do when left to my own good sense. I first experienced drunkenness with Bradley, sharing a bottle of Scotch until we were both sick. There were many similar experiences. And I worry suddenly, as I approach him, whether he can still exercise such power over me. I imagine him addressing me in that insistent manner he used when we were younger, telling me that for my own peace and bliss I must go with him, embrace him, feel my heart beat against his, the flowers growing, the earth turning. And, as ridiculous as it sounds, I see myself agreeing. I see myself shedding my clothing and sitting down on the rock next to him. But I don't. I stand over him with the picnic blanket draped over my arm, appearing, I imagine, to anyone in the house across the channel, like the butler calling his master in for dinner.

Bradley appears to me to be unapproachable, as if he sits inside a giant candle's flame. I am frozen in place, unable to call his name or to touch his shoulder. Small eddies of wind dance through the trees along the shore, rattling the few remaining leaves. Then they skate across the bay, making fan-shaped disturbances on the water. When the sun dips below the tree line, a giant wave of dusk sweeps across the lawn and rushes by us on its way out to sea.

Bradley's back is now creamy white. And it's really cold, all at once. The muscles in Bradley's shoulders ripple and his rigid back collapses, suddenly. He begins to sob, and I kneel down beside him and cover his shivering body with the picnic blanket. Still, I do not speak to him. I leave my arm draped over his back, so he knows I'm still there. Other than that, I just look down the shoreline of Pleasant Bay and watch the small patches of fog rise in the coves.

After about ten minutes, Bradley sits up. He has built up some heat under the blanket, and he tucks the front ends under his knees and pulls the sides tighter across the front. For a few more minutes he looks out to the horizon where the color of the sky is a dull gray.

"I once observed a surgery in a hospital operating room," he says, after he glances at me for a second. "The skin on the patient was the same color as that."

"Really?"

"Yeah. I thought it was the bright lighting in the room. You know, sometimes certain kinds of light can make a color look different. But my professor said it wasn't so. He said that the drugs used to anesthetize the patient caused his skin to turn gray."

"I don't remember you taking a course like that."

"But the worse thing was how flat he was," he continues, ignoring me. "He was just a limp, straight line laid out on the table, like the ocean horizon."

His hand moves under the blanket as if he were going to point at the horizon. It makes a bulge in the draping material. He looks at it, and then withdraws it.

"I couldn't pay attention to the surgical procedure. The patient looked so helpless. And all those men and women were scurrying around him dressed in all those strange garments, using all that equipment. What they were doing seemed so hopeless next to that straight, limp body."

"Did he die?"

"Who?"

"The man on the table."

"No, it was just an appendectomy. That's not my point," he says, irritably. "Just forget it. It makes no sense anyway."

I decide not to pursue his point, knowing from years of friendship that to do so would only heighten his irritation, and we sit silently. From across the channel, on Sipson's Island, comes a burst of laughter. Several men and women are standing on a deck that extends out from a house facing across the channel. I can tell that the man on the right is speaking by the way his hands and arms are moving, but I can't make out what he is saying. The light that shines through the two big doors that lead onto the deck makes the cocktail sippers into silhouettes, and their distance from us makes them small, so they look like shadows made by a child's hands on a wall.

My sister Betsy and I used to play a game where we'd invent what people across the room were saying. The best place to do it is in a big restaurant, but there are lots of places to play, and the people over on the island right now would be a great opportunity. I imagine the story Betsy would produce. The woman on the right has recently returned from her bimonthly pilgrimage to New York and she is talking about Dali, Betsy would say. And her husband, acting proud yet secretly jealous of her erudition, helps her with her story, though he did not attend. His words are not his own—they are remnants of her conversation with him the night before. This is the stuff of social chatter, Betsy would say. The other women in the group glow with attention, willing accomplices in this display of spousal hierarchy. This is the stuff of marriage. The men shift their eyes from their feet to their cocktail glasses to the dark landscape across the bay, the sea of black among several lighted houses that during the daylight is a golf course. Theirs is the manner of polite aloofness, their cocktail selves, strutting aboard the deck in their haughty demeanors, callous to the beauty of the late October night, and the dark sky studded with stars. Soon the moon will rise, the air will get cooler, and they will retreat indoors.

"What are you doing here?" Bradley demands, startling me because I had been so wrapped up in my fictional account about the people across the channel.

"I came down from Boston to see you," I tell him.

"To kidnap me, you mean. You and Black Lightning."

"That's not exactly right," I stammer, although I know immediately from the look on his face that I must recant. "No, you're right. That's why I'm here."

"Why not call?" he says, laughing good-naturedly. "Why not just knock on my door?"

"I thought I'd be turned away by the people at the ashram. I thought you wouldn't see me."

"And why would you think that? What possible reason?"

"I don't know," I say, sheepishly, wondering myself why all the things said by Professor O'Neill and Mr. Henry should override what seems so obvious now.

"You thought we'd try to keep you there," he says, quietly. "And perhaps you thought you'd be unable to refuse."

"You're right," I say, knowing, suddenly, that his power over me while we were kids grew out of his uncanny ability to see my insecurities before I saw them. "Yes, I worried about that also."

"Do you remember Dr. Browning?" he asks.

"I do. I remember you going off every week to your session, during which time I would have nothing to do. I was jealous, I think."

"I thought it was queer, going to Dr. Browning. And I hated my parents for it. But I've found recently that I'm remembering, vividly sometimes, the things we talked about. Not that I'm trying, or even that I want to. It's just that they spring into my head, almost like I'm sitting right there on his stupid couch with all those stupid pillows he had everywhere. You never saw him, did you?"

"No. And you really never told me anything about it either."

"I know I didn't. It was an embarrassment to me. And I resented it. I still resent it. If I didn't tell you about it, then somehow it never happened. You know what I mean? If it's only you who knows about something, then it doesn't really exist if you don't want it to."

"Yes," I say hesitantly, unsure of the direction of our conversation.

"Anyway, Dr. Browning used to tell me there were two sides to everything, an outside and an inside. Just a minute ago I remembered, like I was there on the couch, my first discussion with him about the outside and the inside of things. What made me remember it was your saying you were worried you'd be turned away if you came to the ashram to see me, that I wouldn't see you. How could he think that, I thought to myself, and then I remembered Dr. Browning. You were telling me the outside, that you feared I'd reject you. You had no good reason to think that, but I can understand it. Fears almost always are born of things other than reason. And there you get to the inside. Your stronger fear was the inside, that if you came to see me I'd try to convince you to stay and, worst of all, that you'd do it. You'd wind up captured like I was."

"I don't know," I say. "Have you been captured?"

"No," he says, and shivers. "It's cold, isn't it?"

The moon is off the horizon now, like a huge white lantern hanging in front of us. I've studied the moon's rise before, from this very spot, in fact. As it rises its size will diminish, but its intensity will increase. The topography around us is already bathed in white light. But some places, like the backside of the dunes, where I know there are beach grasses and shrubbery, are in dark shadows. And the white light washes the colors out of everything. So what we see is only black, white and a few shades of gray.

The white light seems cold on my skin. The cocktail sippers across the channel have gone inside, as I predicted. They're moving behind the sliding glass door on the deck like goldfish in a bowl.

"You're not the way Henry said you would be," I say.

"Who?"

"Sam Henry," I say. "Black Lightning."

"Black Lightning," he says emphatically and laughs. "We have pictures of him on the bulletin boards at the ashram. And descriptions of the crimes he has committed against us. But his real name is never mentioned. And, by the way, his real name is Patrick, in case you didn't know. I've always thought that amusing."

"I guess if he were really evil, he wouldn't have a name," I say. "Maybe that's the point of omitting it from the posters."

"Even the devil has a name, Larry. The beliefs of the Path are not so Eastern, nor so philosophic, as to dispense with labels. There is no debate as to whether good and evil exist. Evil exists, and Black Lightning is the proof we offer our children. But he isn't what I expected."

"How's that?"

"You can't tell from the pictures what his physical stature is because they are only close-ups of his face. You know what I mean. There's a yearbook picture, and another one is a newspaper pose. So when I saw this little man in overalls jump out of that truck, I almost laughed."

"You mean you recognized him? Right away?" I say, incredulously.

"Oh, sure. The car didn't break down, it just stopped, like someone turned it off. I don't know how she did it. But cars don't break down like that. Lucky for you, young Jim didn't know the difference. And he didn't recognize Black Lightning immediately because he wasn't suspicious. Even if he had been, he probably wouldn't have recognized him. What everyone expects is a big man who breathes fire, not a little guy with glasses. He doesn't have his glasses on in his pictures."

He pulls the blanket tighter around him. The rock must be ice cold.

"Should we go sit on the porch or in the house?"

"No. This is fine," he says quickly. "I don't want to go inside."

As I watch him pull the blanket tighter, I think that in the morning the grass will be wet. The cool night will wring the moisture out of the ocean air, like twisting a washcloth.

"I don't know," he sighs. "I don't know how Josh will live without the ashram. It's his home. You know? I can't explain it. But he loves the place."

"Then we've made a mistake. Is that what you think?"

"It's ironic," he says, ignoring my inquiry.

"What's that?"

"We were here at almost this same time the October before we went to college."

"That's right," I say, unsure of why his thoughts have changed direction so quickly, but nevertheless enthusiastic about speaking about the past, because the past to me at the moment is solid ground, and the present a swamp. "It was eight years ago last weekend. I thought about that yesterday when I crossed the canal. We came down for the weekend to try to make up our minds about what schools to apply to. We were going to go somewhere together. That was our plan. Do you remember that?"

"Yes, I do. We sat right here when we talked about it. I thought we should go to that college in St. Louis. You probably don't even remember the name."

"Sure I do. It was Webster College. But my father would have killed me."

"That's what you said then."

"It was too experimental."

"I don't know. It sounded good. You wrote your own curriculum. Anyway, then there was the University of Colorado. We both applied there."

"And we both got in."

"But we didn't go. Do you remember why?"

"I don't. God, you'd think I'd remember something like that, wouldn't you? I only remember you telling me that you'd been accepted at Berkeley. And I didn't know you'd even applied there. I remember that. The rest is a blur. But that all happened in the spring. And there was so much happening then."

"My family was going to move to Texas," he says.

"That's right. That was happening too. It was a good job. He was going to be chairman of the department. Right? Why didn't he take it in the end?"

"I don't know. He pushed me so hard to go to Berkeley, telling me I just couldn't turn down such a good opportunity. And then he turned down his. I felt betrayed in a way."

"I'm sure that's not right."

"Maybe," he says pensively. "I don't know."

"I doubt that the two were connected at all."

"It was Dr. Browning's idea that I go to Berkeley, you know?"

"I didn't know that."

"Well, I say it was his idea. He never actually told me anything. He would only manipulate the conversation. I remember we talked for almost a month about how frustrated I was with things, and with the people around me. Little things people did would leave me incredibly annoyed. Do you remember me being that way?"

"The only thing you ever told me about Dr. Browning was that you didn't like his sitting behind you and taking notes while you talked to him," I say, ducking the real question.

"That's right," he says, after delivering me a suspicious glance. "That wasn't what I was thinking, but it's the same thing. Anyway, he changed that so we faced each other, and I could watch him writing. Then the scribbling noise that he made didn't bother me as much. But it was sometime later that we started talking about the things that annoyed me. We got started because, although I got used to his taking notes, he had this habit of clicking the top of his pen every time he stopped writing. And then he would click it again when he started. He'd have to because on the earlier click he would have retracted the point. It got to be so irritating to me that I would pause after I finished saying something and wait with my teeth clenched for the click, meaning that he had finished writing it down. And then there would be times when he didn't do it, he'd break the pattern, and I'd want to rip the pen out of his hand and click it a thousand times right in his stony, expressionless face. Just to see how long he could stand it. You know what I mean?"

"I do," I say, disingenuously.

"Well, in the beginning of one session, after his first click, I said to him, 'Listen, no offense, but you click that pen every damn time you stop writing, and then you click it again when you start, and it bothers me so much I forget what I'm saying.' So he held the pen out in front of him and clicked it a few times, paused, and then clicked it a few more times. Then he said, 'Well, what bothers you about it?' And I said, 'the noise bothers me. The noise. That's what I just told you.' And he said, 'Well, you said a lot of things. You mentioned the times when I clicked it, and you mentioned your being distracted, but if you mentioned the noise it was only by implication.' He was always dissecting everything I said. Anyway, the whole thing led into a month's worth of sessions on all of the things that annoyed me."

"What happened with the pen?" I ask, although it immediately seems to be to be a senseless question.

"The pen?" he says, distractedly.

"Did he keep clicking the pen?" I persist.

"Oh. He switched to a fountain pen," he says, chuckling.

"Well, that was progress, wasn't it?"

But he looks at me like he doesn't hear me. In fact, he stares at me for a while, like he's counting the hairs on my eyebrows or measuring the distance from my chin to the end of my nose.

"Well, that's it, isn't it," he says, finally. "I never thought of that before. Dr. Browning accommodated me, didn't he? He did just what you and Sally, my parents and everyone else did. You all accommodated me. That's where my idea to go to Berkeley came from. After we talked about all the things that annoyed me, we talked about how all of you tiptoed around me all the time to keep me from being annoyed. And you know what? It annoyed the hell out of me that you did that. I've always thought that he and I concluded that going off to Berkeley would be good for me because it would put me with a whole new group of people who wouldn't be so tolerant of all my annoyances. I don't know. It seems kind of silly now."

"I don't know," I say, his accusation distressing me.

"It may be that going off to Berkeley was to get away from your annoying habit of accommodating me," he says after looking across the bay for several moments.

"Maybe."

"I hadn't thought of that before," he says.

"I don't know," I say, trying not to sound as defensive as I feel. "You can look back and make up a motivation for anything, if you want to."

"I guess so," he says, shaking his head. "But it all suddenly seems so pathetic."

"What do you mean?"

"Nothing was right. And still, nothing is right. I'm missing something. I try and I try, and I can't grasp these fundamental things. It was why I left Berkeley. I'd just learn the words, or whatever. Everybody did that. We studied the texts. We memorized the principles. But no one ever really understood the meanings."

"You mean things like why are we sitting here right now on this rock. Things like that."

"Yes," he says curtly, after looking at me quickly. "Things like that. Things like why that light across the bay is shimmering in my eyes. And I don't want to hear about waves or particles of matter."

"I don't think you understand those kinds of things," I say softly. "I think you feel them."

"I'm not satisfied with that," he says vehemently. "I won't accept that. I can't spend my life like Herrick does. He knows what time of day it is by how many empty coffee cups are on his desk."

"Herrick gets a lot out of life," I argue. "You can't get distracted by the routines and conventions. Sometimes you fight them, sometimes you go along with them. But you evaluate yourself by the whole, not by each little piece. Do you want to make every moment of your existence meaningful? You'll drive yourself crazy."

"It's a bullshit life, what Herrick does," he says, emotionally. "It's like going to the movies and keeping your eyes closed. And I *am* driving myself crazy. You're right about that. And that's the point."

"Why don't you come back to Boston with me tomorrow," I say quickly, hoping to keep him from wallowing in his bitterness toward Herrick.

"Why would I do that?"

"I don't know," I say, trying to sound as casual as possible, as if his return with me to Boston was a thought that had just occurred to me. "Just for a change. You can hang around at my place. Sally is back from Africa, and still recovering from her illness. You could spend some time with her."

"Does she know you came down here?"

"No. I didn't tell her. I didn't tell anyone. As far as they know, you're still in California."

"I couldn't handle seeing my father right now," he says.

"Why not?"

"Because he'll try to be so understanding, and he won't understand anything."

"Would anyone?" I ask before I can stop myself, causing him to look away from me and to become quiet.

"Perhaps Uncle Raymond would. But, really, I don't want to be understood," he says. Uncle Raymond isn't our real uncle. He was Captain Bradley Wright's best friend. They served together in the Navy during World War II. Raymond visited regularly, and he paid attention to all of us, even thought it was mostly Herrick he came to see. He would watch you carefully when you spoke, and then he would say something that made you think that he'd just read your mind. And he was never wrong about Bradley.

We listen to the water racing through the channel. Just behind us on the lawn, we used to have family dinners after really hot summer days. My grandfather used to come out in his sweater, and my sisters would tease him. But after the sun went down the evening would always turn cool and they would scurry inside, looking for a sweatshirt. He never said anything about it to them. He'd just lean back in his chair and talk about how beautiful the stars were.

The current in the channel is incredibly strong. One day Bradley and I tried to paddle a canoe up the middle of the channel against an incoming tide. Bradley scoffed at my suggestion that we hug the shoreline, where the current was weaker. We paddled with all our strength and made no progress. My sisters and Herrick jeered from the shore. My muscles ached and I wanted to stop, but I refused to quit as long as Bradley continued to paddle. Finally, he threw his paddle in disgust into the middle of the canoe, and the tide pushed us back to the boathouse. I did not decry his quitting, as I suspect he would have done had it been my paddle that was thrown into the canoe. But I suffered the shame that I did not exercise the good sense to retreat when I knew the battle was lost, or to challenge him on his decision to attack the current at its strongest point.

"Your father doesn't have to know you're in town," I say after a while. "Just come hang around at my place for a few days."

"When do you have to go back?"

"Tomorrow. I have to go back to work on Monday."

"I don't think so," he says. "I can't."

"Just for a couple of days. Then I'll borrow a car and drive you back to the ashram."

"The ashram is a comfortable place," he says, quietly. "They would miss me, were I to leave, even for only a few days. And I would miss them, for they help me when the devil comes to me."

"The devil!" I exclaim, startled.

"Oh, the devil," he says, laughing in an unstable manner all of a sudden. "You must know. Each of us has in us a side that is the devil. In my case, he looks just like me. Whatever I'm wearing, he's wearing the same thing. Or if I'm naked, he's naked too."

"What does he do, your devil?"

"Really not much. Until recently, he just told me nice things. Sometimes I couldn't even see him. Like at night, in the dark, I would hear his voice when I was in bed, like he was right behind my shoulder. But recently, he's been more out in the open, and he's been giving me lectures. He's been obnoxious, in fact. He keeps bringing up all these things I talked to Dr. Browning about. He knows them all. Or he imitates my father. I've screamed at him to go away, but he only laughs at me. I've tried to hit him, but I can't seem to connect, even if he's standing right next to me. I've ignored him, but that sends him into a rage and makes him do ugly things, like breaking things, or peeing on the floor right in front of me, and laughing while he does it."

He shakes his head and pulls the blanket tighter around him. Someone in the house turns on the porch light. I look around quickly and see Hal standing at the window, his hands cupped around his face against the glass. Bradley watches me.

"Is someone coming?" he asks.

"No. They're just looking to see what we're doing, I think."

"I don't want to go in yet."

"Neither do I, although sitting out here all night with only this blanket will not be good for you."

"Who's to say what's good or not," he says, quickly. "The truth is that for me what is good is my life at the ashram with my children. At the ashram I deal with my devil by meditating. It works. It was what I was doing out here. I shed myself of all that is worldly and I blend myself into all that is good. It's like walking down a path. That's why we call the ashram the Path to God. It has brought me peace, where before all I had was commotion."

"Did you say 'your children?'" I ask him.

"Yes. They are all my children," he says with a sparkle in his eyes. "I am their prophet, because I alone can recognize the devil and I alone can protect them from him. And for that they really need me; I am not merely an accommodation to them."

"I don't understand any of this, Bradley," I say to him, disconsolately. "It is not true that I or Sally or anyone else merely accommodated you, if that's what you're suggesting."

"And you can't understand," he says, vehemently. "And I can't explain it to you, because the only way we communicate is with this imperfect language. All of the words we use are tainted by the devil. And everything I say, or that you say, is heard behind the veil of past experience, all of which is what the devil has created. It's impossible."

He puts his hands over his ears and shakes his head when the screen door whines and Hal announces that dinner is on the table. I wave Hal off, and Bradley and I sit for a few moments listening to the surf along the National Seashore.

"Did it ever occur to you, Bradley, that all this stuff about the devil and the ashram is only a method by which you avoid dealing with life?" I ask him gently. "Do you think perhaps that you are accommodating yourself?"

"Oh, you are so wrong about that," he says strongly, his voice rising. "Why, it's just the opposite. I am confronting myself. It is why I am the prophet, for I undertake the difficult task for all of them. And for you I will do the same, if you choose. I shall battle the devil on your behalf."

"I'm not understanding again," I say wearily.

"The answer is in here," he says, pointing to his forehead with his index finger and looking at me intensely. "Answers come from thought. The path to the Absolute is a mental one. I start with easy questions, and answer them. As the night goes on, I make the questions progressively more difficult. The answers take longer. But I move down the Path. I move toward truth."

"When do you do this?"

"All night long, I am vigilant," he says. "At the ashram. It is how I find the truth and conquer the devil, because in my inner self and only in my inner self, the devil cannot reside. It is what I have prophesized: My Inner Self Holds All!"

"Your inner self?" I remark out loud, trying to make some sense of what he is telling me. And then I see it.

"Misha is not a person," he says, as if he has just read my mind. "Misha is a state of consciousness that only I have obtained."

"It's such a waste, Bradley," I blurt out, "to spend all of your time being vigilant, or however you characterize it."

"Larry, when I was living on the West Coast I would visualize you sitting in a leather chair at Widener reading the newspaper articles about the migrant workers and feeling sympathetic. I heard babies cry at night from the hunger pains in their stomachs, and you'd be in your leather chair, feeling sorry for them.

And there I was in my despair," he says, and then pauses to look at me, at which time a weird smile crosses his face. "Despair. Leather chair. That rhymes. Ha!"

"What are you talking about, Bradley," I say, some urgently rising in my voice at the strange composure that he has suddenly adopted.

"What I learned from my year with the migrant workers is that humanity is basically disgusting," he continues, now in a belligerent tone. "I came face to face every day with this huge, futile abyss that separates one man from another. There was the beggar sliding his diseased leg down the street while you sat in your leather chair and my father smoked his goddamn pipe in the faculty lounge. What kind of existence is it that suffers such horror right under the nose of all those comforts? You, my father, Sally, and me, enjoy this life of contentment that is more squalid than a beggar's life. And for my part in the comforts, for my very upbringing, I am ashamed. I am ashamed beyond repentance. I am struck by an existential horror so immense that it defies description. Only, it strikes me to my knees and makes me wish that my life would simply dissolve away, like the last few drops of water from a retreating wave sink into the sand."

His face is flush. He pulls the blanket against his shoulders with such force that the stitching at the seams is about to burst.

"I am sometimes unhappy with my life also," I say slowly, "but I don't know if I've ever thought of your life or mine as squalid."

"In the spiritual sense, Larry," he shouts. "It is squalid in the spiritual sense."

He stands up and pulls the blanket around him in a big, sweeping movement, like a matador waving his cape as the bull passes.

"You don't see the squalor I am speaking of because you are not vigilant. Come closer and listen," he says quietly, almost in a whisper, as he puts his arm, with the blanket draped over it, around my shoulders. "Sometimes there's a stately old gentleman who babbles in my ear. He told me his name once. 'Mr. Babble,' he said to me. So I started calling him 'Bab.' I've never seen him because he's too small. Or that's what he says, anyway. He says he is no bigger than a ladybug. He speaks to me from a perch just at the top of the ear. I'll touch the place on you, so you'll know, in case he pays you a visit. It's just here."

When he reaches up to touch my ear the blanket begins to slide off our back. In a flash his hand snaps back and grabs it.

"When he's not with me, he's making visits. He visits cocktail parties, where he sits, hidden behind the knots of the men's ties or perched on the posts of the ladies' earrings. There he listens and remembers all of what they say, which he repeats for me later in an all-night babbling trance."

He pauses, takes his hand off my shoulder and stands up straight.

"He visits the studies of men smoking pipes, the kitchens of women making soup. He listens to the intimate moments in a lover's bedroom, the idle talk of children in a nursery, the bitter talk of enemies, the connivances of law partners, the big talk of little men, the little talk of big men and the queries of a young child on his mother's lap. And he tells me all of this. He tells me of the doctor's new boat, the wife's new necklace, the accountant's new house, the lawyer's new car, the salesman's new television, and a woman's new dress. He tells me of the dreams of promotion by the company man's wife, of publication by the young professor, of the judge's order by the young lawyer. He tells me of the subway motorman with a second job in the evenings who struggles to stay awake in the cool darkness of the tunnels. He tells me of a broad-shouldered man in an unemployment line on a hot summer day who worries that his baby will climb out of the fifth-story window in his tenement building. He tells me of the young mother who bends over an old, scarred kitchen table in the same tenement, her tears falling upon a scrawled list of creditors on wide-lined yellow paper."

He speaks loudly now.

"Bab slips under the doors of women's closets. He climbs through the keyholes of diaries. He sits in the folds of handkerchiefs, in the collars of coats, in the hems of nightgowns. He watches from an old lamp the quiet movement of the line in a soup kitchen."

He pulls the blanket tight around him, climbs up on the rock and stands over me.

"I am lecturing you," he cries, and bows to me for a moment. "You are fortunate to have the Vigilant One talk to you so. I have taken what Bab has told me and I have rolled it up like a ball of yarn, and now I offer you its end to pull across the lawn."

He flings his arm, and the billowing blanket, out in a sweeping gesture toward the house.

"And when the ball of yarn is unwound, when you can see all these parts of life for what they are, when they are naked, so to speak," he shouts, and drops the blanket so that he now stands naked on the rock, with his arms outstretched and his eyes unfocused. "Then you will see the devil's work."

"Bradley, get back under the blanket," I implore him when he suddenly starts to whimper. I hold the blanket for him and he leans against me.

"You see that in my vigils Bab shows me the truth," he says in a voice laced with despair. "Yet I fail! For I still spend my days struggling with a desire to return to you and to all of this," he says as he motions with his head toward the house. "And I have begun to suspect that Bab is really the devil, come to taunt me, and that he stands before me upon his cleft foot and summons a wind to blow me from myself."

"Bradley," I say. "You are not making sense."

We sit down together.

"My life is all so futile. I paddle against the current," he says, looking over at the water rushing through the channel, and then at me. "Do you remember that, Larry?"

"Yes," I say, nodding my head.

"I was stupid and you accommodated me."

"No, Bradley. That's not true. We were just young. That's all."

"That's a bullshit excuse. I paddled against the current then. And now I blow against the wind. I spit against the rain. I look for my answers in the darkness," he cries, putting his head in his hands and then yanking at his hair with his fingers. "And the path I follow is narrow."

"Bradley, you're talking in circles," I say, quietly. "You speak of nothing."

"You're right. I'm not making sense," he responds, with his head bowed. "I'm not as much the Vigilant One as I pretend. Somehow with you I cannot successfully carry the persona."

"You've spent too much time with yourself, Bradley. That's all it is," I say in the most positive voice I can muster. "Your thoughts have no bounds."

He doesn't respond and after a few moments, I plead, "Come back to Boston with me, Bradley."

"I cannot," he says. "At least tomorrow I cannot. And I cannot tell you why. I just know that tomorrow I must go back to the ashram. And you must not attempt to stop me."

"And what about Josh?"

"Josh will leave with you. From the time I met his sister at the ashram I knew one day he would depart."

"That was you who talked to her?"

"We shall go inside the house now," he says, pulling the blanket around him and taking a step onto the lawn.

"And when will you come to Boston?" I persist, speaking now to his back.

"First, I follow the narrow path. After that, if it's time to go to Boston, I'll go," he says, wearily.

"And you'll know when that is?"

"I'll know."

He walks across the lawn like an old man would, watching the ground and shuffling his feet. On the porch, after he enters the house, I turn around and see our course marked by the leaves our feet pushed aside. The moon is bright, and I recall, suddenly, the cold cream glowing on Sally's face. Our lives have changed dramatically since that night in a way I could never have imagined. We should never have left home, I think as sadness overwhelms me. We should have moved into this house and lived here together forever, as we once planned. Tonight we should be assembled on our backs out on the lawn, poised to catch the falling stars.

14

IN THE LATE AFTERNOON OF the Tuesday following the weekend of my meeting with Bradley at the Narrows, the little piece of sky that I can see through my classroom windows is gray. In the city there's no horizon; everything is enclosed by borders, as if I'm constantly standing inside a photograph. It's a regimen that holds me tightly in its grasp. I made myself appear to be insanely busy when the dismissal bell rang so that none of my students would hang around, as they often do. I struggled to keep up the facade when one of them stood in the doorway, looking at me desperately, but I managed her departure without breaking my resolve. I needed to think.

When I walked into Millie's house on Sunday evening, I was hoping for a compassionate ear into which I could speak of what had transpired between Bradley and me. Unfortunately, what I received was a lecture about how irresponsible it had been for me to go to the Cape in the first place, followed by a magnanimous display of forgiveness and instructions regarding the manner in which we were going to spend the upcoming summer. It was during the summer instructions that I stood up and walked out. What was funny was that Millie was so involved in delivering the instructions that she didn't realize I was leaving until she heard the front door slam. I hadn't intended to slam the door the way I did. Something came over me at the last second, and I could not bear the thought, suddenly, that the motivation for my departure would not be crystal clear to her. She shouted at me from the porch, which I coolly ignored, and the phone rang incessantly Sunday night until I finally took the receiver off the hook.

I thought in the middle of the night how my feelings for Millie were really all about what I wanted her to be, and how continuing in a relationship with her would be as impossible as catching a falling star. Suddenly, all my life was a swamp of impossibilities, from returning to that time when Bradley, Sally and I were such close friends, to Bradley's Mr. Babble whispering in his ear, and to my being granted tenure by the school board, which seemed as likely as impregnating a mandrake root. I know about metaphysical conceits, of course. And as the night wore on, my cynicism collapsed into despair.

A rumble of thunder makes the big classroom windows rattle and brings me back to the present. I received a message from Melvin Lardner this morning that he planned to stop by my classroom this afternoon. Lardner is the assistant superintendent of the Medford Public Schools assigned to my tenure review. The school board met yesterday evening, and I am guessing that their decision regarding tenure for me is the reason for his visit. Lardner and a school board member visited my classroom yesterday and, much to Hal's relief, I taught a lesson around an Asimov short story.

As I sit, staring out the window and waiting for Lardner, I suffer pangs of anxiety over my wasting time—although it won't make much difference once Lardner gives me the bad news. Spread around me are my plan book and papers to grade, but I have forsaken them. It occurs to me that often I am manic about time's passage. It's as if time is a depleting asset, like oil or coal, which I am shamefully wasting. But I resent, suddenly, the ethic in me that compels me to fill every minute with tangible productivity. I resent the common teaching that time lost is lost forever, like a marble dropped down a deep well. Time is completely fungible, I theorize; if I can't use a minute now, I can use it later. One minute is the same as another, after all, and their supply is endless. Unlike air and water, the lack of which will cause death, time is only extinguished by death. In that sense, it occurs to me, time is like food that you can't finish at the restaurant. You can wrap it up and take it to go. Then later on, when the circumstances are better, you can use that minute that you couldn't use before. These thoughts make me smile. I can see that some clever rationalization has crept into my new philosophy. And I chuckle to myself at the concept of "time to go." How modern!

Bradley told me last Saturday night, after we had gone inside and sat in his room, that after long periods of meditation he believed he could roll time up into a little ball and do what he wanted to with it. He was, I suspect, continuing his analogy of life being a ball of yarn. You can carry it around with you, he said. It occurs to me now that he was saying that by his meditating he could make time stop. That distresses me, suddenly, because what a person who wants time to stop really desires is for life to stop. It is also why a depressed person only wants to sleep; time, and life, appear to stop while he sleeps.

I worry that Bradley is suicidal, that his wanting to stop time is only a code for his desire to end his life. He mentioned to me that when he was particularly vigilant he would hear mermaids singing, and that their voices were a great comfort to him because, he believed, hearing the mermaids' song was the stage just before one reached the Absolute. Of course, T.S. Eliot connected the mermaids singing to drowning, and Bradley's descent to the Absolute may be only that: a drowning. I am concerned that his promise to come to Boston was a hollow one, or, even if sincere, that being convinced in the interim that he has reached the Absolute, a leap to the conclusion that life is superfluous will be a short one. This logic would not appear strained to one who believes, as Bradley says he does, that conventional life is futile.

We were a restless household on Saturday night. Several times during the night I awoke, thinking I heard someone stirring in the hallway. On one such occasion I heard Bradley and Henry conversing in quiet tones. To my amazement their voices sounded friendly, although I could not discern the content of their talk. The hour being so late, I rolled over and fell back into my hazy sleep.

At dawn on Sunday I was jarred awake by a pounding downstairs on the porch, just below my room. The pounding was so heavy that all the small objects on the nightstand seemed to jump off the surface with each beat. Downstairs, I found that a group of men, several of them police officers, were gathered outside of the porch door. It was a strange place for them to be since they had to walk halfway around the house to get there. Most people think of the main door as the one on the north side of the house underneath a portico that extends out over the driveway. There were police cars parked in the driveway, their lights flashing through the windows. An early morning fog shrouded Pleasant Bay.

"Where are they?" a man in a dark, stylish suit demanded when I opened the door.

"Where are who?" I asked sleepily.

"Oh, come on," he said rolling his eyes and acting exasperated in a dramatic fashion for the benefit of the others. "Let's not play any games here."

"Just a minute, Ralph. Let me handle this," one of the others said, politely stepping in front of the man who had just addressed me.

This man wasn't nearly as well groomed as Ralph. He reminded me of the detective I talked to briefly when I tripped over the corpse at the Lars Anderson Bridge. I looked at Ralph and the others more carefully. Ralph had perfectly combed black hair with a razor-sharp part that made a bright white line across his head, like the white line in the middle of an asphalt highway. Next to Ralph was Jim, the guy we left by the side of the road. His lips were moving, but his words were not audible, like he was saying a rosary.

"What's the matter with him?" I asked.

"Nothing," Ralph growled.

"Mr. Brown," the man in front of Ralph said. "Are you Mr. Brown?"

"Larry Brown," I said, briefly shaking his extended hand.

"Mr. Brown, I am Mike Morse, the assistant district attorney on the Cape. We're sorry to disturb you so early, but we have some urgent business."

"Urgent business, nothing," Ralph shouted and pushed his way back to the front. "We have a search warrant."

He pulled a neatly folded paper out of his coat pocket and flipped it with his wrist so that it opened in front of me. The paper had a big red seal on the bottom of it. The other man stepped in front of him again.

"Mr. Brown, this is Ralph Bedell. He is an attorney for a religious organization called the Path to God, which has a residence near here. They have sworn out a complaint against you and several others claiming that you have abducted two of their members and are holding them here, in this house, against their wills. The paper he is holding is a search warrant, which grants me authority to enter the premises to ascertain whether the two members of the Path are here and whether they were abducted."

"Can I read it?" I asked, trying to sound innocent and hoping that Henry has heard the commotion.

"Oh, come on," Bedell shouted, taking a step toward the doorway, as if he was going to push me out of the way.

I became irritated and took the uncharacteristic action of grasping both sides of the doorframe, which made it impossible for Ralph to walk by me. He stopped. Morse took a step forward and faced him.

"Mr. Bedell," he said sternly. "This is police business. We serve the papers. You observe."

After a nod of Morse's head, the policeman standing next to him handed me the warrant. Bedell paced around the porch with a disgusted look on his face. When I looked at the warrant the first thing I saw was my name and Patrick Henry's name at the top. I couldn't read more because I was thinking all the while what I was going to do. Just when I determined that I had no choice but to let them in, Jim cried out something unintelligible and rushed by me to Bradley, who had quietly come up behind me.

"Oh, Vigilant One," Jim cried until Bradley gently pushed him away.

The men on the porch and I looked at Bradley in astonishment. He was wearing a long, white robe and he stood quietly with his hands clasped together in front of him.

"Are you Bradley Wright or Josh Barrows?" Morse asked, finally.

"He is the Vigilant One," Jim said quickly.

"Yes. I am Bradley Wright," Bradley said.

"Mr. Wright, Mr. Bedell, here, has sworn out a complaint on behalf of the Path to God against a Mr. Henry and others stating that they abducted you and that they are holding you here against your will."

"I am here voluntarily," Bradley said.

"Perhaps I could have a few words with my client in private," Bedell said after overcoming his incredulity.

"Your client?" Morse asked.

"Uh, Mr. Wright," Bedell said.

"The Vigilant One," Jim said.

"Yes," Bedell said, looking carefully at Bradley.

"It is unnecessary, Mr. Bedell," Bradley said.

"Yes," Bedell said.

"Mr. Wright," Morse said. "Forgive me but I feel that I must ask some additional questions. The affidavit that Mr. Bedell and Jim here swore out described some fairly serious matters."

"Of course, there has been an unfortunate mistake," the Vigilant One said, facing Morse, looking like a holy man, with each hand holding the opposite elbow beneath the robe's sleeves. "I assure you that no one has been abducted. This house is owned by my family and Mr. Brown's family. Certainly I am not a prisoner in my own house."

"According to the affidavit," Morse said, "You were tricked into leaving the ashram with two unidentified individuals and driven to a place along the side of the road, where the accomplices, with help from Mr. Henry, beat this young man and left him, forcing you and Mr. Barrows to depart without him. Is any of that true?"

"What is truth is in each man's heart," the Vigilant One said. "Our young brother," he continued, motioning to Jim with a sweeping white-clothed arm, "I am sure told you what he believed, but often the line between perception and reality is not straight."

"I'm not sure I fully understand," Morse said politely, after shaking his head and looking again at the paper in his hand. "Are you saying the affidavit is not correct?"

"May I speak?" Bedell asked.

The Vigilant One nodded his assent.

"The Path to God would like to withdraw the charges," Bedell said officiously.

Morse was perturbed. He snatched the papers from my hands.

"Withdraw the charges?" he said hotly, waving the papers in front of him. "Ralph, you got me and the judge up at five in the morning with this affidavit about kidnapping, and battery, and, what did you say, here it is, 'feared torture,' and now you want to withdraw the charges, just like that."

"On behalf of my client, I apologize," Bedell said. "The mistake was unfortunate."

"Your client," Morse shouted. "Just who the hell is your client? I'm not withdrawing any charges until I see with my own eyes your client retract this affidavit."

"I retract the charges," the Vigilant One said.

"You?"

"He has complete authority to speak for the Path to God," Bedell said after Bradley nodded. "When I go back to my office I can produce for you a certified copy of their charter."

"Okay," Morse said, disgustedly. "We'll drop the charges. Just let me look around and speak to Mr. Barrows, so I can put it in the report."

"You are free to look around," the Vigilant One said, "but Mr. Barrows is not here."

"What?" Morse and Bedell and I all said together.

"He departed this morning," the Vigilant One said. "I wished him well on his journey."

"This morning?" Morse said.

"Early," the Vigilant One nodded.

"And the others?" Morse asked.

"They accompanied him. Mr. Henry and Jenny," the Vigilant One said.

"Who the hell is Jenny?" Morse asked, after looking back over the papers for a minute.

"Oh, sorry," I said, when Bradley didn't speak. "She was one of the 'accomplices.'"

"She is Mr. Barrows' sister," the Vigilant One said.

Morse's face evolved through a small series of contortions as he grasped the significance of this information.

"What? Miss Barrows is the woman referred to in the affidavit?" he asked Bedell.

Bedell looked sheepish for a moment and then said, "Yes, she is."

"You mean you swore that Mr. Barrows was abducted by his sister!" Morse screamed.

"The law makes no distinction that a perpetrator of violence cannot be a family member," Bedell stammered.

Before Morse could respond the Vigilant One said, "What you argue about does not appear necessary since the affidavit has been retracted."

"Okay," Morse said. "Just let me look around for the record."

"I am honored," the Vigilant One said and stepped aside.

Bradley stayed behind when the police entourage departed. Jim complained when Bradley instructed Ralph to take Jim back to the ashram. But Bradley's confident, self-possessed appearance prevailed and Ralph and Jim departed at last, with Jim craning his neck for a last look at the Vigilant One as their car turned the corner. Watching Bradley play this role, it occurred to me that he was no longer the Bradley that I knew, my Bradley, my confidant, my friend. And perhaps he never was such a person. One can fictionalize his past, I think, and he can fictionalize the people in it, so that when he brings them into the future they compensate immediately for his changes, as if they had lived his life with him every step of the way. Bradley had been gone from my life for some time, and the recent events had demonstrated that my life was as foreign to him as his was to me.

Just before I left the Narrows on Sunday, I moved the old car back into the garage. When I got to the key rack on the kitchen wall, however, I hesitated with the keys in my hand. Should I take them with me to keep the car from becoming Bradley's transportation to the Absolute? In my mind's eye I saw the rails of the Sagamore Bridge drawing closer and closer. I heard the roar of the old car's engine. The rails blurred gray. Against them the metal of the car scraped, and shrieked, and screamed. An explosion pushed the breath out of his lungs and his shoulders lurched forward. Then, the world became quiet, and he saw a spinning display of topography. A gentle whistle of air rushed through the car. It was a sweet release from the loud commotion. His shoulders slackened. Blank white and blue whirled around him. The mermaids sang.

I saw that Bradley watched me stand in front of the hook with the keys, like he knew what I was thinking. I felt guilty and quickly put them on the hook. When I turned around he was gone. I feared that he hadn't the strength to overcome what might be an easy solution to his frustrations. But I left the keys on the hook because I couldn't tell him so. Like so many times in the past, I accommodated him.

The thunder rattles the whole classroom now, and the rain starts. At first, it just makes tiny pings on the windows. Then the noise becomes loud and sustained. I walk over to the window. The rain is coming down so hard, it's like a plastic curtain that distorts the schoolyard.

For the lesson I taught yesterday morning for Lardner and the school board member, my 7A class read a story about a group of children who lived in a colony on a distant planet where it constantly rained, except once every seven years for a short time when the world's twin suns broke through the clouds. One of the children in the story was particularly anxious for this to happen. On the day the suns came out, the other children in the colony locked her in a closet and she missed the event.

The official curriculum states that oral reading in the classroom should be preferred over silent reading. I asked them to read the story out loud, even though I looked around and saw most of the students flipping the pages ahead. I couldn't make myself go through the questions and answers in the teacher's guide. That was too much to ask, even if tenure depended upon it. Instead, I assigned each student a character in the story, arranged several chairs and a table into a set one often sees on a television talk show, made myself into Dick Cavett and asked for volunteers to be interviewed.

Of course, every student knew why my guests were sitting in the back. Kids have an uncanny way of figuring out what adults are up to and then acting like they don't see it. Only I knew that they were putting on an unusual performance. At one point one of the most outgoing of the girls, Darcy, who of course had volunteered to be the little girl who missed the sun, and Tony, who played one of the crueler boys in the story, got into a wonderful name-calling act after Tony said to Darcy, "So what's a few minutes of sunlight, anyway." And Dick Cavett somehow managed to ask all of the questions in the teacher's guide.

"That was a damn good class, Brown," the school board visitor said. "They really got involved in the story, didn't they?"

"Yes, sir," I said.

"That's one of the better stories in our anthology," Lardner said.

"Yes, it is," I said. "The children love science fiction."

"It's a strong part of our curriculum," Lardner said.

"What bullshit," I wanted to say to the two of them. Instead, I just stood there, smiling and nodding like a fool.

My thoughts turn back to Sunday again. Bradley stood on the lawn and watched me get into the car with Hal. I thought about staying a few more days. What stopped me was the intense look on Bradley's face and my inability to make sense out of our conversation the night before. It was like trying to imagine the ocean being hung up to dry like a wet towel, or the stars turning to geese that fly away into the darkness.

The indecipherableness of Bradley's soliloquy symbolized to me, as I closed the car door, how separate Bradley and I had become. I once believed that would never happen, and it was too much for me to continue to experience it. I had to go.

As we left, I glanced over at the old rocking chair on the porch. I used to sit in my mother's lap there when I was very young and she would read me fairy tales. In one short moment, as we headed down the driveway, I remembered all the fairy tales she had read me. All of them ended happily. They were intended to be a life's promise to a child.

But the whole thing was a lie, I think now. What my parents told me about life when I was young, in those formative years, had no more truth in it than there is water in a sieve. They'd never mentioned that Herrick was actually Bradley's cousin, that he'd been rescued from a mission in French Indochina as a young boy after my Aunt Betsy and Uncle Bradley had been murdered. That news had come from an older man, who'd mysteriously appeared at my dorm room in college, an honorary Uncle Raymond he'd called himself, a friend of my Uncle's from the Navy. I become furious as I remember this. And then my anger dissipates when I hear steps in the hallway.

"Mr. Brown. Are you here?" Lardner says from the doorway. "Oh, there you are. They said downstairs you were still up here, but I didn't see you at first over by the window." He's all wet from the rain, and he has to keep wiping water off his forehead so it won't go into his eyes.

"I like storms," I say, walking back to my desk to greet him. "I was just watching the rain."

"As long as you're inside and dry, it's fine," he says, brushing some water off his sleeve. "Otherwise, it's just nasty weather."

"I suppose I'll change my mind when I go out in it."

"Well, I'm glad I've made it here before you left. I dashed over here from the high school. MacCreary told me you often stay late."

"I was just about to go."

"Well, I didn't want to wait to give you the good news that the School Board last night voted to offer you tenure."

"Oh," I say flatly, confused by my sudden ambivalence to what he has just told me.

"Well it is good news, don't you think?" he asks, perplexed at my demeanor.

"Oh, yes. Yes, it is," I say, regaining my composure. "I'm sorry. I'm just surprised it happened so fast."

"Well, we're trying to get this done early this year, rather than waiting for the spring like we usually do," he explains. "There are so many of you up for tenure, it seems. We took up five teachers last night. Only two of you made it."

"I'm sorry," I say, not quite sure how to react to that piece of news.

"Yes, it is unfortunate," he says, shaking his head. "But the profession has become so competitive. We have at least fifty applications for each position. And with all the boys coming back from Vietnam, it will probably get worse. Anyway, congratulations to you are in order."

He reaches into his suit coat pocket and takes out an envelope, which he hands to me. Inside is a long piece of dull-green paper, the same kind of paper bank checks are printed on. I unfold it. At the top in big letters it says, "Contract for Tenure." It's good stiff paper, the kind that's best for making a paper airplane, one like I've seen made so deftly by Louis, a boy from my 7H class. For a moment I imagine myself making one out of the contract and soaring it across the room.

"Sign it and hand it in to MacCreary next week," Lardner says, and then notices what must appear to him to be a blank expression on my face as I turn the contract over in my hands. "Are you okay, Mr. Brown?"

A gust of wind rattles the windows.

"Oh, yes. Sorry. I'm fine," I say, quickly and put the contract on the desk.

"Nasty weather," he says, looking behind me. "Oh, well, no time like the present. They'll worry about me at home soon."

He turns on his heels with a parade turn and marches through the door. Just before he turns into the corridor, his right hand rises up above his head in a kind of salute. He holds down his fourth and fifth fingers with his thumb, and moves his hand, with its two fingers pointing, to draw a check mark in the air. I can see only his back and, just as the electronic school clock on the wall ticks away one more precious minute and his body disappears, his voice reverberates in from the corridor.

"Good luck, Brown," I hear him say, as if he knows.

THE END

A NOVEL

A LION IN THE GRASS

MARK ZVONKOVIC

"Fans of Ludlum, Clancy, and other writers who hold the ability to craft high-impact spy scenarios within the broader scope of world events and interpersonal relationships will relish the attention to detail and the realistic action and perceptions cultivated in *A Lion in the Grass*.

"Its strong ability to weave thriller and suspense elements into a historical saga steeped in spicy psychological entanglements makes *A Lion in the Grass* a top pick for those who like their spy novels sweeping, embracing changing times, changing relationships, and characters who grow into their duties and abilities."
—Diane Donovan, Midwest Book Review

Acknowledgements

WHEN THE EVENTS IN THIS novel took place, the world paid scant attention to cults and their practices. The mass suicide at Jonestown had not yet occurred. In 1976 Ted Patrick published *Let Our Children Go!* (EP. Dutton), which brought attention to practices utilized by some cults to keep their membership. In 1989 Marc Galanter published *Cults—Faith Healing and Coercion* (Oxford University Press), which explored the psychology of cults. Both of these works proved invaluable to the understanding of cults I needed to write this novel. For the reader who wants to learn more about cults than my work of fiction depicts, I recommend both of these books.

I wrote several versions of this novel before I relegated it to a box in the attic in 1996. The encouragement of John MacWilliams and Leonard Groopman led me to rescue it from the banks of the Acheron in 2007 and continue work on it, and I am truly indebted to them for that. I did not appreciate how valuable an editor can be until I met John DeAngelis and I am very grateful for his excellent work on this novel, as well as his patience and support through so many versions over the last few months. Finally, my life would be too empty to write even one word were it not for Nancy, Kate, Sarah and Andie. They have made my endeavor worthwhile.

About the Author

MARK ZVONKOVIC IS A NOVELIST and recovering lawyer who lives in Baja, California with his wife Nancy and their two dogs, Finn and Cooper. When he's not writing, he and his dogs watch pelicans fly.